FREE

F R E E

Todd Komarnicki

D O U B L E D A Y

New York London Toronto Sydney Auckland

PUBLISHED BY DOUBLEDAY
a division of Bantam Doubleday Dell Publishing Group, Inc.
1540 Broadway, New York, New York 10036

DOUBLEDAY and the portrayal of an anchor
with a dolphin are trademarks of Doubleday,
a division of Bantam Doubleday Dell Publishing Group, Inc.

Book design by Viola Adams

Library of Congress Cataloging-in-Publication Data
Komarnicki, Todd.
Free / Todd Komarnicki.
p.   cm.
I. Title.
PS3561.04523F74   1993
813′.54—dc20   92-38396
                                                                  CIP

ISBN 0-385-46849-0

1   3   5   7   9   10   8   6   4   2

First Edition

ACKNOWLEDGMENTS

Peace and gratitude to my sister, Kristyn Anna Komarnicki, without whom this novel never would have been worth reading. And to my sister, Robyn Komarnicki Hubbard, who believed long before I did.

To Jjet, Tim Nett and Victoria Brett, for more than they know.

To Dr. Jill Baumgartener, miner of deeply hidden talent.

To Kenny and Laurie Martin, for giving me New Orleans.

To Ruth Pomerance, an angel along the road.

To my uncle, David Komarnicki, who ignited the very first spark.

To my wise and generous editors, David Gernert and Bruce Tracy.

To my agents, Ginger Barber, Mary Evans and especially Jennifer Rudolph Walsh, full of surprises and magic.

And to the artists whose poetry lit my way; Frederick Buechner, Rainer Maria Rilke, Tom Waits, and Declan MacManus.

—T.K.

For George & Marigrace Komarnicki
my parents,
inspiration
and best friends

FREE

The shots were loud and dull, like a stripper I used to know. And I was alone. I spent all my time alone, looking in mirrors and store windows, just to prove I still existed, and on most nights, when the dark was too black and the curbs reached up to trip me, I found myself in an adults-only nightclub. Maybe it was boredom, or the mystery. A priest I knew called it self-destructive, but it was the only way I knew how to live.

Wong's Exotic Dance Club, despite the neon promise of All Live Nudes, was never crowded. I knew I could get a free refill from Dent the bartender, and I only looked at the girls when I was too drunk to be polite. But these gunshots made wine into water.

Dent had already hidden in his customary spot, under the floorboards. The stink of old urine and fresh blood steamed the air. On the pool table in the back room, the game was over.

A Chinaman, with the cue ball stuck in his mouth, lay spread out on the table. The killer had taken the time to stuff the Chink's hands into the pockets and rack a new game between his legs. I admired the work. It seemed familiar. The room was empty, and the jukebox coughed out Howlin' Wolf like a prayer. The Chinaman had two clean shots through the chest and no money in his wallet. My bad luck. I didn't work for anyone. I wasn't a private dick or scam runner, no grifter with a sauce to sell. I just chose to fill my hours with other people's tragedies. To better prepare for my own.

The victim, one Dao Tei Cheng, was carrying three Louisiana state IDs and a set of copycat keys. By the time I got his shirt off to examine the bullet holes, the sirens began to wail. On his left shoulder blade was a fleur-de-lis tattoo. Not prison green or tattoo blue. Red, and getting lighter every minute, as if it were filled with blood. He was hairless, of course, and his belly button was half gone. Knife fight. I got his shirt back on as the cops busted in, took a handful of talcum powder and eased out the back. Some uniforms chased me a couple of blocks, but I lost them at St. Peter, above Jackson Square. I always could run like hell.

I used the talcum powder to soak up the blood and washed in the bathroom of a Texaco. The mirror was nearly black with graffiti. My face peered back between the bars of the letters. They kept me from seeing how beaten I really looked. I could make out the scar that ran like a tributary from the top of my skull to my ear. The doctors had shaved my head, so I could see the reminder. It was fat with regret and teeming with glass shards that couldn't be removed, small speed bumps in my head. This slowed me down. Enough to survive. Enough to listen. Almost enough to remember.

Rock-a-bye-baby in the treetop. When the gun's fired the cradle will rock. Back. Back to the front. Back to the beginning. In the beginning was the word. And the word was . . . Bang. Listen, Jefferson. No one has to know. No one ever has to know about. What happened. No one. Not even you.

There was no one to tell about the killing. Just my slow thoughts and the early morning paper. The front page of the *Times-Picayune* Metro section showed the bloodstained pool table but no body. They didn't even list the victim's name. I threw the paper away and walked two blocks before the thought limped over the speed bumps. Back in my print-stained hands the photo made the promise. Dao had left a bloodstain on the green cloth of the table. It stretched long, with its short arms reaching out. For help? To embrace? To invite? My dead man had bled a fleur-de-lis.

My name is Jefferson Alexander Freeman. I go by Free. People learn it fast after I repeat it, and it reminds me of who I want to be. Rather, how I want to be. Dao Cheng was free. Of this mortal coil. And now he lay on some city coroner's gurney, a pincushion for a lot of overworked, undercurious professionals. He wouldn't be drinking tonight. But I would down a few to his memory. I went back to Wong's. Dent was alone, finishing up the payroll.

"No Friday night fun doing the books."

"It's okay," Dent hummed. His mouth was so small that his tongue pressed up against his palate. When he spoke, he buzzed.

Wong's wasn't exactly a home, a place to be accepted. But it was the last safety net for those who lived on the wire. It was there for the fallen. And we all had fallen.

"Find anything last night?" I probed.

"I was under the floor. Didn't go back there yet. Let the cops dig."

"You know the guy? Dao Tei Cheng."

"Never seen him." That was Dent's standard response.

"He has a tattoo. A fleur-de-lis. Like the Saints."

"Everybody in New Orleans has that tattoo."

"Everybody?" I asked. "How about you?"

"Never seen him."

In the poolroom, some blue corn lackeys were dusting for prints.

"Don't you guys get any time off for good behavior?" I slurred. It was better to let the cops think I was drunk. That way I could wise off without getting much heat. Maybe even pick up some important information.

"Go home, rummy," one of the bulls said. He had tiny ears that barely held his hat on. It kept sliding down over his eyes when he leaned forward.

"Good thing you have a nose, copper."

"Beat it."

"I heard the spike was a China boy," I tested.

"Read the paper. Believe anything you want."

"Guess he should have stayed in China." I was having a good time. Cop One, with regulation ears, stood up and hobbled over to me. His kneecap swam around in his pants, a crazy fish.

"What do you know, skinhead?"

"This haircut is courtesy of Charity Hospital. It is not a political or fashion statement."

"They left a few chunks in there," he said as his finger rumbled over the scar.

"I asked them to. To remind me."

"Remind you of what?"

"Not to dive out a church window."

Felulah Matin stepped into the breach and took the officer's hand off my head. "He's had an accident. He's a little funny in the head. He don't mean no offense."

"None taken, ma'am." The cop swiveled back to work, and Felulah led me to her dressing room. As lead stripper she commanded the nicest dressing room, and she took advantage of it. The walls were painted sapphire blue, or so she said, and the carpet accepted my feet like quicksand. Unlit candles were everywhere. "They burn down if you light them," she explained, and neither of us wanted to see that happen. Felulah was illegitimate, irrepressible and irresistible. The only stripper I ever kissed.

"Why do you talk to them?" She pouted. "You never ever talk to me, and I'm a whole lot more talkable."

"Following a lead."

"Bullshit. Dent said you took off running."

"Something like that."

"And what are you following it for? Ain't no job. Ain't no money."

"There's always money, Felly. As long as I stay awake during the important hours, there's always money."

"You're a thief."

"And you're a stripper."

"Your head looks nicer."

"Nicer than what?" I laughed. "Did you know the dead man?"

"He was here only the last couple weeks. A few times. Lousy tipper. Very quiet and a lousy tipper."

"You wouldn't kill a man because he was a lousy tipper, would you, Felly?"

She swung, but I ducked. "Free, how could you say a thing

like that?" Her face flushed magnolia pink. No one was above suspicion in New Orleans.

"He had a tattoo. A fleur-de-lis."

Felly didn't seem to care. She leaned closer to me, still in her stripper's uniform. "Free."

Dent broke in, and Felulah pulled away, tugging on a T-shirt. He stopped two steps inside the door, like he'd broken into a tomb. "Hey, Dent," I said.

"Sugar, you know I need you to knock."

"Miss A. says no customers in the dressing room. You know that, Felly."

"Dent, this is Free. He ain't a customer. He's a friend."

"Don't say anything I might regret," I said.

"Boss says," he repeated.

"I can't believe your actions sometimes." Felly's face folded like a handkerchief, and she turned to the mirror for comfort.

"I don't know what I'm saying." Dent retreated. "I didn't know it was just Free. I thought—and then I was all set to say something. So I said it." He looked terminally sad. "I just want you to be careful. Things and all."

"Too late now, Dent." Felly's trembling voice pushed him out the door. He left it open. "A woman can't get a decent moment alone. Even with a man. Not in this town. Not in this place."

"I have to go, Felulah." I was already standing.

"I know," she whispered. "I know. Can I come with you?"

I didn't want her to come. I needed more time to wash the blood away. But before "no" came out, we were walking through the Quarter. The streets were crowded with happy drunks visiting from anywhere. The circus was in full swing.

"Everybody's having their sport tonight." Felly smiled. A businessman fell hard against a shopwindow, leaving fingerprints on the window. Fingerprints. Always wipe off the fingerprints, I thought. "You hear the shots?"

"Like I was in the room," I answered. "Loud. Dull."

Felly stepped behind me and covered my ears with hard hands. She was peeling me back a layer at a time. I pulled away. "Just trying to make the noise go away, Free. Wouldn't you like it if all the noise went away?"

"I like the noise."

"I had a vision," she said to the ground. "Maybe. I know I had something."

"A vision," I repeated.

She spun in front of me and walked backward, staring me in the eyes. I looked down. "Look at me," she said.

"You'll walk right into a lamppost."

"But I have you to protect me. I don't have anything to fear." Felly's tomato-red hair spun tight circles around her face. Something black pinned my thoughts. "I had a vision, Free. I did. Don't you want to hear about my vision?"

The wail of a horn. Not a trumpet or sax escaping from the Absinthe, but a car horn, as Felly backed right into the intersection. I grabbed her wrist, the thin end of a rope. A Chevy paused to catch her fall. An inch away from metal and flesh. She ricocheted into my arms, giggling. Drivers popped out of their cars, their fingers stabbing the air. "Fuckin' bum! Watch where the hell you're going?!?"

"Stupid bitch."

"Goddamned sonofabitchwhorebastarddrunkenscum!"

"Thank you," I said.

Felly was still laughing, pressed against me. She was hold-

ing on so tight, it seemed she'd pass through me like a ghost
and come out the other side. I wanted to pop into some bar,
any bar, for a quick shot. But Wong's was the only place that
would take a skeleton like me. I swallowed dry. Something
had me dizzy. We moved on, Felly again walking backward.
"I don't believe in death," she proclaimed. "I think it's been
done, if you sense my purpose."

"It has been done. Keeps getting done all the time."

"That's what I mean. Aren't you a tiny bit tired of all the
dying? I say it should stop. Right now."

"Just like that?"

"Just like that." Felly looked convincing. As if she might
have an idea. A vision.

"I wish you the power to make it all stop, Felulah Matin."
If death would have stopped for anyone, it would have been
Felly. Her body all curves and surprise. Her eyes wicked and
wise.

"The gift. The power is in the gift."

I wanted to change the subject. "Let's talk about the dead
Chinaman again."

"You keep changing the mood, Free. You have to allow a
girl her mood." I didn't know the rules. The conversation
needed to end. I palmed my gun. It felt like murder. I
shouldn't have done it. "I . . ." Felly started.

"Will you walk face first, now?" I asked as we turned onto
Toulouse.

"I don't do anything face first."

"That's how you get run over. I shouldn't have been here to
catch you. I won't be."

"I had a vision."

"I heard."

"I'm serious, Free." She tried to get me to stop walking. To lean against a wall and listen to her. But I shook free. She caught up. "You don't want to hear."

"There's nothing to hear. You don't believe in death. I don't believe in visions."

"I saw something. My grandmother." I was getting desperately thirsty. Needed a bar fast. Needed a river. Needed to drown. "I've never seen you scared before." She hung a disappointed laugh in the air. A question mark.

"You've never seen me."

"I watch you when I strip." Felly's hand reached for my shoulder, so I quickened the pace. "I see your back. I know you won't turn around and watch me, even though I wish you would. No one else I want to dance for. Do you understand, Free? I watch you. I imagine you turn around."

Out of the corner of my eye, I spotted a streetsweeper headed toward Decatur. "You get home okay from here?" I asked without turning around. She understood.

"Yeah. Sure. Sorry." I caught the tail of the truck, and left Felly behind like a warning. I didn't even hear her cry.

"Freely you have received, freely give," Father Mobley said from his truth-telling pulpit, Sunday morning. I often went to church after a murder. Something about the candles and waxy floors. I had trouble looking at the cross, with or without the suffering Jesus. I had trouble looking. It wasn't painful, just a focus thing. Even before I dove through the stained-glass window. My church of choice was St. Patrick's Cathedral on Camp Street. It was close enough to the French Quarter to walk and far enough from the decay to feel like an escape. The cathedral had recently been restored, and the black-and-white marble floor glittered. I closed my eyes. The wooden pulpit fanned out like a crab shell, and behind it were three giant murals. Jesus took up most of the space, glowing in one painting and walking on the water in another. He seemed happier then. The organist shouldered into another hymn as I headed for the exit. All the newness bothered me. I had liked it better when rain made its way through the patchwork roof, and the organ sounded like a crying child. The bell still didn't work, replaced by a recording of chimes. They'd sealed off the tower for repairs and then never did them. I saw St. Lucy and St. Anne with their glass eyes and tired faces. They seemed to see me too. St. Theresa guided me out the door, and I landed on my feet under a big black moon.

With too much time on my shaking hands, I headed to Cheng's dwelling. I'd copped the address from his driver's license. Two buses and a transfer to reach the shack, on Numa Street in the middle of Algiers. I knocked six times. The glass in my head shifted. Candy in a box. The last thing I wanted to walk in on was a chicken-stuffing voodoo dance. I listened for feathers. No answer was an open invitation. I used his keys to get in, wiped my feet on the mat and entered. Two quarts of milk and some rock-solid pudding in the Coldspot refrigerator. A half-melted ice-cream bar in the freezer. Tasted good. The rats were quiet as the March morning, and I moved room to room, making noise to confirm my presence. It appeared that Cheng lived alone. Nothing feminine around. Nothing interesting. Except for a bottle of twenty-year-old scotch. I poured it down the drain. Never drink a dead man's liquor. Eat his ice cream, but don't drink his liquor. Caught a glimpse in the bathroom mirror of a lunatic. With my hair poking up like razor stubble over the scar, a three-month beard and a crisscross face, I broke out laughing. Sweet, cackling, curdling laughter. I was booze thin, and taller than I'd remembered. I seemed to be growing out of myself. Trying to shed what was dead. I couldn't keep my eyes open. The tears plopped onto the dead Chinaman's sink. I laughed till my ribs broke wide open, and I sat on the toilet. Crying, laughing, tugging at the long hairs on my chin.

I fell asleep in Dao's bed. I'd even slipped into his pajamas, too small, and brushed my teeth. I looked at the empty bottle of scotch on the way out and regretted my stance on dead men's liquor. He had an envelope stuffed with cash under the mattress. I took half of it, in case he had relatives, and jammed my pockets with the two hundred dollars. It was way too much to carry around, so I put it all back, save a twenty spot. I never liked having money. It meant people would be after me, and I preferred being alone.

Cheng didn't make the obituaries. I had expected that. He was an in-betweener. In between cultures, in between jobs, in between chances. And in-betweeners didn't get obituaries or funerals. They just got buried. Fast.

I dropped in on Felly to see if she knew anything else about the dead man. And for something else. Felulah was nowhere to be found, so I dug through her things. Her address book had six names in it. Three of them were high-paying local johns. When they got sick of listening to their high-society wives detailing Uptown shopping sprees, they took Felly out, so they could bore her. She was the vessel of their rage. These ugly gentlemen were layovers from her hooking days. Some habits are hard to shake. Especially when they pay so well. She also had the name of her former madam, Miss Camille Arnaud. Miss A. was notorious around the Big Easy and equally invisible. And known for her beauty and cruelty. There were always rumors around about uncooperative tricks winding up at the bottom of Lake Pontchartrain. Only the fish knew for sure. Street talk was that she could be anyone, and if you saw a beautiful woman in the Quarter, you called her Miss A., just to cover your tracks. She'd gotten two mayors elected and countless others excited to run. I'd never gone in for politics, but after eight o'clock on election nights, a polling booth was a great place to catch a few hours of sleep.

Felly also had my name written in, with no address, of course. It was scrawled in pencil, in a hurry, and fading to a light gray. It had been a year and a half since I'd made Wong's my new watering hole. Clary's had gone under, and I was hard pressed for a place to drink free in the city. Dent caught me one night cleaning up the service entrance and offered me a drink. He thought I was working for a finger of whiskey, but I was just trying to make a bed for the night. He made me an offer: that if I kept the back area clean, he'd keep my tongue wet. Of course, I never cleaned up again, but Dent felt good about his charitable work, so I became a regular at Wong's. Felly had just started work as a stripper. She said I was cute. It was the one thing I'd never been accused of. She was skinnier back then, worn thin by businessmen's fantasies and her own abandoned dreams. She had the crooked smile hookers wear when they're slipping off their boots. But with time, Felly's edges rounded off. She turned soft to look at and touch, and her smile had crumbled into a leer. It kept the customers confused and Felly off her back. Most of the time.

Felly came in as I shut the book. "What you doing, cutie?"

"I'm not cute anymore, Felulah."

"Going through my things?"

"Yes," I admitted.

"Well, if you find anything interesting let me know, because my life is so boring right now, I could vomit. I need a man. To take care of me." She laced her fingers around my neck. She smelled of bubble gum and scotch.

"Don't tempt a confused man, Felulah. It's not fair."

"You're a little funny, that's all. You're still the same. You're not so confused." Felly prowled the room, a caged cat.

"No one knows."

"Not even you?"

"Not even me. I went there. I slept there. In the bed," I admitted. I didn't even know why I was telling her. I was in the mood to confess.

"Whose bed?"

Cheng's. The dead man, I wanted to say. It wouldn't come out. "It doesn't matter. Nowhere. Forget it."

"The other night," she managed. "The other night I'm sorry. I shouldn't have told you."

"There's a lot of things we shouldn't do."

"The way you caught me from the car. Saved me. I just haven't been held like that."

"I didn't do anything."

"That's what I mean."

"I have to go."

"You always have to go, Free. You're always going and I'm always staying." Felly fell into her dressing-room chair, with its torn pink cover and blistered cushion. She crashed into it, powder exhaling around her legs. "You're always going. I'm always staying." I searched for a word, a key to set her loose from this room and this club. To never see her again. To know she was anywhere but here under the dull glare of strangers' eyes. "You're not taking me with you?" she asked, knowing the answer.

"Where am I going?"

"Yeah. Where are you going?" I headed for the door, but her call stopped me. "Free," she said too softly for me not to hear. I turned. Felly pulled her hair back, letting the pale skin of her face and neck hum in the bare-bulb room. "Will you stand still?" I nodded yes. "I don't know why," she said as the buttons came undone. "I don't know why, but I don't mind. I just don't know why." Her shirt dropped to the floor, and she paused for a moment. For the first time, I didn't look away. For the first time, I took her in. She stepped out of her shoes and peeled her jeans like skin. One last motion, and she stood before me in all her newness, in all her perfection. There was no music. No writhing, no wanting, no lust. There was no stage or props or distance. There was just Felulah, reborn.

We didn't move. We didn't touch. "Thank you," she whispered. A single tear appeared. "You have to go."

"I . . ." I was out of words.

I decided to go back to Cheng's nickel hut in Algiers. Maybe I'd grab a shave and another ice-cream bar. No. I'd eaten his last one. The bus ride was full of bad memories I couldn't quite get a hold of. A sense of unease, the backhanded slap of the past. Bullets. Two bullets. One to put 'em down, and one to keep 'em down. It was running through my head like a nursery rhyme. A couple of stoolies and a lost tourist were my only company.

"Like voodoo?" I garbled to the tourist. He was tall and wickedly thin. He kept moving seat to seat, mercury without a thermometer.

"Too hot," he returned.

"Never too hot for voodoo."

"Don't like voodoo, if that's what you're getting at, Willie." I got the feeling he called everyone Willie.

"Don't have to like it to want to see it." He was in the back of the bus by then, and I had to yell. "I said you don't have to like it to want to see it."

"I heard you, Willie. Quit bothering me. And give me a shove when we hit the Quarter. Wife wants one of those cityscapes inside the glass. Shake it and it snows."

"Doesn't snow in New Orleans," I finished, but he was already asleep. The horseshoe indentation on his chin gave him away. He was missing a chunk of himself. His neck began to betray him on the bumpy roads. The Adam's apple spinning around, a whirling dervish. "Doesn't snow."

"I heard you, Willie. Just wake me when it's time."

The bus stopped, and my thin tourist was fast asleep. I left him there, his mouth yanked open by some trampling dream. Better asleep on that bus than punchy on the streets of Algiers. Look who was talking.

Cheng's place had been gnawed on by hungry hands. The bed was gone, so my planned nap got scratched. Every bit of silver, wire, feather, straw, anything the witches could use for a gris-gris had been harvested. Once the word got out, a dead man's belongings were part of the community, and they knew how to put raw material to use. I found a pair of scissors under the toppled refrigerator. It had been dropped suddenly, the result of lazy thieves. The blades were rusted together, so I broke them apart, a metal wishbone, and trimmed my beard. Just down the sides, with the original whiskers remaining. The sloppy mustache and long goatee were too close to my mouth, so I threw the blade in the tub and started to leave. As my foot hit the porch, something collapsed inside the house. Turned out to be a bookshelf tucked away in Cheng's closet. Mostly Chinese translations of American novels, or so it appeared. American full-breasted women on the cover, nearly impaled by the Chinese letters shouting the title. Books by great unknown hacks like Mack Pendleton, Strafe Bennet and Loring Montrose. The spines were unbroken. Maybe Cheng enjoyed paperback cover art. At my feet were five books in English. A Dr. Seuss story, an account of the Civil War and three books on meditation. Buddhist meditation. It was no surprise that an immigrant would hang on to his past. *Buddhist and Taoist Practice in Medieval Chinese Society, Questions of Milinda, The Tao Te Ching*. These were books of the mind and soul. Maybe Cheng was warding off voodoo spirits. Maybe he was looking for himself. Whatever the case, this was no junkie shooting pool in a strip joint in N.O. My dead hairless friend was looking for something. And so was I.

Amazing grace, how sweet the feel of a pistol, a .38, cocked to shock. Loaded, aimed. Two shots. One to put 'em down. One to keep 'em down. The chest? The head? Freedom of choice is what made this country land of

the bullet and home of the gun. You can breathe now. Go ahead. I dare
you to breathe. (Quip, quip. Dead-on laugh. Same) sound of blood gur-
gling out of a wound. Like in the neck. Like a kiss you keep on giving.

My dwelling at 327 Bourbon Street was free. At least until
someone found out I was living there. Not much living, just
sleeping, getting out of the sun. Nothing anybody could object
to. The building had been condemned for two months prior to
Cheng's death, but the zoning wheels spun slowly through
political mud, and so I had a place. The trick was coming in
and out at low traffic hours. I used to jump out the back
window. It was only one story, and my legs had been bent so
many times they'd become elastic. But since the church fall,
heights weren't my favorite level. Walking up stairs had become a victory. A struggle I didn't need or appreciate. Still,
squatters didn't often get the pick of housing, so I held my
breath, closed my eyes and crawled into my secret. An old
train station bench was my bed, padded by a torn car cover
I'd found in the alley behind Baronne Street. From on top of a
Mercedes to underneath a sleeping man. I tried to read
Cheng's books as I curled into sleep around nine, but I faded
off. I faded off. I faded.

1. Having abandoned the practicing of violence toward
   all objects, not doing violence to any one of them, why
   wish for a friend? Let one walk alone like a rhinoceros.
2. There are friendships to one who lives in society; this
   our present grief arises from having friendships; observing the evils resulting from friendship, let one
   walk alone like a rhinoceros.

5. As a beast of the forest prowls, free, whithersoever he will for pasture, even so let a wise man, observing solitude, walk alone like a rhinoceros.

10. Let a hero, abandoning the ways of the world, and also flinging off the bonds of the household, walk alone like a rhinoceros.

18. There are cold, heat, hunger, thirst, wind, sun, gad-flies, snakes; having overcome all these various things, let a man walk alone like a rhinoceros.

Walk alone. Like a rhinoceros. Cheng's legacy had me thinking. Granted, I could only connect with five out of the forty-one credos in the Buddha's *Rhinoceros Discourse*. Still, I was glad to know I was closer to being a monk than I'd ever imagined. Not that being a monk had any interest. But being halfway to somewhere beat being nowhere. No violence. No friendships. Freedom through solitude. A hero. Overcoming nature. Walk like a rhinoceros. I pictured myself on all fours walking the streets of the city, shunning violence and weather, to be completely and finally alone. Alone I was. More alone than a rhinoceros. Cheng hadn't shunned violence and wound up on the Dutch end of a bullet. He lived alone. He died alone. Like a rhinoceros.

My mind swelled. The glass inside my head pushed and shoved. Pieces of Jesus and shards of Mary. My stained-glass crown resting so uneasy beneath the skin. I was in over my soul, and I needed a drink. I snuck out for early mass.

The sun was bald and quiet as it muscled over the spire at St. Patrick's on Camp Street. I stuttered into a back pew. The cool vinyl of the hymnal felt sweet against my hands and face. The sanctuary was peppered with winos, repenting hoodlums and students preparing for exams. The priest on duty was afraid of my road-map head and handed me the wafer and wine from arm's length. The wine flamed into the top of my chest, where it always stopped. At my heart, I guessed. I fell feet first into the morning. Cars were doing their Saturday waltz. Women locked their doors as I approached. Walking alone. Like a rhinoceros.

"Ever read any Buddha?"

"Never seen him." Dent's consistency steadied me.

"No one has."

"Told you."

"Hey, Dent, do you believe in God?" I was certain of what he'd say.

"Yes." Maybe not.

"I guess you've seen him," I added jokingly.

"Yes."

Back in Felulah's dressing room, I juggled a few candles till her morning shift ended. Spraying her perfume under my arms and behind my ears, I began to feel lighter. I needed to eat. I grabbed her overcoat, walked out onstage, and threw it over her like a prizefighter's robe. The customers were too bombed to care. They thought it was part of the act.

"Have her back in twenty," hummed Dent.

Felly and I took a streetcar to the lake and sat under the Southern sun. Dogs and Frisbees dominated the landscape. The freshly cut grass spiked into the back of my neck. Felly was close enough to kiss, and I wanted to kiss her, but I couldn't. I wanted somehow to vanish with her, maybe into the clouds, and protect her from nothing. Go to a place where we weren't who we were or what we did. We just existed, outside of everything and everyone else. But I was afraid she wouldn't want to come. And even more afraid that I wouldn't want her to be there with me. I looked at her coolly. I moved back, out of kissing distance, out of touching distance, out of harm's way.

"I haven't been feeling well," Felulah whispered as she pressed her hand down till grass shot up between her fingers.

"You always feel the pull after Mardi Gras," I hoped. "It's the change in weather, the end of a season, the removal of all desires."

"Removal of all desires?" Her face crumpled like a sheet of paper.

"Buddha. Never mind."

"I didn't know you were into it."

"I'm not." My words turned to vapor in the heat. "Just some reading. You remember Cheng."

"They got another one last night," she deadpanned.

"Another one," I repeated. As if I already knew. As if I already knew.

"By the back entrance. Blew the little guy away."

"Dent didn't say."

"He didn't want you digging through the garbage. I wasn't supposed to tell you, but I don't see the difference. Anyway, the bulls cleaned it all up. It's over." She bit her lip until it nearly bled. "Maybe I need a change." She waited too long. "Would you take me away, Free? Do you need a change? I don't mean love or anything, but you'd be good to me. And I could get honest work. Would you take me away?"

All the air spilled out of my lungs. "Felulah," was all I could manage.

"I just need a push to do it. Something to call me out of this shitty life. This godforsaken city. You know, something big, like a hope or a vision. Do you believe in visions?" I didn't answer. "My grandmother used to have visions. Before people died, or bought furniture. All types of bizarre visions. That's really all I need. A little push. A vision. Or maybe just a friend. Like you, Free." She looked through me, around me, on top of me and underneath me. My blood began to dry up. "What are you afraid of? It's just me. It's just talk. Dreaming. I still think one of my dreams is going to come true."

"Everybody needs a change, Felulah."

"Yeah. Everybody but you. You're all fine just by yourself. You don't even talk to anyone at all. I guess I should feel lucky to have your attention."

"You shouldn't feel . . . I'm a bum, Felly. That's all I am. I don't have friends. I don't believe in friends. There's nothing there."

"You never let me tell you about my vision."

"Your grandmother," I answered.

"No. My vision. Mine."

"I don't want to hear it. I don't deserve to hear it."

"It's me. I'm somewhere. I don't know where it is, but it's snowing. And it's warm. Warm like Spring and Dogwoods and Magnolias and it's sweet, sweet Spring. And snow." I tried to block her out. "There isn't any sound in my vision. But I'm laughing. I can feel myself laughing. The snow is falling into my mouth. And it tastes like tomorrow." She was building to a frenzy, an explosion. I knew if she got to the end she'd leave us both in pieces.

"Come on, Felulah. No one cares."

"There's a church, not a church really, but it looks like a

church, and I can see someone standing on the steps. I can see him so clearly."

"Don't."

"He's happy. And he's laughing too. But when he opens his mouth, I can finally hear. And he speaks to me. To me. And all he can say is . . ."

"Shut up," I hammered. "Just shut up, Felly. Shut the hell up."

She took my command like a punch to the gut, and stood up, heading for the parking lot. It was filled with cars I'd never own. Cars that would never take me anywhere. Not to a place or even away from it. Nowhere. I was going nowhere.

"Felulah."

"Don't say you're sorry, 'cause you're not. I don't know why I put myself through this. I know you don't care if I'm even alive or not. I don't know why I keep thinking. I guess I just don't have visions like my grandmother."

I grabbed her by the arm and spun her around. We were too close.

"I do care. I do think. It's not how you said it. You are too good."

"I'm a stripper, Free. I used to hook. I'm not too good for anything. I'm not good enough for anything."

"Don't have visions of me. I'm not worth it. I'm nothing. It's like I'm not here. Don't you get it? I'm invisible. You are the one with the dreams. The visions. Have them. Somebody will take you away. You don't want me to take you anywhere. I have nowhere to go."

"Isn't that for me to decide?"

"Do you want to hear my vision?" I seethed. "Do you, Felulah?" I said her name like a curse.

"I have to get back."

"It's me. I'm somewhere. And there's no sound. But there is a gun. A loaded gun."

"Goddamnit, Free, let me go."

"Felly," I called after her, hoping she'd ignore me. Hoping she'd come back. "Felly."

"Do you love me?" she hollered. I didn't even know what the word meant. "I love you," she said.

"You don't love me." I was sure.

"You can't tell me that."

"You don't know me."

"Goddamnit, Freeman. Isn't it enough?! Isn't it enough punishment? Haven't we taken enough?" She wavered, and almost disappeared. "When is it time to just go home?" I had no answer for her. "When is it ever going to be time?"

"Felly," I said to myself. But like everything else, she was gone.

Felly was right. The cops had scoured the kill site. No bullet count or ID. Nothing to tie the murders together except location and race. Coincidence is a tricky fish. With more than one billion in China, a few boatloads were bound to spill onto the Gulf shores. But two kills outside a quiet, barely break-even strip joint. Fingers were pointing every which way but right.

The security guard wouldn't let me into the city library. The homeless were notorious for snatching a few hours in the reference section. So I rode the streetcar to Tulane, where I had a better shot at fitting in. The March air felt good against my scar. The windows of the streetcar opened onto the beautiful homes of St. Charles Avenue. Houses I'd never live in. Houses I'd broken into. I recognized at least five that had given me shelter during their owners' vacations. The soft beds, crisp sheets and full refrigerators of the wealthy. I always did the laundry before I checked out, rearranged the fridge, covering the empty spots with pickle jars and beer bottles. I didn't want my hosts to feel invaded upon their return. Once I even wrote a thank-you note, but decided not to leave it.

Since I'd boarded the car, the few people sitting up front had quietly eased to the back. Some got off before their stop so they could catch another line. Even the driver peered over his shoulder, hoping each stop would be mine. I had a knack for clearing an area quickly. All the homeless did. The cops could have used us to break up riots. No one wanted to be around the remains of a human being. Especially if it was still alive.

I got off near campus and headed for the library. I rubbed my shaved head as I entered, and the university guard even said hello. Eccentric grad student, he was thinking. It took me two hours to get my eye on some information regarding the fleur-de-lis. It dated back to the fifth century when it was believed to have been brought down from heaven itself. Upon the baptism of King Clovis, an angel came down from above to give it as a special blessing from the Virgin, whose symbol had always been the lily flower. It was made up of three formal petals surrounded by a band. Other experts said the idea was a lance head in the shape of a flower. Beautiful but deadly. Although I didn't believe in angels, the idea of a gift from heaven seemed right. But it made no sense that Cheng would wear one, as a Buddhist. And now, there was another shoulder blade I needed to check.

"I'm here to identify a body." Criminal Forensics. The stench was fat as a fist, and too few white coats ran around in some unspoken panic. My lies were coming quicker now. I felt a certain grace. "My buddy got wasted outside a strip joint on Bourbon last night. They just called me this morning." A boyish technician took great interest in my jigsaw head. He really wanted to help, but I was in a hurry. "I have to see him now, you understand, because I'm jonesing." I spoke with quiet desperation. The smack-fiend angle always made the college boys jumpy, so he hustled me down the dirty steel hallways, concern in his voice.

"I can get you into a meth clinic this afternoon. And you should really have that head checked out. Looks like an infection might be starting."

"That's just my hair growing in over the scar, Doc."

"I'm not a doctor."

"Then what do you know?" He got me past a waiting line and had me in the ID room so fast I thought I was dead.

"What was your buddy's name?" His question was simple enough, but the lies were logjammed. Speed bumps. I couldn't think. "Sir, your friend's name, what was it?" Come on, come on.

"Billy. Billy Wong. I mean Chong. But that was his horse name. We never told each other our real names. He's a Chink. I mean he was. Look, he bought it outside Wong's last night around three in the A.M. I know you have him, whatever the hell his name is. Two bullets," I continued. "Through the chest." One to put 'em down, and one to . . .

"What is your real name?" he asked, new wrinkles splitting beside his dull green eyes.

"I can't tell you that, Doc. I'm sworn to secrecy. Government agent. It's for your safety as well as mine. You understand." And he did. Within minutes, he and another tech had the body in the room. I was face to face with Mr. Nobody, my best friend. Walk alone like a rhinoceros. You take comfort where you can get it, and I took comfort in the face of that dead man. I wasn't glad he was dead. I wasn't sad either. It was just comforting to not be looking at my own face. His closed eyes, flat nose, colorless lips. It was a mystical moment. He felt like my friend. As if he'd died in my place.

"Is this your friend?" The tech's inquiry died in midair.

"Yes."

"That will be all, Mr. . . . Jones," the boyish one said, smiling. Like we shared a private joke or a distant cousin. But that wouldn't be all. I needed to see his shoulder blade. I needed to turn him over.

"Can I be alone with Billy for a minute? Only a minute. Ten seconds." I negotiated downward, and it made them nervous.

"I'm afraid that's impossible."

"You're afraid that's impossible!" I hollered with rage. "I'm afraid that I'll never see Billy again. I'm afraid I will have no more friends. I'm afraid. Very afraid. I'll have no one to shoot with. Do you know what that's like? Do you have any idea?" My reflection wavered back at me off the metal door. Blood tripped under my scar.

The other tech whispered to the boyish one and took off. I had to plead before they dragged me out of there.

"Please, Doc. All I need is a minute." Guilt and ignorance flashed in his eyes. Without a word, he stepped out of the room and turned his back. I could see the back of his head through the fogged window.

I rolled Billy Anonymous over and quickly studied his shoulder blades. My fingers paused on the thickening skin to feel any upheaval, the mark of a needle, the thick clot of ink. Nothing. All this for a police escort to the sidewalk. I heard the rubber soles thumping toward me. Then my fingertips found the answer. Billy had been shot twice, just like Cheng. In the chest, just like my Buddhist friend, but unlike Cheng, one of the bullets came out his shoulder blade. I pressed my face close to the dank chill of his back. Death seemed to be tugging at me with formaldehyde hands. There it was. The vague outline of a bent petal, the very top of the bent-lance flower. The color was unidentifiable, but he wore the tattoo like a promise of death.

Listen to me. Listen to me, hush. Jefferson, I want you to listen to me. You are safe here. Always safe. Please. Hush, little baby, don't you cry, wait till the mornin' when the blood run dry. Shhhhh. Knot a word. Not a word. Not a goddamn fucking word. Where there's a will, there's a way, where there's a body, there's a grave. A hiding place. A disappearing act. Time to cover tracks. Pick up the shells. Should be two. One to put 'em down. One to . . . You know the rest. Now, get a grip and we'll bury this thing deeper than hell. No one's gonna find it here. No one alive.

Father Mobley wouldn't get to St. Patrick's till 9 P.M. He slept in the vestry the night before Sunday services. Sort of his big Saturday night out. He was the only priest I'd met who didn't drink, but he smoked Chesterfields like Christ was on the doorstep.

When I first came to the Big Easy at seventeen, Father Mobley sort of took me in. He saw me sleeping on the church steps for a week before he invited me in, so he was no soft touch. And he didn't like being called Father either. Jessup was his first name, but he was so full of his sister's Creole cooking that I just called him Sup. When he was in a good mood. His face was round and hard, a medicine ball, and his great black hands swooshed through the air when he preached. Crows in flight. I felt the dark fury of those knuckles only once, when he caught me eating communion wafers by the handful before mass.

"Son, that's the Lord's supper. You want something to eat, you wait till you get to my house. Lolly will do you up right."

And Lolly did. Six years his elder, and unmarried, Lolly cooked the classic Crescent City dishes. It was her sweat and recipes that made me strong enough to stand on my own. Jambalaya of chicken and ham on Mondays, chicken à la Creole or Mayonnaise of fish on Tuesday. Wednesday was always a blanquette of veal and strawberries with Madeira wine for dessert. Lolly could never make up her mind on Thursdays, so we went to Popeye's. Friday meant turtle soup, potato omelet and a jambalaya of rice and shrimps, with mutton feet and snails on Saturday. Sunday was the Lord's day, and we ate to his glory, with Bouchées à la Reine, creamed cauliflower, roast turkey stuffed with truffles and more coffee than a bladder could stand. I was two days shy of twenty-one when I broke away from regular eating at Lolly's table. I'd stopped going to mass, and being around Jessup and his sister just made me feel guilty. They never said a word, but I knew it was time to start scrounging for meals again. Even if it meant an empty stomach most every night.

I could almost smell the Madeira as I pushed through St. Patrick's heavy doors, and sidestepped back to the vestry.

Mobley was on his knees, so I waited till he'd finished his conversation.

"Evening, Sup."

"It's been a few spins of the calendar, Jefferson." Mobley was the only one I let call me Jefferson. Somehow it didn't seem right for a priest to call the unconverted Free.

"I have a question. A lot of questions."

"I'm off duty." His face beamed in the low light. A shiny black moon.

"Not God questions. Not really. It's about rhinoceroses."

He didn't bat an eye. "Buddhism, you're into? They teaching that at the shelter? The archdiocese won't be pleased." He was being funny. He knew I didn't go to the shelter.

"I dug this up on my own. Actually, it just sort of fell dead in my lap."

"Go on." He looked tired but just interested enough to keep me going.

"I've been reading, barely, and I want to know why."

"Why?"

"Why Buddhism? What's the point to all those words run together?"

"Simply put, Nirvana. Nirvana is the point. To stop oneself from being reborn. A ceasing of bodily existence. Buddhists believe that they never die, just pass from one body to the next. The trick is to become so holy, so detached from life, that you cease to exist. At least in bodily form. Then you reach Nirvana."

"So you must learn to walk alone," I pressed.

"Like the rhinoceros." His fingers stretched like wings as he continued. "It's a somewhat selfish pursuit, in my eyes, but an interesting one nonetheless. Are you planning on pursuing it?" Of course not, I thought.

"Yes. I don't want to be a Buddhist. I just want to walk alone."

"You already do."

"Then I suppose I am a type of Buddhist already." I was bragging. Picking a religious fight.

"A rather shabby one. Is there anything else? I need to prepare tomorrow's homily."

"I'm sorry I bothered you, Jessup. It really is good to see you."

"Come by for supper. Lolly still sets a place for you." After nine years? I almost believed him.

"Sure." We both knew I wouldn't come.

Sup was right. I was a shabby Buddhist. Face it, I was just plain shabby. And so was the connection between Cheng and Billy. I needed something. Felulah. No. Even so, she'd be off for the night, out drinking with some loudmouth numbers runner driving a newly washed Lincoln, with a wad of counterfeit bills in his money clip.

Or maybe not. Felly's vision snowed my brain. The man standing on the church steps. The laughing man, ready to say something. To make something come true. Was it real? Did I belong in her vision? Was there anything left of me to give? I hustled down to Wong's to try to find out.

Felly's dressing room was empty, and Dent had the reason. "She's gone for a drive, Free. Lent her my car. Just leave her be."

I popped out the back door, and saw Dent's taillights disappearing around the corner. Something wicked shot through me. Kicked out the window of a gold LTD that wasn't worth stealing. It had Florida plates and a box full of bait in the passenger seat. I snapped the steering-wheel lock like breaking someone's neck, sparked the wires and sped off. Two blocks up, Felly was stopped at a red light. I stayed a few cars back. I still wasn't sure why I was after her. To apologize, to talk, to finish what I'd started. To be told who I was and why I was laughing in the snow. I grabbed a lipstick-stained cigarette butt out of the ashtray and torched it. Checked my gun, the chambers full as a bank vault.

Felly took Bourbon to Canal, then hung a right. When I turned to keep up, she'd nailed me. She was waiting, engine running. She'd sensed a tail, and she'd found it. The street was dark and I ducked low. It wasn't me she saw, but the car, the strange car in pursuit. It didn't matter who was behind the wheel. Just that she was someone's evening entertainment. She buckled her seat belt, and took it as a challenge.

She swung left onto Rampart, barreling through lights, scattering people like pigeons. In a stolen car, with nothing but intuition pressing the gas, I bolted after her. I admired the darkness. I never knew Felly could push it so far. Fishtail onto Lafayette. East like a demon to Magazine. Crashed onto Howard, spun out onto Tchoupitoulas. All the way up to Poydras for a spine-stretching left, headed straight for I-10. Blood thudded against my skull. My scar grinned at the chase. I flashed her over and over again. Not to blind her, but to say slow down. It's Free. The ride's over. Nothing. Then the crash.

A man in a brand-new Cadillac ran a stop sign at Baronne and Poydras. Felly just missed his front end. I erased his ass. The LTD did two revolutions and folded around a Sycamore. It wouldn't start. I crawled out from the metal pretzel and limped to the intersection. Felly's red lights said get-away.

"What kind of asshole are you anyway?" Here came the suit. He was short and stocky, with enough alcohol on his breath to open a brewery. His nose was bleeding, but not quite enough. Decked him with a firm right, and laid him down next to the box of worms.

His Caddy wouldn't start either. I called an ambulance from his car phone, and headed back to the Quarter. That-a-girl, Felly. Hell of a job. Maybe I was in her vision. Maybe I was.

Back in familiar surroundings, all I had going for me was Billy. Check Cheng's taste in religious reading against his. I'd nabbed his address off his clipboard at Forensics, so it was time for a little show and tell. It was just past midnight, full of ache and regret, that I headed for the corner of Fourth and Prieur Street in search of Nirvana.

The rain started two blocks from my destination. It hurried down, fat knuckles of wet pounding on my head. I took long leaps to outsmart the rain. Still, its dumb drops exploded all around me. By the time I reached the lobby to Billy's apartment building, I was dipped in Louisiana wet. The main door was open, so I bounded to the third floor. My muscles were tight, lungs rubbery. I knocked. I was sure no one would be home. Even though the weather promised to keep good folk indoors, this apartment felt empty. It wasn't.

A stupid woman, holding two cats and a TV dinner, some-how opened the door. She wore a too beautiful dress, stolen off a department-store delivery truck. It sagged low on her chest, and her collarbones stuck out like cash drawers. The cats were asleep. One had nodded off in the Salisbury steak. Its breathing bubbled the murky sauce.

"No salesman," she said, nearly winking. I couldn't tell if she was flirting or getting something out of her eye.

"Hush, little baby, don't you cry." The lullaby came tumbling out of my mouth like a bad joke. "Mama's gonna . . ."

"Mama's gonna what, sugar? There ain't no apartments for rent, and I don't mean nothing by it, but you'd be a lot cuter if you wore a hat."

"Mary had a little lamb, little lamb . . ." I slapped a hand over my mouth.

The woman grinned painfully. "You haven't missed last call down the corner."

"The shape of the human head is not appreciated enough." There was an overload. A pileup behind a glass shard. A bloody thought accident, sending ideas screaming into the side of my skull.

"I appreciate it, sugar. I just got my hands full. Maybe another time."

"Billy!" I shouted like a cop. The traffic had finally broken through. The stupid woman and her sleeping cats took it in stride. One lolled over into the mashed potatoes.

"No Billy here. Try 326." She quietly shut the door with her foot, winking at me as it clicked shut. Try 326. My confusion had started with the numbers. I wanted 326, that was Billy's address. Billy wasn't his name, it was something else altogether. But with the roadblocks already wreaking havoc on my memory, I'd stick with Billy.

326. Knock-knock. This time the apartment was empty. I'd been right, just three doors short. It took me fifteen minutes to

pick the lock. It had been picked so many times that the lock runner had spun completely around. To break in, I had to lock it all over again and then lift the latch. Obviously, the cops hadn't gotten there yet. Too busy, too bored, too routine, but the place was untouched. Half-empty cans of Bud, old newspapers, girlie magazines. Billy's taste in clothing ran similar to mine, but he stood a full foot shorter than I, so I wouldn't be picking up any bargain items. There were several jackets, with the linings ripped out, and pants as well. Plus soleless shoes scattered like road kill. I found a New Orleans Saints hat, with its fleur-de-lis design, and took the stupid woman's advice, pulling it over my bristled head. It felt strange. There was too much air between the top of my head and the inside of the hat. Room for things to hide and live. I took it off, and tossed it beside a large gray canvas bag. It was unmarked and newly bought. Inside, there was more heroin than I'd seen in a lifetime. Great sand beaches of heroin spilling out over the zipper and disappearing into the addicted carpet. My heart collided with my ribs, and another one broke. I was not excited. Horse wasn't my flavor, and a drug arrest meant a long time in Angola. It was a hotel I'd managed to avoid for too long to get caught with some dead man's dope. I zipped the bag and waited for footsteps. For a billy club to the back of the skull. For my head to split open like a July watermelon and spill its black thoughts like seeds. I slithered around the studio apartment looking for anything to tie Billy to Cheng. No books on meditation. Nothing on medieval Buddhism. No rhinoceros. Under his mattress, I found the first connection. In a light blue envelope a nice chunk of money was hidden. It seemed close to a grand, and also inside the envelope was a Louisiana driver's license, a

Louisiana ID and an American passport. I was about to open it, when the bulls came.

In great herds their black cleft feet pounded into my head. They were on the second floor. I grabbed the bag of horse and poured it out. It snowed at my feet. I grabbed magazines, letters, books, the last two beers, a sneaker, three packs of Marlboro Menthol and an address book. I even took his phone.

The door fell flat, and the shine of badges lit my way down the fire escape. Bullets and thunder guided me toward the street. I jumped the last sixty feet and landed in a pile of blue ruin. No cop in sight. They'd either gotten stuck on the heroin or were coming out the front entrance. I was double right. I splattered the ground in my salty Thom McAns and bolted down the alley behind Derbigny. My feet were changing. I felt a tightening with each thundering step. They were swelling into the wet leather, darkening, hardening. The pain bulleted up my legs and set my knees on fire. I hadn't removed my shoes, it seemed, forever. I felt the laces wrapping up and around the ankles, burning into the flesh, trying to lock me down. I stopped before they exploded.

Under cover of an abandoned pharmaceutical company sign, I dug through the bag, tossing out items to lighten the load. My hand fell upon the fleur-de-lis sewn onto the Saints cap. I yanked it on and took off running. With my lungs and feet a bonfire, I switched to another source of power. Fear. I ran as only a frightened man can, hurdling fire hydrants, park benches and potholes, an outlaw Olympian. By the time I'd realized I was alone, I was lost. I snuck on the first bus I saw and wound up displaced at 8 Royal Street. I was only blocks from my hideaway, but my feet wouldn't allow me another step. I howled inside my head, a dying beast. It was close to midnight, and I stuck my soaking feet into the bag. With the wind at my back, I fell asleep in the doorway of a barbershop.

"Off your ass, killer!" My eyes shot open. I was two feet from a police officer. Caught. "You heard me. Nap time's over. Find another hole to crawl into. Mr. Wassem has to do some regular business. Respectable business."

"Mr. Wassem . . ." was all I could get out before the cop kicked me hard in the thigh. "Mr. Wassem lets me watch the place for him at night."

"Beat it, punk. And get sober. You smell like the state of Tennessee." His compassion was sobering enough. I hobbled off, the imprint of his boot merging with my skin. The dampness had left me stiff. My ribs had melted together. They ached as one. With a few found quarters, I bought a Sunday paper and a cup of coffee. Sitting on the softest curb I could find, I let the sun wake me all the way up. The black wool of the cap circled heat around me. I was glad for it and was slow to take it off for fear I'd never get it back on.

There wasn't a word in the news about Billy's murder, or even any investigation pinning Cheng's death to his. I was really working under cover of darkness. But on the back page of Metro, I saw it. I'd finally made the papers. Not officially, but I knew it was me. This was the kind of publicity any smart man avoided: "HEROIN RING BUSTED—SUSPECT FLEES SCENE," the headline trumpeted. The cops loved to congratulate themselves. I poured a lifetime supply of drugs at their feet, and they claim they busted a ring. But a headline. I was a suspect. The suspect. No description, but seeing the word so square and black on the page made me nervous. It was time to go home.

Home is where the heart is. Or in my case, where the car cover was. But now, I was truly homeless. Some Housing Authority officials had found my little dwelling and cleaned it up. They cleaned me out. The entire second floor was ribboned off as unsafe, and all my belongings, even Cheng's books, were gone. I crawled over barricades to sit by the window that had been my nighttime city view. The rain had stopped, but the puddles still shimmied under tires and a little boy's stone. I'd escaped from Billy's with twelve porn magazines, two blue movies on cassette, a few letters, but no obvious connection to Cheng. Were they working together? They sure didn't seem like partners. Cheng the monk, and Billy choking the monkey. I kept digging. The letters to Billy were from Hong Kong. Billy's IDs looked good, but, like Cheng's, they were probably fake. I rubbed the fleur-de-lis on my hat as I opened the letters. They were written in Chinese. My eyes blurred. The glass stood up and saluted in my brain. Words, characters, they grabbed each other in nooks and crannies, dancing off the page and out the unpainted window. They hadn't been stamped or sent. They were addressed to Billy, written, but never mailed, only handed off. One thing was clear. Each letter was sealed identically. Three formalized petals surrounded by a band. The quiet violence of a fleur-de-lis.

Frère Jacques, frère Jacques, dormez vous, killed him too. Aim. It is all about aiming at the target, pulling the trigger, you understand aim, don't you, Jefferson. Um-huh. Yessir, right again. Dead aim. Focus, see the

bull's-eye, enemy, hatred, let it go. Just let the little bastard go. Easy as
pumpkin pie. Surrender. It's all so much easier if you'll just surrender.
Then you'll be free. You are free.

"Felly? Felulah, it's Free."

"Nothing's free, Sharkey. Not even me." Mae had her
breasts pressed up against my back. She had a way of making
an empty room feel like a crowded bus.

"I'm looking for Felulah."

Mae's fingers spider-walked the back of my neck and
kneaded my scar.

"Felulah told me about your head. How we missed you."

"You didn't visit," I offered, spinning out of her web. Few
things were more terrifying than an aging stripper in full com-
bat dress.

"Duty calls. Dance, they shout, and dance I must."

"You're so committed to your work, Mae. It makes me
proud to know you."

"We really did miss you."

"I need to talk to Felly."

"So does every man in this bar." Her jealousy seethed.

"I really do. It's important. We're friends. No, we're not."

"Remember, Free, you told me there ain't no friends worth
having that ain't dead, and no friends worth killing that ain't
enemies." She was right. I said that twice. To Mae and . . .
I couldn't remember.

"Mae, don't listen to everything I say." My eyebrows
started to peel off. My lips receded, and my head made a
sudden left turn.

"You should maybe lie down in my dressing room. You look

awful. Dent, could you pour Free a nice hot cup of joe?" As Dent poured, I could hear the coffee waterfall into the ceramic. I heard his knuckles crack, and the wild splash of liquid spilling over the edge. Everything got tiny. I cupped Mae in my hand and flicked Dent across the bar with my pinky. I swallowed the stage whole, spitting out the nails and lights.

"Come lie down in my dressing room." Mae's words hurricaned through me, and I fell down in between. They dragged me into her dressing room. I remember the fiery smell of perfume and sweat as I tumbled off toward sleep.

"He's coming apart."

"Too much running around. Look at his head, for God's sake. It's about to crack wide open." I sat up with a jerk, a jack-in-the-box.

"Felly," I hollered, and passed out.

I woke up laughing like a child. Mouth closed, chuckles leaking out between upturned lips. I was alone, and I didn't need the mirror to tell me that I was running out of time. The years, months, days I had left before all the thoughts got tired of the nicks and cuts. When it would be easier not to think at all. My body was already preparing me for that day. Tingling hands and shoulder, an almost permanent cramp in each foot as they folded back upon themselves, slowly and surely. And the visions. Flash points of memory and make-believe. Words and shapes I just couldn't quite pin down. Patches of invisibility. Shreds of myself. There were times I couldn't think at all and other times when the thoughts came so fast they severed at the point of release. Sounds and images wrapped in gauze, and still the fall. Always the fall out of St. Patrick's.

It had been a too cold night in December, just before Christmas, and the church was filled with signs of the season. Advent angels hovered over the altar, keeping a close eye on the manger. There were three-legged camels and crooked cows stuffed into the tight section allowed for the crèche. Hay peeked out from under the animals' feet, and everything looked right, but there was no Mary or baby Jesus. Even Joseph, bearded and robed, carved in silent wood, looking happy just to be involved, stood by the cradle, but no mother and child.

Mobley was in a panic, because the Christmas Eve service was only a day away, and without the statues, it seemed like there would be no Christmas at all. Cries of vandalism and burglary could be heard throughout the parish. Mobley even came to Wong's to ask me if I knew anything about it. He assured me there would be no charges pressed, but I had nothing to say. I was drunk and very sad that night. Cold weather and the familiar face of a bartender can break a man's heart in two around the holidays. So I went back to St. Pat's with Sup. Told him I'd help him look for Jesus and Mary. He knew I'd be in his way, but if it got me off a barstool, he'd make it work.

We tore that church apart, looking under every pew, lifting each starchy choir robe, spying behind every saint from Peter to Alphonse. Not a sign of the Christ child. The idea that Christmas would go forward without the baby Jesus seemed more than I could bear. I stole up to the balcony to think and cried myself to sleep.

I awoke on Christmas Eve morning. The sun through the stained-glass windows splashed diamonds of light onto my face. My head was still thick with drink, and I could barely open my eyes. It was then that I saw them. Jesus and Mary. She was holding him in her arms tenderly, her pale face smiling over the babe. I was so glad to see them, to have finally found the meaning of Christmas for Jessup Mobley, that I ran to greet them. In great bounding strides I ran.

As a child, I had been told that stained-glass windows never break. They're built strong to keep evil out. But I never heard that they were strong enough to hold a bad man in. So as I opened my arms to hug Christmas, I smashed through the stained-glass window of Mary and the baby Jesus and spiraled two stories down. A fallen angel. The impact jammed so many pieces of glass so deep into my head that removal risked serious brain damage. I liked to think that carrying a little part of Jesus around in my head would protect me. But I was running out of time, and the ideas were lumbering now. Wide and cautious, prepared for disaster. Reminding me of something. It wasn't Mary and Jesus chatting, planning, plotting to overthrow my soul. Not the dreams of a homeless man bubbling to the surface. It was something I'd done. Something I was doing. Something I was about to do. Again. It was all about to pop. Like firing a gun. The way a bullet separates bone from skin, muscle from tendon. A slow-motion bullet, tearing everything, creating its own seams, ripping a smile, a howl, a mouth of blood out of a perfect thing. Like a bullet. Like firing a gun.

They found Felly face down somewhere. I can't remember quite, but she was dead. Dent and I identified the body. The young tech remembered me.

"Hello, Mr. Jones."

"Jones?" Dent clicked, looking at me like an off-duty cop. "Just play along."

"Sorry to see you in here again."

"It's not been a good stretch for the people I know. It's a good time not to know me at all."

"She's very pretty," he added.

Tears wanted to burst. Enough to drown us all and wash us into the Mississippi. I held them off. "Just another stripper. Usually end up on the wrong side of the line."

Dent eyed me funny again. On our way out I heard a noise. I let Dent head back to the lobby. I hung around. It was the sound of a body being turned over. It was bitterly familiar. Like flipping Billy to check. To check. Slowly, I returned to the exam table. Felly's corpse was on its stomach. The room was empty. I pulled back the sheet like tearing off a scab. On the dead white of gentle Felulah's shoulder blade was a red fleur-de-lis.

Back at the strip club, I knew Dent didn't want me snooping around Felulah's room, so I spilled a few bottles of well gin when he wasn't looking. His cleanup time was my only chance. Her room was as empty as a tomb. There were even flowers on her dresser where candles used to be.

And just like that, I was totally alone. I'd been on my own for fifteen years, thirteen in the city that care forgot. Weeks without conversation, without a decent bath or a meal that started with me. Nights spent walking till even the cops went to bed. Fitful bouts of sleep ended by the hammer of a nightstick or the shrug of a freight car. I knew alone, but I'd never felt alone. It was all I was, and it was a life. Losing Felly forced me to admit that she had been my friend. If missing and emptiness is friendship, then she was a friend. Felulah

Matin was a two-bit hustler just like me. She knew alone too, and we shared that. It was the air that we breathed, the smiles we forgot, the love we never gave or had to give. And in that barren room, where Felulah's sweet imagination died, I stood. I stood in one spot. For five hours I couldn't move. The carpet was quicksand, and it held me in its grainy fingers. Felly had a vision.

The mirror hissed and glared at me. Everything stopped. I stopped breathing, thinking, hoping. The stillness was absolute. The shameful swirl of customers just beyond the papier-mâché walls couldn't shake the trance. I realized that to be truly alone, apart, separate even from oneself, was a terrifying thing. It had claws and burning eyes, a straggly beard and a shaved head. It was me. Alone. Like a rhinoceros. All I was missing was a callused horn and a desolate outback to roam. New Orleans was barren. It seemed my only choice. I jerked my hand free from my side and rubbed the top of my head. Slowly at first, just at the hairline, and then faster and harder, till the friction heated the scalp. The rough outline of a horn. My legs loosened, and I nearly fell. I couldn't bring Felly back, but I could keep this horn from growing. I had to.

I bought a pack of gum and a disposable razor at the corner store. My feet were curling. Hooves, I was certain. In the Texaco bathroom, I let the water run hot and mad. There were a few squirts of soap in the canister, and I lathered my face like a wedding cake. The razor package said Good News. Good news indeed. The whiskers came in patches at first, clumping the blades mute. But as the shaver dulled, the hair came easier, and for the first time since I'd embraced the glass Jesus, my face was new. I rubbed it for luck, a new crystal ball, and looked into my future. The sink was thick with dirty beard. Scars from the accident striped my face, but they were pink with promise and healed shut. My hair seemed to grow. I felt taller, lighter, and my feet uncurled a few inches.

Stepping into the sun was a baptism. The rays broke like water across my new skin, and soaked me from the neck up. The Salvation Army let me wash up, and gave me a flannel shirt and a 7-Up T-shirt from the donations closet. I smelled good. The hair in my nose limboed to the round odor of soap. I even wrangled a new pair of underwear and newly repaired pants from the Lord's soldiers. All I needed was shoes. No luck. The fire would rage on. I bit the white off my teeth and hoped for feet.

The buses were crowded that day, but no one was afraid. A mother in her forties took her young girl onto her lap and offered me a seat. I was weeping.

"Are you all right, sir?" She really cared. I could see the little girl out of the corner of my eye. She couldn't decide whether to rub my shoulder or suck her thumb.

"A friend," was all I could manage.

"You lost a friend?"

"A friend." I meant Felulah, but also this woman, with the Southern chin that trembled with mine.

"I'm deeply sorry," and she touched me. The flat of her palm lay on the cool flannel shirt. I could feel her life line pulse. The bus stopped. She and the thumb sucker got off. I couldn't speak. I'd ridden buses, streetcars, walked the avenues, slept in the shelters, but I'd never been touched. Felly and I kissed once, but she held her hands back, the way hookers do, and she apologized. But this stranger, with the child on her knee, had left a mark on my back in the shape of a hand. A healing hand, a forgiving hand, a strong hand held out to a drowning man.

"I'd like to see the officer in charge."

"In charge of what?" The desk sergeant at NOPD Vieux Carré Precinct was triangular. Small, pointed head, sloping shoulders, sunken hips. He was an equation I had to figure out.

"I have some information."

"You want personnel. End of the hall, turn right until you run into a wall." He thought I wanted a job. I fought back a roaring laugh.

"About a case, Officer. I think I can help. The murder of a stripper. Felulah Matin." He shuffled some papers on a clipboard. The howls and clicks of the precinct bounced off me.

"You want Li, Aggie Li is the investigating officer." And so she was. I had to wait thirty minutes at Aggie Li's desk while she finished a report.

"It'll just be a second," she said every five minutes. Her nameplate stated Agatha Li. She was a Chinese-American in her early thirties. Her skin was bright, like a Christmas ornament, and her thick black hair curtained black eyes. She typed quickly, with mistakes every other word. Her hands darted like Gulf Coast fireflies, lighting up the keyboard and pushing back her stubborn locks.

I knew cops. Better than most people know their families. Not personally, but their habits, the way they walked, when to take them seriously and when to spit in their face. Li looked too confused to be a cop. All her motion trying to make up for the fact that she didn't belong in blue. The other cops moved in orbit around her, laughing, joking, cursing. And Li just banged away at her report, hammering the minutes away.

"Now, what have you got for me?" Her words pricked, little daggers.

"I'm Free."

"Congratulations."

"That's my name. People call me Free. I knew Felly. The girl that just got . . . They said you were in charge." Her gaze never shifted. Those black eyes never moved, never blinked. "The desk sergeant said I should see you. Talk to you."

"I'm Sergeant Aggie Li, and I am looking into the murder of Felulah Matin, stripper." Clip. Clip. Clip. A news wire report. And still her eyes never moved.

"Do I look strange?" I thought aloud.

"You look fine. I just look at people when they talk. Folks aren't used to that." She was right. It made me nervous.

"Maybe I should go."

"What do you know, Free? You didn't sit here for thirty minutes for the gratis cup of coffee." Maybe I had. "Which you haven't touched."

"Felulah was my friend."

"I'm sorry."

"So am I. I don't know anything."

"Then why did you come?" Her eyes finally raised and spotted my scar, only to quickly avert. She was too polite to stare.

"I don't know about Felly, but she didn't die alone. She was the third." Aggie casually slid out a small notebook, the kind only cops use. Her pencil hurried, then broke. She eased out another.

"The third," she repeated.

"Two Chinamen. Two Chinese guys. Is that how you say it?"

"Chinese is fine."

"And then Felly. They all had the same tattoo. A red fleur-de-lis."

"A red fleur-de-lis." She wrote without looking down. I didn't know how much to tell this black-eyed Susan. "How do you know this, Free?"

"I'm not a suspect. I came here of my own free will. For my friend, Felulah. I can't be a suspect."

"Calm down. It's okay. I just want to get everything straight." I started regretting my decision. I wanted to be back on the bus, beneath the warmth of that mother's hand. She changed tactics to weaken my resolve. "What happened to your head?"

"I fell out of a church."

"Oh."

"Look. I know it sounds weird, but I just know they all had tattoos. If you look in the morgue, you'll see. They all died at or outside Wong's. You must think there's a connection."

"We've been unable to tie the murders together by anything but location."

"And they're both Chinese," I added.

"Yes." She was wondering how I knew.

"This could get really complicated, but if you trust me, I can help you. And you can help me. You see, I'm alone. Like a . . . never mind. Are you a Buddhist?" She blinked at the suddenness of the question.

"No."

"Anyway, I can tell you things I shouldn't know. Do you understand? But it's not because I'm involved. I'm not a suspect. I just pay close attention. And I'm a regular at Wong's. Not for the girls, just to drink. Dent lets me drink. I just know

things that can help you. But I'm not a suspect. I can't be a
suspect."

"You're not a suspect," she repeated without a trace of
encouragement.

"I'm not turning myself in."

"We'll see." We'll see, she said, and it felt good. Better
than the doctors at the hospital saying of course you'll be
okay. Of course you will. Of course. She only believed me a
little, but enough to listen. We'll see. We'll see.

We reached Cheng's hut in Algiers in the squad car twice
as fast as public transportation. Li didn't trust me enough to
sit up front, so I got chauffeured. I stared through the iron
mesh that separated us, the lawless from the law. You'd have
to come apart to go from the back seat to the front, go to
pieces. Aggie's shotgun pointed at the ceiling, and the radio
buzzed with crime. "219 at Chartres and Gallier. Officer
needs assistance at Superdome. 414 at Franklin and Robert
E. Lee."

"Doesn't that radio drive you crazy?"

"Crazy," she deadpanned. I knew what she meant. The
smell of the cop car, the way it squealed around corners, the
death rattle it did over bumps and potholes brought back
memories. "Ever been in one of these machines before?" she
investigated.

"No," I lied. "You?"

"My first time too. Nice American ride, though. I think I'll
take it."

"I can get you one cheap," I kidded. It felt good to walk
along the wire of a joke. It had been too long.

"I bet you could." She had me relaxed, so she moved in for
the kill. "How did you get mixed up in this murder business?"

"I'm not mixed up."

"You sound pretty mixed up."

"Just drive," I shot back. She was acting ungrateful and cocky.

"I'm the one with the gun. Just remember that."

"Drive," I repeated, fingering my hidden pistol.

It had been a week since I'd dropped the scissors in Cheng's tub, and everything was gone. It was as empty as Felulah's dressing room. The looters removed a few walls, and the nails that held the floor down. The fridge was gone, gouges in the kitchen wall announcing its awkward removal.

"While the body's still warm. We already scoured this dump. Looks like the Mothers will have enough Goofer Dust and Man Root to spook the whole bayou."

"You didn't find his books," I announced. "Cheng had hidden bookshelves in the closet." We double-checked, but even they were gone. "Books on Buddhism."

"Are you a Buddhist?" Aggie asked me with an unwanted smile. It seemed funny to her, and neither of us knew why. Her teeth were crooked, a small train wreck.

"Can't figure it out," I whispered, footing the tubless bathroom tile. "They didn't take the tile."

"Maybe they don't like things in black and white."

Billy's apartment was already up for rent. Aggie got the landlady to let us in, and the stupid woman came to her door as we passed through the hallway. She didn't recognize me. I stroked my clean face.

"You policeance come and chasin' me tenants. Prospective tenants," the landlady complained. As if she ran a five-star hotel.

"Shut up, Dolores, or I'll close you down for so many code violations you'll be back in Havana rolling cigars for Castro."

Once inside, I heard the thunder of the bulls, saw my fire escape exit, the shadow of heroin by the couch. Dolores left us alone. I felt like a SUSPECT. The headline typed itself onto the wall.

"I suppose you were here too." The prospect of drug charges shut me up. "Freeman?"

"No. I came to the door, but I didn't go in."

"Why not?"

"It was locked."

"Spare me."

"I'm not a suspect."

"How can I trust you if you won't level? I could have you arrested for breaking and entering right now."

"First of all, you don't have a witness, and second of all, I don't need to be here. I didn't have to bring you back here."

"I already knew about this place. And I could take you in on a confession. The Cheng shack."

"I wasn't under arrest. No rights were read." She thought for a long minute.

"Did you really fall out of a church?"

"At least I go to church," I fired back.

"So do I. It doesn't mean anything."

"Then you shouldn't go," was my quick response. She was starting to like me.

"You ought to have that head examined."

"I've heard that before." We both looked at the scary carpet. "I was in the paper. I was the one who jumped out the window and ran away."

"You are the heroin ring?" she said in shock.

"I told you, it was curiosity. I'm clean as clean," I said, showing her my trackless arms.

"I was here. Why did you run?"

"I was in a dead man's dwelling, going through his things, plus all that smack. I was sitting in the gator's mouth. I had to run."

"You lost me by that drugstore. I don't get lost easily." There was a sudden feeling of dark respect. "Who are you, Freeman? What do you do?" I didn't know the answer to either question.

"I'd seen that Cheng and Billy . . ."

"Billy?"

"That's what I call him. They both had the tattoo."

"So did your pretty friend."

"I didn't know."

"I guess you never watched her work."

"Felly knew how to take care of herself anyway. I was never worried about Felly. Didn't seem like she needed anybody. I guess I didn't look close enough."

"It's okay," Aggie reassured. I leaned over to puke, but nothing came out. "Let's grab a bite at Antoine's and talk this through. You're lucky I didn't catch you the other night." She was right. I was lucky.

Antoine's served the best oysters Rockefeller in the city. I never knew Rockefeller, but I silently thanked him as each bitter pearl slid down my throat.

"I haven't eaten like this . . ."

"Looks like you haven't eaten at all. You're way too thin for your height. How's your health? Where do you live?" Aggie was getting personal. To a homeless man, the place where he stands is his castle.

"Antoine's. I live at Antoine's."

"Come here a lot?" she asked, full of doubt.

"Only when I'm invited." We ate Shrimp Cardinal, and
drank German beer as dark as Aggie's eyes. For a moment it
was my castle, and I the short-haired king.

"The fleur-de-lis is the main thing. Where did they get it?
Why on the shoulder blade? Why red?"

"Some kind of symbol," I said. It felt good to swap hunches
at last.

"Or a signal." She had a piece of shrimp stuck on her lip.

"Felulah didn't know these guys. Except Cheng. She knew
him for two weeks before the kill. Your lip." She wiped it off,
her black eyes flashing embarrassment.

"I need to get back to the precinct. We'll talk more tomorrow." But we wouldn't. I could see the lie. She let her hair fall
into her eyes, and her neck was tight with dishonesty.

"Agatha," I called her. "You'll check your leads, make a
few calls and forget about this whole thing. Two aliens and a
sweetbread stripper get bumped, and it's just another day."
My voice pumped out, gasoline onto fire. "This was nothing to
you today. Tapping a junkie's phone line to get some dirt. Buy
him a meal and hope he shoves off. But I'm not a junkie, and
I know this is bigger than what you want to see." I was nearly
standing, and she pressed her hand on mine, guiding me back
down. Her palm was sweaty.

"Freeman, forget it."

"My friend is dead."

"You're scared. It's natural. Let me take you home." It was
a moment where pride had always stepped in before. I'll walk
was the standard answer. It's just up the street, out of your
way. I'll call you, don't call me. These were the salvation
words of the shamed man. But sitting in that fat restaurant,
surrounded by all that cotton and leather, the song of the

silverware, the security of idle chatter, I could muster no pride. I was too lonely for bravado. I wanted her attention. At least long enough to figure this out. I was seeing fleurs-de-lis everywhere I turned. I kept feeling my shoulder blade for the gentle rise of a lily just etched. But I couldn't reach far enough, and I was afraid I might be the next. I stared at her, tickled my scar and whispered. "I don't have a home."

"Are you in one of the shelters?" Her concern was flat.

"I haven't had a home for fifteen years. I don't have a home." And that was enough. Five words that guaranteed at least enough sympathy to keep me around her. For a while, or long enough to bother her into digging deeper. Long enough for me to feel like I wasn't alone. Her hair swept back, revealing the wonder and sorrow of a woman who knew lonesome. We shared the air for an instant, and then she spit it out. Yet in that moment, my feet uncurled a little more. My back straightened and the horn receded. Detective Li took me in. Like Mobley had when I was a middle-aged seventeen-year-old, Agatha Li came along at the perfect moment. It didn't seem like a perfect moment. Born more out of necessity than anything noble, I allowed myself to be taken care of for the first time in a decade.

St. Agatha was one of the earliest saints. She was a beautiful woman who refused marriage with a powerful governor in Sicily. She was martyred. Agatha was the saint who protected homes from fire. I had no home, but I was burning down, and this New Orleans Agatha was saint enough to try and douse some of the flames. She took the rest of the afternoon off and drove me to Charity Hospital for a checkup. As was often the case with the homeless, they'd "misplaced" my file. In the trash can, I was sure. So we had to start from scratch. New

forms, new nurses, new doctors. And Aggie Li was patient as
a flood, sitting in waiting room after waiting room. She read
fourteen magazines cover to cover. Everything from *Women's
Wear Daily* to an undated *Popular Mechanics*. Aggie had a
hard time convincing them of the urgency.

"Do you want me to smack him with my gun? Then his
head will rip open and you'll have to do something."

"With all due respect for yourself, Detective Li, and for the
patient, without a present danger . . ."

"Feel his head," Aggie growled, grabbing the nurse's hand
and dragging it across my head.

"Oh, my," said the nurse, losing color.

"Oh, my is right. That bubble you feel is getting bigger. I
assume it's full of pus and broken glass. Or am I overstepping
my medical expertise?" Aggie was a terror, running wild over
the poor young woman in white.

"Pus is as good a guess as any," the nurse managed.

"Get this man a doctor!"

"That's really not my decision."

"Do it!" The nurse tried hard to smile, but her face had
frozen. Aggie's black eyes could immobilize a person. So began the endless process of being bounced from test to test,
needle to needle, all due to the kindness of strangers and the
guts of one lady cop. They gave me two vitamin shots and an
enzyme injection.

"Your body is a car, Mr. Freeman. Car can't run without
fuel." The nurse who said this was built like an Olds 88.

"Don't get to do a lot of grocery shopping," I offered. She
didn't care for excuses and rammed me hard with the injection. A doctor, or so I guessed by his easy manner and thick
hair, drained the pus from my head. He put a bandage on my

head and took me into his office. The walls were sparsely filled with diplomas and degrees. He didn't look as smart sitting down.

"Do you want your guardian to hear this?"

"I don't understand."

"Detective Li."

"She's not my guardian. She's just . . . I'm helping her with an ongoing police investigation. She needs my head in working order. She's not my guardian." He had gotten my quills up.

"I can call her in."

"No. No, just you and me, Doc. I know what you're going to say." I was sure I knew. They'd said it before. A few empty lines of good intentions and hope. A pat on the back on the way out. Everything will be all right. Standard doc talk. I knew exactly what he was going to say. But he didn't say it.

"We have a problem."

Fire. Almost. Now, fire, fire, fire, fire. One left, but you're still doing it wrong. Sonofabitch, what the hellsafuckinmatterwithyou! See her. See her. Aim at her. Her head. Chest. Anything. Relax your hands, and let me get in around, and now . . . Goddamnit, somebody's going to have to answer for this mess. Mother? Pick up the goddamn phone it in and write it down. Just so you don't forget. It's so easy, so routine, so elementary, elemental, like blood. Just like blood. Don't cry over spilled blood. Don't cry over blood, don't cry over spilled blood,

"Good news, I hope." Aggie looked less like a cop, and more like a . . .

"Good news." I was just repeating her. I liked the sound of those two words together. Mobley talked about Good News on Sundays. The kind of Good News that didn't shave but saved. But that wasn't good news the thin-lipped doctor had told me. So I latched on to Li's hopefulness, and got in the squad car.

"Bet you've spent more time in a squad car today than you'd want to in a lifetime."

"I need work, Detective."

"Let's get you a place to sleep first. Is there a shelter you like the most?"

"I don't go to the shelters. Except for a pair of pants or such. Maybe once a year. They don't like me there. I don't want to get off the streets. I'm making it without them, and that pisses them off. They like to feel necessary."

"They are necessary, Free."

"Yeah, I guess so. I'm not worried about sleep. I need a job."

"Money."

"I've been getting it here and there, but . . ."

"Not legally," she said matter-of-factly.

"I just need a job."

"I pay my snitches one-fifty a week. If they're honest and consistent. That fit the bill?" I caught a chill like a punch.

"I don't snitch."

"You know too many people, right? It could be dangerous for you." That wasn't the reason. I didn't know anyone.

"I don't snitch."

"Then I can't punch your ticket. You got to work to earn."

"How about just this case? I do legwork, help you get another stripe on your sleeve. I already know the angles. I just needed a quicker brain. And the law don't hurt."

"I can't pay you one-fifty. The captain needs to see results."

"Just meals. I'll find a bed, even if it means the shelters. Aren't you curious? Heroin, illegal immigrants, tattoos."

"Crime is not interesting."

"It's your job. You don't like your job?"

"I like it fine." She was lying. She'd have been just as happy helping homeless blood jockeys with infected heads for a living. Reading those magazines, waiting hopefully, taking charge, that was her thing. She wasn't on some lady power trip to bust people. She was a good person who wound up a cop.

"I won't get in the way. It'll help me pass the hours faster than sleeping in St. Patty's until mass."

"You go to St. Patty's? I didn't know it was still . . ."

"So it's downtown. You probably go to church outside the city. You know, God didn't move to Metairie. He still likes New Orleans. There's plenty of sinners to keep him occupied." We drove for ten minutes without a word. I was trying to picture the suburbs. Houses, lawns, cars but no people. I couldn't see any bodies no matter how hard I tried. Aggie's hair crouched around her face. I could just see the bottom of her chin, beaming out of the darkness.

"Okay." Okay was all she said. Okay. I had my first job. I wanted to punch my fist through the roof of the car.

"Thank you, Agatha."

"Thank you."

That night, I went to a shelter. Desire had nothing to do with it. I preferred the steady bones of a park bench to the uneven squeak of shelter cots. Somehow I always woke up sore. And with the late-night crazies wandering in, celebrat-

ing invisible victories, it was Mardi Gras every night. I went
because I'd promised Aggie. I hadn't broken a promise since
I was a boy, but I hadn't made any either. I guess I stayed
there as a sort of test. If I could keep my word, maybe some
good news would start coming my way.

There isn't much community in the streets. People are
fighting for beds, for decency, for the very last hair on the
dog. I don't dislike the other travelers and DPs, I'd just rather
stay to myself. Less said, less trouble to get into. I'd seen
death shake its rattle over bottles of whiskey or arguments
about art and philosophy. I liked making my own trouble on
my own terms. Keep everything in front of you, and you never
get chased. Shoot before you get shot. Don't be afraid to pull
the trigger. I had learned that years ago. One of the few things
I'd carried with me beside my gun. But now I'd changed the
game. I was working for someone, with someone. There were
new rules. Rule number one, keep your word. That's how I
ended up tossing and turning all that ugly night. At least it
reminded me of why I slept on the streets and in abandoned
buildings. There's great comfort living outside the lines. Not
physical, but mental, maybe even spiritual comforts. My
memory was as jagged as my scars, but I recalled Sup Mobley
talking about living outside the lines. Nowhere to sleep, nowhere to eat, but going on. Following a greater . . . good. Or
a greater bad, danger, murder. Still, it pulled you forward,
kept you alive.

Around 4 A.M., I went into the back alley to grab a smoke
and a minute alone, away from the hacks and rampant insom-
nia inside. An oval-shaped woman strolled up to me and took
a seat on an upturned trash can. She had beautiful white hair
pulled tight into a bun, and her clothes bore the brown scars

of street life. She was new to the area, to the Quarter. Thirty years before, she had made men cry. Now, only she cried. "You're lovely," I said, exhaling a nicotine rain cloud.

"Are those your teeth?" Her voice was the sound of falling rocks.

"Yes, they're my teeth."

"It's good to have all your teeth. What are you?"

"What do you mean?"

She scooted closer. "I mean, what do you do? Are you anything? Does anybody miss you tonight?"

"No," I said flatly. "I'm just a bum."

"Just a bum," she said. It sounded like a prison sentence. She had something long rolled up in her hands.

"Show me what you've got."

She folded to her knees like a bandodeon, and laid out a collection of ragged drapes stolen from every transients hotel in the South. On each she had made a crayon drawing. One had the face of a young girl. Self-portrait? Another showed a vase full of flowers, roses maybe. The pictures were crude and childish, worn from years of traveling, rolling and unrolling, her museum in motion. Still they had the undeniable beauty of creation. They were hers and hers alone.

"Ten bucks."

"You know I don't have any money, ma'am."

"Gambling money? Nothing? Panhandling?"

"I don't beg."

"My name's Leigh. Wait here." She had my complete attention, but she stood and walked away. "Say a prayer for me, cowboy. I'm flying away." She folded her paintings up as she backed away, and stumbled into the thankless night. "Wait here," she said again.

In the morning, a trio of scrub-faced college kids cooked us water-swelled pancakes that bounced and barking sausages. They were so proud of doing their part. I didn't know who I felt more sorry for, the homeless or them. I drank enough coffee to ricochet my heart around a few hundred times and reentered the comforting danger of the city outside. I fought my way past the twenty-four-hour drunks and beggars. These were men and women who somehow managed to stay lubricated every waking hour. A sort of dark fame went along with it, a filthy awe among more sober street dwellers. They looked up at me with toothless, hopeless faces and begged. I wasn't much for beggars or drunks. I didn't believe in retreating from the horrors of life. If you resigned to live on the streets, it took just as much concentration and discipline as any other way of life. I can't say I never enjoyed the pleasure of washing the night down with a bottle of booze, but as a daily habit, it turned my stomach. I'd smelled every smell a man or woman could collect. Seen open cuts the color of Japanese plums, body parts hoping to fall off to avoid the shame of being attached to such a destroyed owner. I'd seen eyes cloudy with glaucoma, tongues swollen up like carpet rolls, yet I still believed in the possible dignity of the gutter. Self-preservation until the day it all went away. Lazy, sloppy living made me hollow, and I left the shelter behind with no regrets and no plans to return.

I took a quarter out of a musician's hat and called Li.

"Where do we start?" she said professionally.

"The tattoo. I'll steal a phone book and score all the tat shops I can. Today and tomorrow. I'll call you when I'm done."

"Steal?"

"How else am I going to get my hands on a phone book, Detective?" I knew she was smiling with those serpentine teeth. "And, Detective?"

"Yes, Free?"

"Under what, I mean by what authority, oh, screw it." I already knew the answer. I'd been lying longer than she'd been a cop. And with the new shave, I could be anybody I wanted to be.

"Howdy, Detective Mark Falgout, NOPD."

"Ken Martin, insurance investigator."

"Stephen Nagel, district attorney's office."

"Kyle Curry, tattoo-needle salesman." And so it went, up and down, north to Lake Pontchartrain and south to the river. I poked my false face into every hole in the wall that had a sharp stick and some ink. Not everybody bought my line. I wound up on the rubber side of a boot a few times, but for the most part, I did my job. I saw more fleurs-de-lis than I thought could possibly exist. Maybe I was seeing double. Big ones, small ones, multicolored, glow in the dark, backward, sideways, on the heads of snakes, the tails of fish, on every dime-store tattoo design from Algiers to the lakefront. I even found one in a Cracker Jack box. I threw it away.

It was near the mighty Mississippi that I noticed the short guy. He was no taller than a mailbox, perfectly designed for his career as a tail. I'd heard footsteps and seen a reflection at the last few shops, but as I turned this corner, I doubled back to see him shuffling behind. His hands were buried in a shabby navy-blue overcoat, and he wore a hat like a fifties gangster. I nearly laughed at his size as he burrowed past me down the street. We both knew he'd been nailed. Now, I got to follow him. We walked less than fifty yards apart, gun-shy duelers, for three hours. He hated to believe it, but he knew I was relentless, stepping on his shadow, trampling his hopes. He didn't exactly circle, but he finally wore out and popped into a no-name joint for a beer. I sat down two seats away. Only a round, stubble-covered chin rolled out beneath his hat, and he took his beer like bad news. It felt good to be tailed. Somebody was paying attention to me, tracing my steps. I didn't know who he was, but I toasted him from down the bar. I was important. I was somebody's job. Follow Free, they told him, and he did. It wasn't so bad being followed.

I finished my Dixie and slid the empty toward my short friend. The bottle hit his elbow, but he didn't move. I stood and took a few steps his way. Take off his hat and reveal the stranger, I thought, but he was out the back door before I reached his stool.

I spent two more days searching the streets and shops, and no sign of the little blue man. I kept whirling around to catch him removing his hat for one stupid, identifying moment, or checking the sky for rain clouds. I began to obsess on that round chin with the five days of pepper, catching glimpses of him in car windows, magazine covers, postage stamps. I got dizzy looking for this ghost, never finding him, always sensing his image. There in that puddle, up on that rooftop, wrestling a squirrel, a robin, a fox. Maybe he'd been fired for incompetence or transformed into a tall, thin woman with voodoo-brown eyes and a purse full of bones. Maybe if all the cars stopped, I could hear her rattling up behind me, I could hear him swinging in a tree. It wasn't so fun being followed.

By the time I'd toured the entire city, it seemed everyone was watching me. I'd been stared at for years, but these eyes said something different. They weren't amazed, amused, even afraid. These eyes knew where I was coming from, what I'd eaten, where I was headed. They knew who I was and what I'd done in the dark. These eyes were on the back of my head, and I couldn't shake them, close them or tear them out. Too many eyes. All looking for the same man.

Then I saw Jefferson's eyes. I was in an alleyway, looking in garbage cans out of reflex, when a two-dollar bill slapped against my shoe. I hadn't seen one for years, and I stared at the man on the bill. Thomas Jefferson, the man I'd been named after. I felt caught, like I'd let him down. I'd never wind up on a piece of currency. I hadn't amounted to much of anything. He seemed to know it, peering out from the green frame. His thin top lip curled in disgust, fluffy sideburns, white curly hair parted down the middle, high collar protecting him from the likes of me. "I'm sorry I didn't turn out much," I told him. He kept on staring, his eyes unmoving. "I don't tell people Jefferson is my name. No one knows. A few people." On the back, countless men stood in fancy dress doing something for freedom's cause. Fighting, writing, dreaming of freedom. I laid the bill exactly where I'd found it. I didn't want his eyes burning a hole in my pocket. I watched the Gulf wind steal it, drawing it upward, a tiny kite.

My tongue was dry. I kept sober on the job. That was rule number two. I was making them up as I went along. My voice was too hoarse to talk to Aggie, so I dropped in on Dent. Once inside, first stop was the men's room. That's when I heard it. The noise was going down in the handicapped stall.

"We're going to be quiet for a while. Get the picture?"

"Promises were made. This isn't a child's game. A bloody rainout." The voice was foreign, maybe British.

"Three dead is enough of a sign, don't you think? Relax.

Have yourself a vacation. New Orleans is an easy city to fall
prey to."

"That wasn't the purpose of my expedition."

"Maybe it's time to rethink your associations." The voices
were hushed, but I heard every secret word. I wanted to see
their faces, but in this deep, an ID could have meant a bullet.
I stared straight ahead, reading the nonsense scratched on the
dull brick wall. They shuffled out and saw me. I heard them
stop. The bare bulb stung my vision. I tried to talk my way out
of it, but the sound came to a helpless, gravelly halt. Last
thing I saw was the wall hurrying up to meet my face. Saints
Rule, it said. Saints Rule.

*Turn to the left. Turn to the right. Don't forget his fingerprints. Honey,
it's just how it is. Nothing here for you. Now, run along. Get. Get going.
Catch a train to somewhere before dark or there'll be dogs and troopers on
your peach fuzz in a whole lot of hurry. 'Cause this time you really gone
and done it. Jesus hisself couldn't plug up that hole.*

"Freeman? Freeman! Can he hear me? I don't think he can
hear me."

"He's been in and out of it all afternoon. He asked us to
call you."

"You did the right thing. Free?"

"Don't hurry him, he'll come awake fully in time."

"But she's read every magazine in the hospital," I pushed
out.

Aggie was standing over me. "Do you remember anything?"

"I remember everything. I just have to remember it. You know?" The wall had broken my nose in two. It rattled when I talked. The impact had also opened the bottom part of my head scar, and bandages were wrapped over the top of my ear. "Hear no evil, smell no evil," I joked, feeling the new gauze.

"Free, who did this?"

"I don't know, but I went to all the tattoo shops. Nobody has one like ours." She held my hand as I continued. "Close, but none so detailed at the base, and nobody would do it in red. Plus, I had a tail."

"No." She seemed sure.

"A little fire hydrant with a blue trench coat and a thrift-store fedora."

"Free, let's wait till your head's clear."

"You can ask him yourself. I caught him. We had a beer together. He's not working for you, is he, Agatha?"

"You had a beer with your tail?" Aggie said, unbelieving.

"Not actually with him. Anyway, I think I shook him. Unless he was the guy who gave me the third nostril. Do you know him, Ag?"

"Slow down, Free. No one's following anyone. This is a simple investigation. And no, of course not. Of course he's not working for me, this mystery tail. You're just groggy."

"Yeah. That must be it. But I think this tattoo has something to do with Hong Kong."

"Hong Kong?" I hadn't told her about Billy's letters from Hong Kong. I'd forgotten the whole connection until the wall shook it loose. It cost me a straight nose, but my head felt clearer. The room was cold, and I sucked air hungrily through my mouth.

"Hong Kong. You have to find out . . ." I was drifting

again. Aggie looked tall and white. Far away like an iceberg. Her hand turned frigid.

"We'll talk when you wake up, Free. Go to sleep. Go to sleep."

"Find out," I spat. Blood filled my mouth. "Find out if Felulah ever went to Hong Kong."

"You knew her, Free. Did she ever go?"

"I only knew her a year, year and a half." The blood rushed out of my mouth. It felt like drowning. My tongue folded as they suctioned me to safety. "We weren't really friends. I never let her . . . We didn't talk about anything like that."

"Let him sleep, Detective. He's draining like the Mississippi." Aggie let go. She floated out of the room like a popped balloon. Everyone's head shrunk as mine swelled. I passed out.

"All I know is that I didn't recognize the voices, and one of the pugs was foreign. British or something. British."

"You're sure." It was two days later, and I was finally alert enough to hold a real conversation.

"I'm sure he wasn't American."

"British fits with Hong Kong," Aggie said, leaning over her coffee. The steam rose and separated at her chin.

"Did you check about Felly?" The bandages strapped across my nose held it in place. It wanted to disengage any minute.

"No one was talking. Your bartender friend was a broken record."

"Never seen her, right?"

"Right. I mean, the woman stripped in front of the guy every night for eighteen months and he's never seen her."

"That's Dent."

"You look like hell." The way she said it made it seem all right.

"I'm okay. You're not married." My sudden switch surprised me. I'd been staring at her hands, and to my crooked brain, it probably seemed natural as rain. It surprised Aggie too. She folded her fingers and spoke into her coffee.

"No, I'm not. Where did that come from?"

"Sometimes the thoughts high-jump over the glass, and get to my mouth before I'm ready. That's all. I just wondered."

"Never been married," she volunteered. "You?" I laughed so hard I dropped my doughnut. Her smile ended the conversation. Like a rhinoceros, I thought.

"Freeman, I need to tell you. They found a dead Brit two blocks from Wong's this morning. He didn't have the tattoo on his shoulder blade." I was more than a little surprised, but Aggie slapped me back on track. "It was on his left hand."

"The Brit I overheard. He must have been looking for protection. Promises were made."

"What type of promise?" Aggie asked.

"Billy had a bunch of letters from Hong Kong with the identical flower as the seal. That flower's coming from Hong Kong. These ducks are getting marked and mailed from Hong Kong." The thoughts were weakening again. "Billy had a bunch of letters. Bunch of letters."

"Slow down, Free. Take it easy." She wiped the sweat off my brow with a torn napkin. My nose slipped right. "The question is who is doing the hit."

We need to go to Hong Kong, I thought. Slowly the words formed. "We need to . . . go . . . to . . . Hong . . . Kong."

"I can't do that. The whole department's buzzing over this now. I'm just part of a team looking in from the outside."

"But you have me, and I'm not. I'm not for sale." She knew what I meant. This was our promise. Rule number three, never back out on a deal. She slid me three hundred dollars in an envelope. "I thought I was getting one-fifty."

"Let me do the thinking. We can't go to Hong Kong. It's too visible, and what would we look for?" Her eyes fluttered. "We really need to get a look at those letters today."

With Billy's letters from Hong Kong, we dropped in on the University of New Orleans' Foreign Language Department. Professor Caine Mordenne was waiting for us, which is not to say he was looking forward to our arrival.

"I hope I can help you," he mumbled through his tired beard. He wore no mustache, just a thin gray strap of hair. He read the letters, pausing only to mutter or occasionally giggle. Apparently Billy had an interesting pen pal. But when he finally looked up, he seemed puzzled. "I don't know what you want to obtain from these correspondences." His volume twitched and wavered like a bad AM radio station. Aggie and I leaned close, bumping shoulders. "They miss him in Hong Kong. 'Come home soon,' says his sister. They seem harmless."

"These are letters from his sister?"

"Yes. Mary is her name."

"Strange name for a Chinese," Aggie said.

"Not quite as strange as Agatha, Detective." Mordenne smiled. He was so happy with himself, I wanted to whack him with a shovel.

"We're investigating a murder, Doc. A bunch of them, and these letters could hold some clues, so if it's not too damn hard on you, could you take this a little more seriously?" I jabbed.

"All right, but I still fail to see how one's personal letters . . ."

"When you're dead, Professor," Aggie said, "nothing's personal." Mordenne shifted in his chair and looked at his watch as if it were a life preserver.

"Goodness, I have a staff meeting across campus in five minutes. I'm terribly sorry."

"We're sorry you'll miss it too." Aggie's toughness was like a good meal. "Now, look closer. What stands out, even in the most minor fashion?"

Dr. Mordenne leaned back into the letters. "There are some rather explicit directions, but they don't pertain to anything in New Orleans. He seemed to be doing some traveling."

"Give."

"For example, after a nice, flowery section . . . 'We miss you, the New Moon Festival was such and such,' and then this: 'Don't forget to pick up souvenirs for everyone. The best place to shop is at Drillo and Gilbert. To get there, take the second right after McGee Avenue until you reach Parker Court. Then ask for directions. They'll tell you how to get to the shop.' But you see, none of these streets are in New Orleans."

"No name of the shop?"

"Just these rather specific directions with unfamiliar street names. He must have been coming from somewhere else. He just happened to be unlucky in our fair city. Do you know that crime has nearly tripled in the last year and a half in the greater metropolitan area?"

Aggie gave him that no-kidding look and he shut up, re-membering she was a cop. "Can you translate these letters by hand, Professor?" she asked harshly.

"I hardly have time to do police work, especially when it's so inconsequential, but I could check to see if some of my grad students want to give it a go."

"I'll expect them tomorrow by three. I'll be by to pick them up myself." Mordenne's jaw dropped like an imploded build-ing. "I'm dead serious. Three o'clock." And with that we were gone. No thank you or goodbye.

"What's the big deal about tomorrow, Ag? You heard him. They're not connected."

Aggie turned on me in the parking lot. Drizzle couldn't cool her concentration. "Don't you get it? Those streets are codes. Billy wasn't some globe-trotting tourist. This was his only stop. And those letters were written before he ever left Hong Kong."

"Codes for what?"

"That we'll have to figure out. Once we get the translations, we'll have a much better shot at it. Poor Professor Mordenne will be up all night translating. Let's see if we can dig up some parking tickets to hold over his head. These college types are always good for a few hundred bucks."

The computer showed that the good professor owed more than seventeen hundred dollars in parking fines. "Wow! I'll give him a buzz from the precinct, and I doubt we'll have any problem getting those letters translated on time."

"So are we dealing with some kind of dope drop-off?"

"Looks like it, considering the amount of smack left in his apartment. The souvenir shop probably supplies or finishes the deal. Maybe IDs are involved too. The question is, if they did come to Wong's to see Felly, why?"

"She was clean," I hurried. "She never shot a bag in her life."

"Okay. Relax."

"Maybe it was cash too," I said, thinking of the envelopes beneath both victims' beds. "Once we get the translation, we can trace the dump sites and tie things up on this end." I was excited but wrong.

"The chances of breaking an erratic code like that are near zero. But still, Billy left us with something in his will. Something we didn't really have till now. Clues."

As we thought, the translations did nothing but frustrate. One little note did make us smile. Each letter had the words "burn" or "destroy" hidden in the text. Billy was supposed to torch his mail. Professor Mordenne sent along two UNO T-shirts. It was his way of saying he never wanted to see us again.

"Aggie, we can draw his fire." The thought intrigued her, but I lost the words. I pounded the table till they sputtered back to life and willed them over the hump. "We can draw his fire. You're Chinese." That was it. That would make it fly.

"I don't speak Cantonese or Mandarin."

"It doesn't matter. You don't have to. Show up at Wong's. Ask around about Cheng, Felly. Yeah, ask for Felulah. Tell them you were sent to ask for Felly. You'll be in the area, say. Around the block, in the bar. Be available."

"They'll come after me?"

"Once you get the tattoo." We both knew it would work. It hurt to think so hard for such a sustained period. Jesus dug in. Mary cut me again.

"I'll have to get clearance. I'll have to tell Captain LeMaire more than I have."

"It's okay." It bothered me, but it was important. "Get

backup, get what you need to be protected, just don't make a lot of noise."

"I need to think about this, Free. This is my life I'd be playing with."

"You're a cop. Don't pretend you don't do that every day. Don't pretend you feel safe with me. Or I'll do something to remind you that you should be afraid."

We wound up at Darian's Tattoo Parlor on Airline Highway, and started looking for the fleur-de-lis. There were tigers, naked ladies, tigers on naked ladies, naked ladies on tigers, the Koran, Superman, peace signs, but no fleur-de-lis.

Out came Darian, a man of singular stature. He was disproportionate; a large head with small features, a huge chest, stork legs and enormous hands. Hands that hold a man down when angry. "What can I paint for you folks?"

"I am looking for something in particular, and this is Angel." Aggie was all whored up. Fat red lipstick, a blond wig, stake-through-the-heart high heels and a dress cut up to her belly button. "Darian, my friends recommended you. Maybe they were wrong. But I don't have time to look around."

"What'll you be choosing, Miss Angel?"

"A fleur-de-lis." I'd done my research when I'd been on the scout before. Darian's had the only design in town close to Cheng's, Billy's and Felly's. The tips of the outside petals were a little sharper, but I'd get him to adjust. "In red."

"I only do it in black," Darian stated before catching my eye. I felt a wild surge below my eye sockets. "And red," he stuttered. "Black and red. You want yours in all red?"

"Yes."

"You got it, Angel."

It was a beautiful and excruciating experience watching

Darian paint Aggie forever. I felt sorry it wasn't me. Not because I wanted a tattoo or wanted to be a target, but because it would have hurt me less. Aggie's face was still, yet beneath the skin a grimace was forming, and her whole body spelled it out.

"Almost done, Angel."

"You have a gentle touch," Aggie lied. This cop dressed as a prostitute had the gentle touch.

Felly's apartment. In the grief of the moment, and the trips and turns of the police investigation, I'd forgotten. She hadn't lived alone. And since she had a roommate, a young girl named Kate or Kelly, the place wouldn't have been raided by cops or looted by night crawlers. I'd finally have a chance to see what Felulah was doing in this deep.

"Who is it?" the voice wavered.

"Free. Detective Freeman. I was a friend of Felulah's."

"Friend or customer?"

"This is official police business."

"Bullshit. Besides, she don't live here anymore."

"I know, honey. She lives with the angels now. Could you please open up, before I get a court order." Best two words for getting a whore to let you in. Court order. Katie Kelly, that was her name, and she opened the door like she was opening my heart. Very beautiful, very quiet, very exhausted. She was a quadroon, with the perfect mix of ingredients. She was every dessert I'd ever been denied.

"You don't look so good, copper."

"Had a fight with the wife. Can't take meat loaf every Thursday night for more than five years. Understand, Katie?"

"How do you know my name?"

"We got a file on you thick as a brick, Miss Kelly, but this ain't about you. Some of our men missed a few things when they were checking out the joint. Won't take but a minute. Coffee would be nice." I had to squeeze the trigger fast while the muscles still worked. Katie made me a cup of instant. It tasted like sand. "Shame about Felly. She was a cooperative score."

"What exactly are you looking for, Jim? I can help you get out of here quicker."

"Got a Johnny on your spot, Miss Kelly?"

"None of your business."

"I'm afraid it is my business. Maybe another time." I was nonchalantly leafing through papers, books, clothing.

"Hey, that's my collection. Maybe I should see a badge or something." I turned on her faster than a crooked judge.

"Listen, Kelly girl, I just want to do my job and get out so you can do yours. Don't piss me off."

"No hurry," she softened, throwing a leg my way.

"Thanks for the offer, but I ain't got the time, the cash or the stamina."

"Too bad, Jim. I like a man with scars." I took a stack of papers, a few books I'd never read, more than my fair share, including a couple of T-shirts I could use. Katie threw me a kiss hard as prison bars. It almost broke my nose again.

Feeling guilty for too many lies and something unspeakable, I busted in on Mobley during a session meeting. His staff, weary from the battle, barely turned a head.

"We're almost done, Jefferson. If you'll wait in my office." Patience always scared me. It reminded me of all the other important things going on that I would never know or understand. Patience made me feel small.

"My friend died, Mobley."

"You admit to having friends? That's a long stride from our last chat about rhinos. You're getting fickle in my old age."

"We used to be friends, didn't we? You, Lolly and me?"

"Sure. I think we still are." His fingernails were dirty. He'd been digging up carrots in their garden for Sunday dinner.

"I don't know. I'm all confused."

"Looks like somebody confused you," he said, pointing at my nose.

"Rabbit ears, Sup. Always gets me in trouble. I'm not sure why I'm here."

"A friend died." I knew if I cried, I'd bleed all over his floor. I bit the inside of my cheek and swallowed hard. "I know it's wrong. I know it is to lie and steal. I want to know if it's okay."

"If it's okay to lie and steal?"

"I have trouble speaking, Sup."

"I'll be patient." Patient.

"If it's for a friend, even a dead friend, is it okay?" His knees seemed powerful and ready, as if he were about to spring high into the air.

"You're thinking about justice."

"I don't know, Mobley."

"You don't want to go to jail."

"I'm not going to jail, I'm just doing things I don't understand because . . . because they're right there to do."

"You're doing what comes naturally."

"No. I have no idea what I'm doing." I was desperately hoping he could understand me through the code.

"Look, boy, you know what you're doing. The same thing you've been doing since I was young enough to care about you. Surviving. Fighting back boredom like some mortal enemy. You'll fight anything, anybody, just to prove that you are alive. Well, I've got news for you. Whether you try to tackle a freight train or lie in a hammock drinking scotch all day, you're still alive." He pressed his thumb on my nose. "Hurt? That's proof that you're alive. I'll do it again. I'll smack your glass head to prove you're alive. Come here. My old black hands don't move as fast as they used to." With steady steps he backed me into the corner, his violent sermon spanking off the ceiling, his great crow hands flailing about my head and face. My words were stuck, and my tongue useless. "I'm not going to hit you, Jefferson. That wouldn't be okay. But for God's sake, man, haven't you taken enough blows to get the message!?" There was anger in his voice. Anger at me for being broken, anger at God for leaving such a giant task to such a simple man.

"I have to go," I managed. My nose hammered with pain.

"No, you don't."

"I have to go." He put his finger, wide as a thumb, over my mouth and walked me toward the bed he kept for Saturday nights.

"I'm going home, boy. Lolly's expecting me." I lay down as if in a cradle, surrounded by hay and dumb animals. The great hulking priest tucked me in like a real father.

"I'll try not to bleed on your pillow, Sup."

"This is a church, Jefferson. You can bleed anywhere you want."

Whiter than a thousand oceans,
Greener than a thousand seas,
Bittersweet the salty potion.
Drown your sorrows at His feet.

At His feet, child, at His feet,
Where the holy ones do meet.
Bittersweet the salty potion.
Drown your sorrows at His feet.

I have lived a thousand murders,
I have died a thousand deaths.
I have shaken loose the girders,
I have breathed my final breath.
In that hour of sweet forgiveness,
Sweet forgiveness I have found.
Taste the grace that Jesus gives us,
Child, we are glory bound.

Whiter than a thousand oceans,
Greener than a thousand seas,
Bittersweet the salty potion.
Drown your sorrows at His feet.
At His feet, child, at His feet,
Where the holy ones do meet.
Bittersweet the salty potion.
Drown your sorrows at His feet.

Lovely service, don't y'all think? Thank y'all for coming. Potato salad. So young! She's just so young. So much promise and so pretty. Always smelled so good. Do you think he'll ever? Will he ever be the same?

In the middle of the night I awoke. Guilty. The entire church was empty. Mobley didn't let anyone stay overnight. First thing in the morning, the bent rush of streetwalkers, junkies and travelers would crash through the open doors, but not yet. I tiptoed, trying not to wake the saints. They were already awake. The same expressions on their bronze faces, candles cold around their robes. I circled the sanctuary, eyeing each one. They didn't seem to want to be there. Trapped icons, ready to break free. All that heaviness, spilled wax and Catholic tears eroding their feet. Especially in the dark, they seemed lost. I wanted to take them somewhere they belonged, but my head was clumsy and they were too much to bear. The light in the balcony was broken. I grabbed a handful of candles and Mobley's lighter.

I hadn't been to the balcony since the fall, and as I neared the window in the blackness, I almost kept walking. It seemed natural that I repeat my mistake and tumble down through the new Jesus and Mary. Something stopped me. I lit the candles inches from the window. The hole I'd opened had not been repaired. There was thick brown cardboard taped over the void, the job done in a hurry. A slim draft snuck around the edges and flickered the candles. Two blew out. The patch started at the chin of a shepherd, like he was being punched. It shook straight down to the innocent foot of a mule looking on. The hoof was amputated. The tail of Mary's covering pointed out from beneath the bandage, and at the top, the sky had fallen, except for the star that guided the punch-drunk shepherd in the first place. And there, standing in perfect silence, whole in every way, was Joseph. Joseph, almost smiling, and still waiting for Jesus and Mary. His staff shone bold blue in the candlelight, and he looked important standing next to all that nothing. His wife and God's son had disappeared in a violent embrace, but he never knew. He never knew.

It began to rain outside. A sort of sideways rain that

knocked against the cardboard. It needed to get in. With the candles fading, I peeled back the skin on the window and let the wound gape. It was a mouth, thirsty for weather, and the rain quenched it hard. I stood there dripping. Raindrops tore the adhesive off around my nose, and I removed the bandage, tossing it out the mouth, down into the puddles. I wanted to pray, but I didn't know to whom or what to ask.

I relit the candles and pulled out the papers I'd snatched from Felly's apartment. Many contained rough drawings of a fleur-de-lis, some with lightning or squiggled lines shooting out from the lance head. For the first time, this beautiful image looked powerful, violent even. The circle was shrinking, and in the dancing light of the church balcony, I felt it tighten around my neck, around my callused hooves and horn, and my great gray belly churning with hunger. There were posters announcing musical guests. Ma Rainey, Bessie Smith and Jelly Roll Morton. The last piece of bounty was a fragile magazine called *The Blue Book*. Its cost was twenty-five cents, and it was dated January 1916. Inside were listings of what appeared to be fancy hotels or clubs, but there was an unsigned note on the inside cover that answered my questions.

"Dear Felly, here is a treasure of New Orleans' romantic past. This book helped Yankees and local men of influence in selecting the Sportin' House of their desire. It was a time of jazz, sex and magic, the flavor of which may never return to the Crescent City. Take good care, and believe in the Gift. It has power over all things." It was sealed with a fleur-de-lis. The Gift. The Gift. Believe in the Gift. It has power over all things. The rain spit harder as I tramped downstairs and broke out of church.

It was after three, and I followed the trail of cigarette

smoke to Cafe Istanbul. It was packed. Mostly musicians done for the night. They came by to hear the dying sounds of the evening. New Orleans folk never put a night to rest easily. They dragged it kicking and screaming, howling and jamming. I wasn't ever much for music. After fifteen years on the streets, the sound of traffic relaxed me more, but this was right. I bought my own drink with my own money. Even threw in a twenty for the band. When a poor man has a dollar, he is rich. When he has three hundred dollars, he'll soon be poor again. Then it snuck up on me. I missed Aggie. I missed Detective Agatha Li? So it appeared. I didn't know what it was to miss someone, but I started seeing her face on other women's bodies. She was talking on the phone, delivering drinks, kissing the saxophonist. I dragged an empty chair to my table. I almost spoke. She had taken the ink of this case under her skin, given me three hundred bucks, and believed me when she had little reason to. Was that her job?

"Hey, copper." The purr sounded familiar.

"Kelly Katie."

"Katie Kelly, you drunk fool. Your face is undone." So was her dress.

"I just got the bandage off." She took my nose between her fingers, and I choked.

"Then it's all better. Your eyes are still black."

"I like black eyes," I said, pulling away breathlessly.

"So do I." She sat in Aggie's chair backward and rested her chin on her knuckles. Her legs were flapped open in invitation, a cotton dress falling softly between her knees.

"Who do you work for, Katie?" My cop voice sharpened.

"Whoever's willing to pay. You ought to know, Detective. I must be doing at least half of the boys in blue. You are an insatiable group of individuals. That's probably why my file's thick as a brick. Full of adjectives." Her jagged smile sawed through the haze.

"You seem to know what you want. What you need." She batted her eyelashes and bit her lip like a slice of orange. "Don't make me take you for a ride in the squad car." I was going too far out on the limb. I felt the branches buckling.

"I'd like that." She slid closer. "And I do know what I want. And what a man wants." Either she knew I wasn't a cop or this was a policeman's privilege.

"I've got a wife at home." I pictured Aggie at Antoine's, hair over black eyes. Black eyes.

"All you bulls do. And it's a long, lonely drive out to Kenner." She sat back and thought for a minute. "Hey, how come I never saw you working Vice around here before?"

"I was working undercover. As a priest."

"I like the way you look now. Nothing against priests or anything." She was just throwing me a line. I'd looked in a mirror. I was road kill.

"Miss Kelly, what is the Gift?"

"You don't have to buy me something till after. I always get better presents after the vacation."

I pulled out *The Blue Book* and opened the front cover. "I mean the Gift. It has power, doesn't it?"

She fell off her chair into the hard lap of the night. I couldn't move fast enough to go after her. My feet were heavy, and my thoughts were minutes behind my actions. But I knew I'd stumbled onto something. It was the Gift I'd been looking for.

Detective Li spent the next few days securing backup, keeping an eye on things at Wong's. After her day shift, she'd slide into the strut and pop in and out of the bar at least twice a night. In between, we'd grab coffee at Kaldi's, while her temporary sidekick, Sergeant Kevin Derry, spied for a response. Derry was a good kid, but he looked too clean-cut to be hanging out at a strip joint on Bourbon. He traded me a pair of his Levi's and a white cotton shirt for my more realistic outfit of flannel and holes. I had a hell of a time pulling the jeans over my shoes, but taking them off was now an impossibility, and I didn't want anyone to see what I was becoming.

There I was. Sitting across from a cop that I was starting to miss, wearing my first-ever white cotton shirt, feeling the rough brush of Levi's on tough skin and drinking coffee, not whiskey. Murder wasn't such a dirty business after all.

"I'm worried your friend will recognize me from snooping around about Felly." Aggie's wig bobbed when she got concerned. I adjusted it.

"Forget him. Dent never looks anyone in the eye. He's terrified of recognizing people."

"Your face looks good. And your head. You must be feeling better." I wasn't.

"The words are coming a little easier." That was true. Some realignment was taking place. I scratched my scalp in gratitude.

"You do. You look really great." It made Aggie feel good that she was helping me. It took her mind off the job. She wore an ugly gold dress covered with sequins, with a small cut in the back to show the tattoo.

"You look pretty, Agatha."

"The name's Angel, big boy." She blushed and fumbled her gaze.

"Don't you get tired working all day, and then making this crazy thing happen?"

"Don't you get tired walking the streets all day, and never lying down on a clean cot with a hot meal?" Her question was tough. She'd called the shelter to check up on me. "We had a deal."

"I stayed there the first night," I answered. "I can't sleep there. The noise. The beds are uncomfortable."

"I suppose the streets are more friendly, less crowded, more comfortable."

"Yes." My response shut her up. "I don't like being around people. It makes me feel I'm part of something. I'm not a part of anything. I'm just. I'm . . ." Something powerful was moving through me. I had to take my time. "I can't stay there. If that breaks our deal, then I'll give you your three hundred dollars back and disappear." I wondered how I'd get back the money I'd spent.

"Hey, hey, hey, slow up, Free. Don't overreact. You don't have to do anything. You've held up your end of the bargain. You've been terrific."

"I'm not a suspect?"

Aggie laughed like a little girl. "No, you're not a suspect."

"Maybe you shouldn't be doing this. There's a place on Canal that removes tattoos."

"This isn't some whim, Free. This is police business. A quadruple homicide investigation. This is my job, and I take it very seriously." She eyed my plate. "You're not eating."

"Here and there," was my reply. "I have money."

"But you're not spending it on food."

"Sometimes I forget. I'm not used to eating. Not at any one time. I don't know. I forget."

"And sleep?"

"I slept in St. Patty's last night. The priest is a friend of mine. He let me sleep in the vestry."

"I've never been to St. Patrick's."

"You should come." I didn't mean it as an invitation.

"Okay. This Sunday I'm off. We'll go to church together."

"We" and "together" in the same sentence.

"Together," I repeated.

"What time should I pick you up?"

"I'll meet you there. Ten o'clock." There was a long pause. I imagined the faces of all the saints watching me. They weren't smiling. They weren't frowning, just watching. Their bronze-green eyes still as a church, and me not being able to return their look. Together. Felly and I had done things together. A few things. Never worked out. I always burned it down. Together was hard, a nail through the day. An obstacle in the passing of time. But together was what Aggie and I were at that moment, and that wasn't tearing out my lungs. My organs shifted. Together. The word wouldn't fit in my mouth. It ran inside my head and stuck out of my ears. It was too wide to say. It was too much to think. "Maybe not," I heard myself say.

"Why, do you have plans?" Aggie joked. And that was it. Plans. No, of course I didn't have plans. I didn't want plans. That's why sleeping in the shelter was so hard. I'd planned it. I didn't want to know what would happen next. I couldn't stand knowing. I couldn't go to church with Aggie, there was no possible way.

"Maybe I'll go. And maybe you'll go." It made perfect sense to me.

"What are you afraid of?"

"Nothing. I'm not afraid. Aggie, I'm afraid of plans."

"Plans? That's ridiculous. That's how people . . ." and she stopped. She saw that it wasn't ridiculous. It was the only way I knew how to live. "Maybe I'll go," she said, "and maybe you'll go."

"That would be great. Maybe I'll see you there."

"Let me tell you a story," Mobley started. His hands were in full flight. I couldn't take my eyes off them. The fingernails seemed as beaks, the pulpit a tree. "Once upon a time there was a man. He had nothing. Nothing in his pockets, nothing in his house; in fact, he didn't have a house. Sort of a home-less man, if you will. He had nowhere to lay his head at night, no friends he could really trust. He had great dreams, but none of them seemed to come true. He worked hard, without much reward. People never left him alone. They stared at him, pointed, were afraid to be near the man. He ate when some people were kind enough to invite him for a meal, but he spent most of his waking hours on his feet. Always on the move, a boxer who just won't quit, no matter how many up-percuts and low blows he endures. Does anyone here know this man? Does anyone want to know him?"

Aggie squeezed my hand hard. As hard as I swallowed.

"This man is here today. He's right here among us, and for all our righteousness and holiness and prayers, we still don't want to take the time to spend with him, to talk to him, to hear what he might have to say. He is an outcast!" His shout echoed off the stiff saints. "He is an outcast in the place he should feel most at home." The congregation squirmed under the palm of Mobley's words. "Once upon a time there was a man. Once upon a time there is a man. His name is . . . Jesus Christ." I exhaled like a Mississippi steamer, and Aggie let go of my hand. My eyebrow caught a single bead of sweat.

"He's not pretty, acceptable, mainstream, Southern, he's not even Catholic. He just happened to save your soul. All I want to say to you today is get your hands dirty. Put your feet down on the mean streets. Get to know your Savior. Once upon a time indeed." With that, he closed his Bible and sat down. Coins dropped in the poor box stole the silence.

"I want you to meet someone," I said to Mobley's back. We were in the vestry, and he was disrobing his mountainous frame. The sweat paddled across his back and over his shoulders. "She's got dirty hands." I said it by accident. I didn't even know what I meant, but Aggie smiled so wide that her teeth straightened from the force.

"Always a pleasure to shake a dirty hand. I'm Jessup Mobley."

"Pleased to meet you, sir. Thank you for the homily."

"Somebody was listening. That's encouraging."

"I've never been to St. Patrick's before." Aggie looked so tiny next to Mobley, like a forgiven child.

"The Sundays are running short. At least for this preacher."

"No!" My anger surprised me. I wasn't myself.

"Vandals, derelicts, repairs, upkeep. I'm running out of energy."

"That's my fault," I admitted.

"This is the church you fell out of?"

"Yeah."

"Anyhow, the muscle to keep it up just isn't there."

"Where would you go?" Aggie asked the question I was afraid to ask.

"I ain't going nowhere but to my sister's dinner table. At sixty-three, the call to the dinner table is the noblest calling a priest can receive."

"Aggie's a police officer." I felt proud.

"He's not in any trouble, is he?" The fat of Sup's cheeks almost touched his eyebrows as he laughed. He slapped me on the back. We got along better when we weren't alone. "How about a little Creole cooking for the two of you? Lolly always makes extra. Come on, steal my leftovers." Sup was too jolly to turn down, and Aggie was so excited she took my hand again. On the way out, Mobley lagged behind with me and asked, "Are you two . . . ?"

"No. Come on, man, no."

"Too bad."

Lolly had her Sunday special filling every part of the house. She hugged me so hard I lost my breath.

"Child, you've been running so long you finally snuck up on yourself." She had a way of talking that sounded good but didn't make any sense. I hadn't seen her in at least five years, yet the curl of her hair, the solid power of her forearms and the yellow brightness of her teeth were unchanged. "You look more different every time I don't see you."

"It's the hair," I explained. It had been long. She touched me like a favorite toy just rediscovered in the attic.

"Keep on looking at you, again for the first time. Jessup, brother, look at him. Isn't he just two sights for a sore eye?" Sup smiled and ate. Aggie just smiled. "It's a direct pleasure to have a peace officer in our domicile," said Lolly while serving the creamed cauliflower.

"I'm a bit overwhelmed by all the hospitality."

"This is the only way we know to do things around here.

And any friend of Jefferson's is a friend of ours." Mobley paused. "That is, assuming you two are friends."

Sup smoked all through dessert, and the harsh tobacco smell mixing with the coffee took me back to age seventeen. Those first meals with a thinner priest and his angelic sister. They had never asked me any questions, just kept filling my plate, packing my starving belly with care. They cared. They still did. Enough to take me in, and even more, enough to never force my hand. It was the greatest gift a boy, a man, could receive.

"I'm really glad we did this." Aggie and I were alone in the den. Louis Armstrong scratched across the phonograph.

"Funny how we just happened to see each other at church," I said.

"Yeah, funny." She didn't know what to do with her body. She kept crossing and uncrossing her legs. She caught a glimpse of my shabby Thom McAns. "Maybe we should pick up some new shoes. Now that you've gone Uptown on me."

"These are fine," I covered up, pulling them sluggishly under my chair.

"You have money. You're supposed to spend it. We'll stop on the way back." She didn't understand.

"Maybe another time. How about some more dessert?" My feet got caught as I tried to stand. A pained grimace betrayed the truth.

"Free, let me see your feet." She squared to me, her black eyes shooting from shoe to face. "You really do need shoes."

"It's not the money." I leaned in low to whisper. "My feet aren't . . . they're not able to . . . I can't take my shoes off. Not in a shoe store."

"Why not?"

"They're not fit to be seen. Aggie, I've had these shoes on for months. I don't think I can get them off. I don't want anyone to see me like this."

"We'll go right home. Are you in pain?" I didn't answer. "We'll go right home." Home, and that "we" word again. At least it hadn't been planned.

Aggie's apartment was Uptown on Richmond, near Loyola University. There were only four large units in the building, and it was a classic of New Orleans architecture. Wrought-iron balcony overlooking the street, sky-high ceilings, French doors and batten shutters. The walls were papered, but no paintings hung, and the hutches and other antiques weren't cluttered with trinkets and souvenirs. It was clean and stark, like the hospital without the waiting. I tried for twenty minutes to take off the shoes, but my feet had swelled into them. Even into the eyelets.

"I don't want you to see this." It was a private misery.

"You don't have a choice. Sit back, and I'll get a knife."

Like meat off a bone, Aggie slowly began cutting away the soldered-on leather. The stench was unspeakable, but she never grimaced, never hurried. With the sole gone, she began peeling off the top and sides, but they were taking skin with them. I soaked in warm water till the leather went limp. Finally, the hide shook free, still taking a few layers of dead skin as bounty. I hadn't been able to watch for fear that my feet had finally become the cleft paws of a rhinoceros. I felt utterly alone, humiliated, ashamed. Aggie poured me a tall scotch. "I don't want you to look yet."

"What does that mean?"

"They don't look much like feet." I jerked forward and looked. The tops of my feet were gray with violent patches of red and black across the toes. Much of the skin was gone, and great boils rose like tumors all along the sides, stopping at the ankle. The soles of my feet were blood and blister. Fist-sized bubbles jutted out and up. Aggie wept. I wanted to comfort her, but I couldn't move to the doorway, where she shook with grief. "Why didn't you tell me?" Guilt wobbled her knees.

"I didn't know." I hadn't known. Pain had been so constant all over my body for so long, I never imagined the wreckage below.

"I'm calling an ambulance."

"No! Aggie, please don't do that." I knew if I went back to Charity, the thick-haired, thin-lipped doctor would admit me and never let me out. My glass top and clay feet would be the end of me. Shattered at both ends.

"You have to see a doctor. They're infected. You could lose them." I'd been losing them for years.

"Agatha, please, I'm asking you. I've survived this long without doctors."

"If you call this survival. Look at the trap you're caught in." She was right, but it didn't matter. I was so certain that I couldn't go back, if I had to crawl out onto the street I would have. "Are you afraid of the hospital?"

"I don't have to tell you. I don't have to go. I'll walk. I'll crawl out of here, and that will be it." She was too shaken to argue.

"This is what you've done to yourself."

"It's part of living on the streets, Detective Li. I've had bloody feet before. I have glass swimming upstream in my head. I'll survive. That's the whole point. Don't you see? I don't care if I go out on my hands and knees, at least I survived till the real end." The street logic I'd made up with the raw edges of fifteen years without a home didn't make any sense to Aggie. It barely made sense to me. But I knew it was the only way. Not right or wrong, just the only way. "Could you help me into the bathroom so I can wash my feet?" Without a word, she moved off and returned with a basin of warm water and a first-aid kit. We did not speak. With a sterilized needle and kitchen knife, she popped and peeled each silver blister. The skin tore easily, like wet paper. She got me to move my toes for circulation, and the gray spots warmed up. My right foot tingled, and the last two toes wouldn't move. They were dead. She washed my feet, held my gruesome feet, soothed them, smoothed ointment on and bandaged them. I sat there with my legs straight out, useless white swabs at the end. Without warning, my mouth yanked open and the tears came. They came for all the years they hadn't come; for the murders, for Felly, for Jesus and Mary, for fifteen years of dirty feet and unheld hands. Fifteen years alone. Like a rhinoceros. This our present grief arises from having friendships, I thought as the tears pummeled me. This our present grief. My eyes were too flooded to see Aggie slide up toward me, but her lips stilled my quivering. She kissed me as gentle as a flower. She drank my tears and gave them back to me. We wept together, mixing salt and our awful loneliness. We kissed till my feet flew away, two gauze doves. We kissed. We wept. Together.

I drank my third whiskey just before the door opened. It was five-thirty in a seamless afternoon, and Detective Li had just finished a punishing seven-to-five shift. In five hours, she'd be back on her feet. On her heels to be exact. High heels, with the darkness pressing into her flesh outside Wong's. When I said third whiskey, I meant since lunch. There had been a few when I woke up to keep my feet from shaking, and then two more waiting for my TV dinner to cook. It was a strange meal to be eating since I'd never seen much television. Even sitting all day in Aggie's apartment, I didn't turn on the set. I preferred the flat hum of the traffic. So as I set the empty glass down, Aggie came pounding in. The city had been cruel again, and I knew not to speak. The two weeks I'd spent healing had been eerily quiet between us. We hadn't kissed again. I was beginning to think it was how she treated anyone who had been shattered. We didn't know what to say to each other. Nothing had changed at Wong's. Her late-night escapades were giving her strong legs and sleepless nights but no clues. She seemed to regret having listened to me that first time in the police station. Sometimes I'd catch her scratching at her tattoo, wishing it away. I kept to the guest bedroom, the kitchen and the living room. Not much living went on there. Only me scooting over to the window to watch the hopefuls go by. Aggie had borrowed a chair with wheels from work, and that gave me access to everything but the highest cupboards. Even on my elbows, rising out of the chair, I couldn't reach the top cupboard, which is where she headed after entering. She had my whiskey bottle in her hand. As she put it out of sight, my tongue went dry.

Without a greeting, she vanished into her bedroom. In the streets, to be ignored was to be happy. Anonymity was the last treasure a man had. But this invisibility made me hate my feet for slow healing. I should have gone to the hospital, I thought. I should have left this whole mess alone. My beard had grown back in. Whiskers pointed in all directions from my constant rubbing. My nose and head felt whole, or as whole as they were going to get, but the feet were still a tragedy. Pus blisters had replaced water blisters, and they needed daily draining. The two deadened toes hardened in their absolute numbness.

Felly and Cheng, poor Billy's corpse getting rolled in the Forensics lab, even my bathroom bashing seemed miles away. I didn't want to know anything about anybody. I was imprisoned. The French windows and fancy doors were the bars, my feet the chains. I lit a cigarette and rolled to Aggie's door. She didn't allow me to smoke in the house. I ashed at her doorstep and knocked. I could hear her groan and the bed whine. She opened and saw the cigarette first.

"What am I doing here?" I exhaled up to her. Her face moved like pressed putty. The bags under her eyes were colorless, but heavy. She took the cigarette and inhaled deeply. Her eyes crossed as the smoke snaked into her lungs. She didn't say a word. "Aggie, I need to go." We both knew I had nowhere to go, that there was no way I could go. "Aggie."

"Jefferson," she finally said. The name came slow, like a child imitating a parent.

"I don't like to be called that."

"I'm sorry." She seemed to be inching backward into her room, crawling into bed, rolling over. My vision buckled. She hadn't moved.

"Can I have my cigarette back?" She took another puff. I was sure she'd put it out in her hand. She looked that careless.

"I'm not supposed to care about you," she said, waving the cigarette like a tiny lantern. "This is all very complicated. You're not supposed to be here, smoking outside my bedroom, eating my food, scratching my floors." She was half inviting, half repulsing me.

"I don't care about anything but leaving. Maybe you should take me to the hospital."

"You wouldn't let me."

"I changed my mind." It was our longest conversation since the kiss. It felt good to raise our voices.

"Okay, I'll take you." She started to put her shoes on, and I rolled after her into the bedroom. It was the first time I'd been inside, and it smelled like rain.

"You can sleep first. It's on the way to Wong's."

"I'm not going to Wong's. I'm off the case." She laced her shoes as I winced.

"No, you're not."

"I have to meet someone for dinner over that way, so I'll drop you."

"No, you don't." I don't remember if I knew she was lying or was just hoping.

"You don't want me to take you to the hospital, Free?"

Suddenly, with the smell and the shade of the dark room, her sturdy feet ready to march me out of her life, the dull sheen of her black eyes pretending, suddenly I didn't want to go. I couldn't. I wanted to dive into her cool sheets and roll around, a child in a sandbox. "Aggie?"

"Yes?"

"Is it because I'm hurt? Because I'm homeless? I'm not helpless. I've survived for fifteen years." She studied my face like a cop. Trying to recognize something she'd seen before, a feeling she could ID.

"Are you hurt?" she asked me. "Are you homeless?" She straightened my whiskers with the back of her hand.

"No," I husked. "Are you?"

"Yes."

I rose up, a fountain of strength, and pivoted onto the bed. We sat side by side, not touching, eyes dead ahead. She kicked the chair away. We lay down.

"I'm not off the case."

"I know," I responded.

"I'm having dinner with you."

"I know."

"Free, what are you doing here?" We curled into sleep.

The midnight wind dented Aggie's bedroom drapes. We'd fallen asleep in a half-embrace. I woke inches from her face. I said her name in my head. I'd never woken up with anyone in my arms before. She felt so fragile, and my hands seemed very important. As if they were capable of great things. Having held this life so close, they could do whatever they faced. My lips pushed against her forehead.

"Agatha." She eased out of my embrace and snuggled with a pillow. I watched her sleep. The curve of her leg into hip dove through my eyes. A perfect swirl of woman, never ending, repeating itself over and over in her hip. Her hip bone peered out slightly, a beacon, and I was sure that I could have lived the rest of my life on the sweet bend of her hip.

I ran my finger along her back like a question mark and asked myself where I learned to be gentle. Her ankle was puffy, and I squeezed the fatigue out through the toes. Her calf had the whispering shine of a new shave, and I smoothed her skin into mine. My pain sat in a sidecar, waiting its turn. For five flawless minutes my cracked head sealed, nose breathed, feet walked, thoughts bounded. I wanted to remember, to compare the glory of the moment, but there was nothing to compare. That was my moment. It was new, unfamiliar, unfrightening.

I lifted her T-shirt. The stomach sank with life, the belly button a perfect circle. Discovery. Ribs framed her belly, and I warmed my hand at her hearth. Her mouth slipped open, lips just parting. Before Aggie, eye contact had been an affair. Now, beneath my callused fingertips stretched the beautiful body and soul of this woman. I kissed her puckered knee and slid out of bed.

It was muggy, even for a New Orleans midnight, so I shut the window to keep out the heat. I went into Aggie's drawers, laid out socks, shirts, old movie tickets at the foot of the bed. There were three packages of photographs, the pictures stuck together from the constant murmur of humidity. I couldn't tell what they were photos of, just large groups of half-smiling people. They frightened me. People frozen, trapped with leers yanking on their faces. Like caught fish, surprise lingering in the corners of their dull eyes.

I picked up Detective Li's service revolver, unloaded and reloaded it. The hammer glistened, bullets purring in antici-pation. The muzzle was cold to the touch, and it cooled my forehead, neck and lips. All that heat and all that cold, I thought. All that heat, and all that cold. I cocked the gun and aimed it at something. I couldn't quite make it out in the darkness. A fallen stuffed animal, a painting of the river, the face of a clown. Then in the center of the blur, I lined up Aggie. She was in my cross hairs. In my way. Like others before. "Bang," I whispered. I remembered the first time I'd fired a gun. Almost. I didn't remember where or when or even why, but I remembered the sweet jolt, how the metal vibrated in my hands. The smoke crawling out the end, spelling something wicked in the air. I remembered how good it felt. The feel of a pistol, cocked to shock. Loaded. Aimed. Bang. Aggie jerked tight in bed. Her jaw flexed in defense. A dream ripped through her. I stroked her hair with my free hand.

In the bathroom, I turned on the light. The mirror did its usual cruel reminding. I hung a damp towel over it, turned on the tub water and undressed. In the simmering tub, sweat became water, and water turned to sweat. I sat there, spilling out and back into myself, the gun teetering on the island that was my knee. I shook out two bullets, and swallowed them with a handful of bath water. Or sweat. They went down like fat aspirin, racing to the pain, shooting out my lights. There were four bullets left, spinning in the chamber before I locked it into place. I slid all the way down, so my head was under-water, and my back stuck to the porcelain. Then I raised my feet up into the air. Liquid pushed into my ears and coated my eyes. I could see the dripping hooves shimmer and shake above me. I took aim, dead center, where the flesh met the ugly rhino skin and calcium. I crossed my eyes and pulled the trigger. Wet fingers didn't make any difference. The trigger fell back like a curtain. "Bang," I bubbled from my un-derwater spot. "Bang." The two bullets I'd swallowed went off in my stomach. Two empty chambers rolled into sight. No smoke. No vibration. I sat bolt upright, sucking air like a baby bird, my belly searing with lead and gunpowder. I lay the gun on the bath mat, beads of water sliding off its nervous body. I let the water drain and fell asleep in the tub.

"Give evil nothing to oppose and it will disappear by it-self." So it said in one of Cheng's Buddhist offerings. I guess

Buddha never went to a strip joint in high heels and a tattoo.
The bullets we'd been waiting for finally got fired. It was three
weeks after I had my shoes surgically removed, and Aggie
and I dropped by Wong's for a drink. Actually, we were just
dropping in to give Derry the night off. He'd been casing the
joint and its customers almost nonstop. He either loved the
assignment or just didn't know how to complain. Aggie was in
plainclothes, a baseball cap pulled low. She went in first, ten
minutes before I did. That would give her the chance to ease
into a casual chat with Derry and make sure Dent didn't
recognize her. I was sort of nostalgic for the old dive. Dent
smiled when I limped in.

"Free, at last."

"You almost sound glad to see me, you old son of a
gun."

"Never got a chance to apologize. Hate to see a guy get
beat in the bathroom. Especially a regular."

"I'm not so regular, Dent."

"Not anymore. I have people who come in here now, actually pay for their drinks." He almost smiled again. He liked to
keep his tobacco teeth out of sight.

"Whiskey and water." I went for my wallet, but throwing
money around would mean a lot of questions.

"On the house. Looks like your nose healed. Sort of." It
was crooked as a poker game. "But your leg. You're walking
like you got a sock full of quarters."

"Going to Vegas," I kidded. It felt good to be back on my
stool, with my bartender, my drink. Looking over at Aggie
closing in on her partner, she felt like a stranger. There was
still only one life I knew.

"Spin the wheel for me," he finished.

Aggie was into it with Derry. I could down my drink and leave. Something was in the air. Something new. The cheap barstools were the same, the dull hiss of the speakers still whistled over the stripper's head. Dent looked as familiar as a reflection, but something was off. I felt watched. Like a mute voodoo priestess was rattling bones in the corner. I scanned the walls for a poster, beer sign, telephone, anything that could have been making me feel strange. It didn't feel like Wong's anymore. I asked Dent what was different, but he didn't hear me. He was stacking glasses and singing along to the music. Everything else was quiet. The music stopped.

Then the shots. They were fired out back. A blond hooker wearing a gold dress slammed into Wong's through the back hallway that led to the kitchen. I had to look at Aggie to make sure, and then I understood. This look-alike blonde was taking the heat for our scam. But the killer was sloppy. The hooker dove behind the bar, landing on top of the floorboards that were hiding Dent. Instinct carried me over and behind the bar. The shooter entered firing, a symphony of lead and shattered glass. Shattered glass. I covered my head and shivered. St. Patrick's loomed up at me. The glass rained down, tearing our clothes. I screamed. Jesus and Mary. Jesus and Mary. I didn't see what happened next, but I heard it.

"Drop it! Police! Drop it!" Loud, laughing gunfire. Nothing. The jam of footsteps meant it was over. I shook the glass like a hangover and walked to the site. Aggie leaned over the dead gunman and closed his eyes. His shoulder had been dislocated by the hail of bullets. I went to speak to Aggie, but she pressed a single finger to her lips. Silence. She backed away, no gun in sight. She hadn't moved a muscle to waste the guy.

Derry had taken cover by the stage, and deposited his magazine in a V pattern across the man's right side. The shooter
had died holding his weapon. It was pointed at me.

"Hate to see a body, but now we're closing in," Aggie spat
between tough bites of a Popeye's drumstick.

"Where's the girl?"

"Down at headquarters. Derry's filling out his report. We'll
have ballistics by morning. Should match the bullets that
killed the others." Her voice was hard, sentences punching
the air.

"That's not it, is it?" I didn't want it to be over.

"Not by a long shot. Hopefully, this will lead to the send,
because this clown was no pro. He missed a blonde in high
heels and only got off two shots before Kevin cleaned his
windows. Definitely not as efficient as the others. The pool
table was masterful." I took it as a compliment.

"You know, Cheng on the pool table, he bled a fleur-de-
lis."

"Come on, Free. Get over that flower thing." I was right,
but I didn't push.

"They were gunning for you, Aggie."

"Yeah, good thing I have a boyfriend to keep me out of
trouble."

"You say funny things."

"I do?"

"Like boyfriend."

"I was just kidding. It's an expression."

"Then I'm not your boyfriend?"

"Do you want to be?" She laughed. "It's just a word."

"I don't like words much," I answered. "I don't like being called anything, being known by anything other than my name."

"Not even that."

"My name. The name I chose to be called. I don't know. I should just shut up. I open my mouth, and I can't say it. What I want to say. It's all that goddamn glass." I whacked my head with an open hand, trying to jar the culprits loose. Aggie grabbed my wrist and brought it down.

"Free, don't punish yourself for being happy."

No one spoke forever. Finally, she added, "Besides, it was me who almost got killed tonight. You should be comforting me." I wanted to be in her bed with her perfect hip and her candy mouth.

"Let's go home."

The body was a disappointment. No ID, nothing to prove anything. Either the guy was a ghost or he went out expecting to be killed. According to the final police report, we couldn't even be sure that the guns matched. The tattoo theory was neither confirmed nor eliminated, but to what end? The blond hooker turned out to be at the wrong bar at the killing time. She was lucky to be alive, but no help to the case.

At about eight o'clock that night, a Tuesday night, I went out for a six-pack. The air felt inviting, and with the cold Bud in my hand, I was in no hurry to get back to Aggie's apartment. There was a spinning in my head, even before I took my first swig. I was dizzy and lost. My shoulders kept my face from hitting the walls I'd run into. Two beers were gone, and I'd lost track of time when I found I was standing in the middle of a tennis court. It had to have been on Loyola's campus. I let the net catch me at the waist and flipped over to the other side, a drunken acrobat. Two bottles broke on impact, and I drank the other two lying on my back. Beer spilled over my mouth and into my ears as I stared at the starless sky. The sky looked like a downtown building being cleaned at night. A few scattered lights, but most everyone gone home for the day. Home to wife, kids, dog, cat, television, drugs, newspapers, hatred, whatever people went home to. The asphalt surface was cool, and I took off my shirt to roll on its sweet face. I wanted to peel the lines up and wrap them around me like taffy, to hold me together, to seal me up before I poured out onto the ground.

Just before daylight, I woke with a shock. A spasm shot through me, standing me in one motion. An empty bottle spun at my feet. I heard a rattling, and turned to see two men in gray suits entering the fenced-off court. There was a sick yellow gloom in my lungs. The men were faceless, and they walked with black rubber soles onto the court's greenness. I clearly saw a sign that read: TENNIS SHOES ONLY ON COURT SURFACE. THANK YOU. I was about to warn them, when they came after me. Dull silver bullets tore up the space that separated us, their teeth flashing, lips stretched in inhuman directions. I was over the fence in seconds, leaving them scrambling up after me.

Their suits restricted movement, giving me a head start as I darted across with aimless purpose. There was a distant shout from only feet away, then gunfire. The day yawned and rolled back to sleep. Every building I tried was locked, so I scampered up a drainpipe and onto a rooftop. Bullets tore shingles in half, and sparks lit up around my hooves. Where was Aggie? Why was she letting this happen? She was supposed to be taking care of me. It was her end of the bargain. A look behind, and they were gone. I shimmied down a set of windows and landed in a patch of dewy grass. I slipped twice trying to get up. They were on me again. A wooden windowsill splintered under fire, and I dove behind a string of bushes. On hands and knees I hurried, tearing my pants, tearing my flesh. I wondered where my shirt was. I had nothing between me and the naked bullets. Up ahead was a clearing, and I ran all out. It was an access road, leading back to the street. Unhappy traffic drifted by, cracking the morning open like an egg.

The sun was rising behind my enemies, burning their outlines into sight. They were reloading, cursing at each other, and I bolted for the company of strangers. I jumped into the back of a pickup, quiet as a squirrel, and lay low. Peering over the side, I saw six, ten, twenty men in gray suits laughing after me. At a red light, I shed the truck and ran across the honking hoods of waiting cars into a sleepy backyard. A child's pool tripped me up, flooding me and the lawn. I laughed out loud. And still behind me, more laughter, the ammunition, the black soles pounding, gray suits swooshing. I cut my arm wide open on a nail that was escaping from its fence. Outside an unopened restaurant, I climbed into the trash Dumpster and waited. My heart bounced from hips to head, as I fought back screams and sighs. Blood poured from gashes. Sweat stuffed pores. Within minutes, the Dumpster was surrounded. The men, how many now? Forty? One hundred? They swarmed the area, clicking antennas to share information. But they'd never find me where I was hiding. People were afraid of trash. Whatever had been thrown away became suddenly poisonous, diseased, even people. One day in the mouth, or in the house, next day in the garbage. But I

felt at home. The dark perfume of yesterdays calmed me, and
I settled in.

An hour later I was awakened by a busboy's first delivery.
Eggs, bacon and soggy toast stung me to life. I sneaked a
look, and no gray suits were in view. In the trees? In their
gray cars? In my imagination? I was alone, and I limped back
to Aggie's.

"Pack your bags, Free." Aggie was as calm as a summer
night until she noticed my bloody condition. "What happened
to you?"

"I didn't come back last night."

"You told me not to worry if you didn't make it home every
night."

"But you do worry. I know you do." I wasn't so sure, as she
stood half in and half out of her closet. "Last night was the
first night. I'm being followed again."

"Not your infamous tail?"

"Twenty, maybe fifty men. They were wearing gray suits
and black shoes. Do you have any alcohol?" I showed her the
tear in my arm.

"What did you do to yourself?" She quickly led me into the
bathroom, and began washing out the wound. It was what she
was best at doing.

I didn't do it to myself, I thought. "They chased me. Not
the little guy from before, but large men. Gray suits, like I
said." I could tell by the wrinkles in her forehead that she
didn't believe me. She was looking for the best way out of the
conversation. But she was holding a bloody arm, and she
didn't have much choice but to hear me out. "I slept at
Loyola. On the tennis court."

"Sounds comfortable."

"It is on hot nights. The asphalt gets cool at night, and there are no bugs. Why am I packing my bags? Do you need to get me out of here? Do they know where I am?"

"Now, Free, just calm down. I know it may be a lot to ask, but just pull it together for one second. Nobody knows where you are. Nobody cares where you are. I didn't mean that. You know what I mean."

"They followed me. You're sure it's not the cops? They looked like cops. They ran like cops. They shot like cops."

"These people shot at you?"

"Real bullets. That's why I ran. Because they chased me first. Then they shot."

"If they were cops, they probably wouldn't have missed."

"You don't know me, Aggie. I don't get caught."

"Look, I don't need to know what you were doing last night. I give you that freedom. I know this isn't easy for you." Aggie was talking like a counselor at the Salvation Army.

"Aggie, I won't try to explain it. It never works to explain."

"Maybe you were followed. But you got away, right? And here you are, and we'll patch you up and be on our way."

"Where?"

"We're going to Hong Kong. I convinced Captain LeMaire to send me on a little fact-finding mission. He's extremely pleased with what we've been digging up. He's starting to see stars." Aggie poured alcohol into my cut, and I bit down on my tongue till it almost cracked in half.

"What you have dug up," I corrected.

"We. Department can't pay for your flight, but I can handle that. Your knees too?"

I nodded yes. "When do I get to pay my own way? I do

want to get a place of my own. Three hundred bucks a week doesn't give me much of a choice."

"I'm taking you on an Asian vacation, and you want a raise."

"I'll trade the trip for a raise."

"No dice. I need you. Besides, this is your job. This case is it."

"Oh, yeah," I admitted. "But you almost lost me again last night. Maybe you should keep a better eye on me."

"Maybe you should keep your ass at home and not go sleeping on tennis courts. Maybe you just got mugged by a couple of college kids trying to get in a set." Her joke made the gray suits seem a million miles away. In another place, another time, another fever dream.

"Aggie, I've never been anywhere. Far, I mean."

"Where are you from?"

"Nowhere."

"Nowhere?"

"I'm fromless. I came to New Orleans when I was seventeen. That's thirteen years ago, and it's all I remember. I did go to Baton Rouge once, by accident. Something about the off-ramp. I didn't know they could close it down." Pause. "I forget why. I just need a little help, you know, leaving."

"Don't worry, Free. I'm good at leaving. You're younger than I am. I didn't know that."

"I look old."

"You don't look older than thirty. You look wiser. You are wiser." She gently put on bandages, and it was as if it had never happened. I thought of broken Budweiser bottles on the tennis court, bullets in the windowsill. How crazy was I? I was beginning to find out.

Next day was passports, so I shaved and had my picture taken. The place was right across from St. Pat's. I'd never seen a photograph of myself. Not one I could recall. I looked surprised, startled, in trouble. Aggie liked the picture, but I felt hemmed in.

"I look like I'm running away."

"Maybe you are," she said, rubbing my stomach.

Aggie took care of the details. I didn't have a birth certificate, or any real proof of who I was at all. I hadn't gotten a government check in years. As far as the United States of America was concerned, I was invisible. I was lucky just to remember my name. I didn't even want Aggie to give them that information. I preferred being the unknown soldier. She used her address, and with a few well-chosen cop strings pulled, things fell into place. It all seemed so easy. Like I was getting away with something.

The night before we left, I snuck back out to Numa Street in Algiers, to Cheng's shack again. It had become the property of the city, and huge padlocks hung on the doors like sleeping bats. I climbed the drainpipe and sat on the roof. Mosquitoes flew by in drunken circles, whistling through the corduroy air. I thought about freedom. Cheng had counted on this house to give him freedom. New Orleans was supposed to be freedom. Maybe it had been before the killer cut him down. The same place that was my prison was freedom to him. And now I was going to Cheng's home, his prison. Would I find freedom there? Did I even want it? Did I have any idea what it was, what it cost? Cheng's search for freedom got him dead. But in the end, everything got you dead. It didn't really matter if it was a surprise visit from a .38 slug, the lingering cough of emphysema that barked through the shelters, or even the quiet desperation of a man disappearing into a rhinoceros. It was still death, faceless and hungry, flat as Highway 10, relentless as the night. So I sat there, waving blindly at insects whose flight I envied, thinking about freedom.

Aggie wasn't free. She was chained to her job, shackled to New Orleans as much as I was. Maybe I was her way out. Was she mine? I imagined her spine as a ladder to heaven, angels ascending and descending, her back a pathway, an escape. I threw a pebble at a black cat. His green eyes flashed in the moonlight, protesting the pebble, hissing that he'd left me alone. Alone. My shoulders were boxier, and my posture slumped a bit. Being away from the oil of city streets had hardened and cracked my hands. I was too clean. I shook my thick neck and listened to the night chorus.

Crickets scratched their wings insanely, while nappy-headed teenage boys rolled dice in doorways and ten-year-olds manned drug posts. All of Algiers was inhaling. Crack, cigarettes, poisonous air. "Breathe out," I mumbled. "Exhale." But they couldn't and they knew it. The city would catch fire and disintegrate. We'd burn like flags, wicks, fuses, tourists, we'd evaporate in all the carbon monoxide. The black sky would smile orange and swallow us whole. We'd burn like hell.

Pitch dark. The night, Aggie's eyes, her hair, her dreams as she lay in her bed. And I was perched on the dead man's roof, wondering what I knew and why I knew it. What I'd done and why I'd done it. Would I do it again? What it felt like to kill. Dead. The dead of the night. I leaned back to trust the dead of the night. Teeth and sneakers lit the children's way as they sparked back home, their jobs completed, fresh cash in the elastic of their underwear. The dope dealers gave them something to look up to, to reach for, a way out, like freedom. Like more chains.

The bough of a magnolia tree scooped low to tell me a secret, but it got lost in the wind. I heard it crash off a sycamore and slide down its trunk, a belt of wisdom. "Talk to me." But she had spoken her peace, and my war was too loud to let me listen. "Good night," I said, shaking down the drainpipe. Laughter tore through me, almost ripping me in two. I shot off the padlocks, kicked in the first-floor windows and walked to the bus station.

Row, row, row your boat, gently down the stream. Merrily, merrily, merrily, mea culpa. Mea culpa? Come on in, oh, sweetheart, you look . . . . . Out!!!! She bought it in the throat. Sonofatwitch shot her in the throat. Need perfect aim. Had perfect aim. What the hell did she ever do? No matter. Her last words were . . . It's something I'll never forget. I don't think we have space for this. I want it all erased. Blip, blip, blip (laughter in the sun leaves no shadow) blip.

Airplanes. I'd seen them, heard them, imagined them, but I'd never been close to one. Never heard the empty complaint of the engines, not seen the dead whiteness of the body and wings. It looked too heavy, hooked up there to the gate, a fat New Orleans mosquito.

"I can't go up in that. It can't go up."

"You pick now to be ridiculous?" Aggie scolded me.

My heart flexed tight. "Isn't there a train to Hong Kong?" I wasn't really afraid of the airplane. I was pretending. I didn't fear crashing, suddenly losing fuel, barreling into a flock of geese. It wasn't the plane, it was what the plane did. It took people away. And now, it was going to take me away.

I knew New Orleans. It wasn't a hometown, a steady comfort. I didn't belong to it or owe it anything. But I knew the loud, sunburned tourists in the Quarter, the starved smiles of drunk locals, the street painters and reality shakers. I'd fallen wasted into the arms of the Mississippi, stolen crawfish from the bowels of Pontchartrain, fooled the cops from the bitter end of Esplanade to the coffins of Martin Luther King Avenue. I'd slept in more doorways and lean-tos than a stray dog, and I knew the flavor of every minute of my life. The slow dance of the mules down on Jackson Square, high on Bute, dragging fools around till death. I'd guzzled beers left unattended on the docks where thirsty stevedores wasted their days. Even watched the sunset over the lake, pollution turning bright brown in the sickening light. I didn't want to leave. I was terrified of a new city, with foreign buildings, alien streets, untraceable smells. New Orleans might disappear.

New Orleans was my prison, but still, I knew its face. For the first time, I was faced with the dim, invisible prospect of freedom, and I was terrified. In another place, how would I act? What would I do when I needed to make a quick getaway? Where would I hide? There would be no maps of secret alleyways and no destroyed buildings for sanctuary. Not only would I be alone, but stripped naked. All my safe houses and escape valves left behind, down on the Louisiana ground. The airport even seemed to say nothing would ever be the same. Words like "terminal" and "final destination" rammed into me. The stale grin of an airline employee was the last straw.

"I can't go."

Aggie froze in her tracks. Her ears were reared back, ready for flight. "I could get mad."

"Aggie, they'll change everything. I have to stay to keep a lookout."

"Who will? Change what?" She was trying to calm me down while inching me toward the plane. I grabbed the slippery podium.

"New Orleans will be gone when we get back."

"Free, this city has been around for over two hundred years. It likes Louisiana. It's not going anywhere."

"I'm not afraid. I'm . . . alone."

"You're not alone. I'm with you all the way to Hong Kong and back." Her smile was drowned out by the final boarding call. "Now, get on the plane, damnit. I need you there." Being needed had never been one of my strong points. Being needed was noble and blinding. It blotted out everything on the horizon. And somehow, it got me on that plane.

Once on board, I let New Orleans slip away. Sure I'd never see it again, I thanked it for its education and tolerance. The stewardesses acted like the shelter volunteers. They leered till their lips cracked behind lipstick. They waved plastic cards and oxygen masks. It was odd, all this preparation for disaster. A plane crash was something I didn't want to survive.

"It's okay if we crash. I don't mind if we smash into a mountain or the ocean. It doesn't matter. Why do they keep telling me about crashing? I'll never need to know."

Aggie settled in quickly, able to ignore the desperate warnings. "It's like visiting a relative, only thirty-five thousand feet in the air. Just sit still, eat a lot, and it's over before you know it."

"I don't have any relatives," I countered. And if airplanes were the equivalent, I wasn't missing much.

"Everybody has relatives."

"What about your family?" I prodded. Aggie stiffened, then relaxed.

"Nothing special. Mother, father, the usual."

"I don't know anything about the usual."

"I don't suppose I do either," she said. Her eyes ricocheted behind closed lids.

"You going to eat your peanuts?"

"I'm saving them for the movie."

"We get a movie?" I'd only seen two movies in the Big Easy. One on television at the police station, and one during a hurricane, when I snuck into the Joy.

"On the way to L.A. we get one, and then two more going to Hong Kong."

"That's more than I've seen in my life. I guess visiting relatives ain't so bad."

"You going to eat your peanuts?" Aggie said playfully. I fed them to her one at a time.

The ride to L.A. was bumpy. We were hitting clouds left and right. My head bobbed uneasily. The glass tangoed across my mind. Aggie slept, her mouth closed tight as a cell. I looked out the window. A light on the wing blinked at me. We were hanging up above everything, yet nothing waited below. There were no people, no bars, no cars, no cops, no knives, no churches. Just the yawning group of us, riding on the shoulders of God, visiting relatives, eating peanuts. I wondered if Buddha would have flown. Alone like a rhinoceros.

"You missed the movie. You slept through the entire thing."

"Why didn't you wake me?" I grumbled.

"You looked so peaceful. Sort of dreamless."

"Sort of dead."

"I didn't say that."

"Stewardesses, please prepare for arrival and cross-check." The captain's voice was salty and wet. He'd knocked back a few fingers during the flight.

"We're in L.A."

"Why are we here?" I couldn't remember. All the babies were quiet. They'd forgotten something too.

We had a three-hour wait in Los Angeles, but I couldn't believe we were still in America. The people who roamed the halls were bigger, darker, they smiled and slapped each other on the back. They wore bright colors, flags of unknown countries. Their hair was bright. Their teeth were bright diamonds, scalpels. They were so bright, I bought sunglasses in the gift shop. They didn't glow, they stung. I hid out in the men's room until our flight.

"I've sent three guys in there looking for you. We're going to be late again."

"You sent those guys in?" I asked. "I thought they were cops. I kept moving from stall to stall."

"I can't get over you." Aggie laughed. She had been losing her ability to look serious week by week.

"These people are really shiny."

"Not enough rain."

"We have sun."

"Yes, but we also have jobs, families, responsibilities. They just have sun."

The flight to Hong Kong was forever. The babies remembered how to cry with a vengeance and kept reminding each other every fifteen minutes. The stewardesses began to droop, the movies were boring and Aggie stuck me with her elbow, like she was telling me a joke in her sleep. It seemed we'd never arrive. Hong Kong felt chased and was hurrying away, our plane in hot pursuit. Aggie assured me we'd make it, but as my eyes grew tattoo red, I got ornery.

"Agatha."

"What, Free?"

"Aren't you tired?"

"I'm asleep."

"You've been asleep this whole damn trip."

"I would have been if you didn't keep waking me up."

"Just don't expect me to come running next time you need me to fly to Hong Kong." Aggie laughed at the absurdity of it all and burrowed her perfect head in my chest. I shut up. We landed.

The airport was surrounded by great electronic billboards screaming the need for cigarettes and furniture, beer and more cigarettes. I lit one. The thousand lights burned the haze away. The air was New Orleans heavy at our midnight arrival. Was it only New Orleans remodeled while we flew? Was it all a perfect circle? We moved easily through customs and into the Hong Kong night.

"Cheung Chau, please. The ferry," Aggie intoned to the cabdriver. He thought she spoke Chinese and rattled off a necklace of words that wrapped around Aggie's throat and left her mute. The hack frowned and drove on. Cabs and cars crowded each other in the airsick night. Everything was exhausted. We banged through tunnels, took red lights as invitations and slashed a wake across the city.

The ferry docks were awake. The day's hardest workers were finally making it home. It seemed like the Quarter, folks jostling for position, pressing on to some unknown destination. But there was one clear difference. Everyone was Chinese. Aggie didn't blend in at all. She had the same hair, shape, size, twists and curves. These were her brothers and sisters. Yet she seemed tacked on. A new patch on an old pair of pants. She didn't belong here. Neither of us did.

We boarded the boat and headed for Cheung Chau, an outlying island, an hour's ride from Hong Kong Island. Aggie had an aunt living there. To be less conspicuous, this would be our home during the investigation. A hotel was too easy to trace. It was a chance to stay anonymous. The ancient ferry scooped its way forward, and we counted the minutes till bedtime. The raw smell of garbage and tobacco muscled in.

"My aunt's a friendly woman. I met her once when I was eighteen. She was very nice."

"All I care about is our bed. I hope it's very nice."

"You're getting spoiled. I should make you sleep outside."

"Okay."

"I'm just kidding," she apologized. "She's a little old-fashioned, that's all. From China, Shanghai. I'll have to tell her we're married." A wave punished the boat and sprayed us with dirty water.

"I'm old-fashioned too," I whispered, kissing Aggie's damp forehead. "I'll sleep outside."

We docked at 12:30 A.M., but the island still stirred like a pot of gumbo. Street merchants selling Pepsi, bald meatballs, ice cream, jewelry, fish, all crowded the street.

"It's twelve-thirty, Aggie."

"These people don't seem to understand that."

"They just wear a different watch. I understand." I knew

how to night-crawl. How to trick the sun and eat the moon. Maybe these were my people. Aggie led the way, following her aunt's scribbled Pidgin English directions. This was the most difficult part of our journey, the walk to her aunt Mei Ling's apartment. Cheung Chau was one giant hill, and Mei Ling lived at the top. We walked past two Buddhist temples, the sweet sting of incense waking me up.

"Joss sticks, Free. Like prayer."

"Like candles to the saints." She nodded. My legs burned as we fought our way toward bed. We passed schools, apartments, shacks.

"Look familiar?" Aggie asked.

"I lived better on the streets."

"People make their own paradise." And with rice and bamboo, these Chinese had made theirs. The roads wound and rose, a stupid staircase, but it all seemed familiar. I wasn't afraid anymore. There would be places to hide. Nooks and crannies. Trapdoors and escape routes. No one could catch me. I was invisible. Just before two, we stumbled upon Mei Ling's dwelling. It was cement, painted army green, with a useless gate between us and the door. Her laundry was hanging out to dry, a congregation of ghosts. Before we knocked, the door opened. She had the soft orange glow of someone who tried to stay awake and failed. Her smile was weak, but her eyes welcomed us. In her late fifties, she was a sturdy woman, with boxy shoulders, wide wrists and a confident shuffle. Her pink slippers slapped the bare concrete floor as she backed in, and we entered.

"Agatha, please, my child." They kissed.

"Mei Ling, I can't thank you enough. I know we woke you."

"No, no," she lied. The apartment was thick with books and magazines. She hadn't cleaned up for our visit, and I was grateful. "I want your holiday to be the special."

"This is Jefferson, my . . ." Aggie started, but I dove in.

"You live very high up. You must have strong legs." She lifted her robe to expose a marbleized, veinless calf.

"Nine years I have walked that walk."

"I'm impressed." Aggie was so happy her aunt and I hit it off that she let the introduction drop.

"Tea?"

"No, Aunt Mei Ling. Thank you."

"Coffee."

"No, really."

"Soda. I have some nice Coca-Cola or some, yes, I might have some. I bought it special. Lemonade. For the Americans."

"Honestly, we're not even . . ." Aggie was weakening.

"A beer, I might have beer or two beer." Her onslaught was relentless.

"I'd love a beer, Mei Ling," I said. "Come on, Agatha, have a beer. We're in Hong Kong." Saying Hong Kong felt funny. Like a ball bouncing up and down in my mouth.

"I think that's my last one." Mei Ling shrugged. She peered deeper into the fridge, as if another beer might appear any minute. She seemed like a magician, meeting us at two in the morning, with her magic pink slippers and her magic laundry keeping watch. She had opened before we knocked.

"Here's to strong legs, beautiful Chinese women and Hong Kong. Let it leave its mark on us."

"Hong Kong Chinese are leaving at the rate of two thousand a week, maybe more," Detective Liu Hai spat. He was a disgusted and disgusting man. Aggie and I were making our first contact with the Hong Kong police, and they weren't rolling out the red carpet. "I don't envy you one bit," he managed between bites of sugarcane and puffs on a Kent. "In this city, it is easy to play a game with the law. And in America, it is easy to disappear." His teeth were yellow with erosion. His mouth looked like the Mississippi Delta. His eyes were black like Aggie's, but misted over. Cleaning his ears with a free hand, he swiveled in his oversized leather chair. "I just don't want any cowboy dealing and wheeling. This is not John Wayne. This is Hong Kong." Aggie's patient face was leaving. Detective Hai had been rattling on with his doomsday speech for nearly an hour. He'd littered the floor with sugarcane skin and rained on us with promises of a failed investigation. "This is in no way to say that we won't be able to assist in some small way, but as long as no crime is being committed in Hong Kong, there is little we can provide."

"You don't call exporting heroin a crime?" Aggie shot back.

"Miss Li, I could walk outside and grab the third person I see. We would have your precious heroin bust. We're getting it from Thailand, Burma, Laos. It comes on planes, fishing trawlers, taped to men's testicles. It comes in a million different ways, but it comes. They bring it overland through China as well. There is a large world market. The number one consumer is America, home of the brave. Congratulations." Hai spoke casually, and his easy manner pissed me off. I'd seen heroin clog the veins and brains of too many street idiots.

Junkies shed needles like memories around alleyways and streetlights. In the shelters, they'd stab underneath the sheets, in the dark, hoping to find an entryway that hadn't sunken with regret. Their eyes leaning far back in their heads, so as not to see what they'd become.

Aggie stepped in. "So I take it you do nothing."

"Watch what you say, Miss American. Much of our work is silent. Not flashy. We dig in."

"I bet," she mumbled.

"The fifth modernization," Hai began, "is underway, and it is something you will never understand."

"Try me, Detective."

"It is Chinese term for freedom. That's why people are running, swimming, flying, smuggling to America. That is why. Freedom. They think China will take that away in 1997. Now, they gamble to get out. Some get caught. Some wind up dead. Some make it. Some people will do anything."

"And some will do nothing," Aggie fired back.

"I don't understand the principle," Hai said. "America. You are not free, are you?" We didn't answer. "I didn't think so. But still everyone goes to America to be free. It is sad, really. Don't you agree?" I understood him perfectly.

"So you just let them go. You might as well buy their ticket on a commercial airline. It'll save everyone a lot of trouble."

"You speak fast, and say little. You anger quickly." He smiled.

"With all due respect, Detective," Aggie said, rising. "I find your attitude appalling. Your fellow Chinese are selling their souls to a moneybag in New Orleans and winding up dead. Doesn't that concern you?"

Hai spoke with his back to us. "This is not John Wayne. We

take what we can get. It's just a matter of time before '97. There is only so much we can do, so much we can control."

Aggie found her composure by the door. "Okay, we'll keep it simple. Tattoo shops. Where can we find a tattoo shop?"

"Wan Chai, Miss Li." He didn't like her, he didn't respect her. He shut his eyes.

"Your fellow officer deserves a little respect," I offered. Aggie glared at me.

"Respect is not for sale, for loan or for everyone, Mr. Freeman. You are in Hong Kong now. We are a city in transition, turmoil. One doesn't always have time for respect."

On our way out of the station, Agatha punched me hard.

"I don't need you to stick up for me."

"That guy was an idiot," I answered. The blood was clotting in my arm.

"I can take care of myself. I don't need . . ." She almost walked into a moving streetcar. I caught her.

"I'm sorry. Look, I held back. The guy was pissing me off. When someone gets under my skin like that, I shoot off sometimes. It's just the way. It's not a choice or anything so simple. Sometimes I just pull the trigger."

"There's more to this than getting pissed off and lashing out. You have to use your head."

"Or what's left of it."

The Wan Chai district was a curious mix of culture and sleaze. Two blocks from the Hong Kong Academy for Performing Arts and the waterfront Convention Centre was what amounted to Bourbon Street East. We walked down Jaffe Road, jammed with strip joints, bars and our favorite haunts, tattoo shops. I felt perfectly comfortable.

"Maybe we should get a place near here. Mei Ling is so far away."

"Getting homesick already, Free?"

"No, I just thought we should get a better idea of, you know, how things work around here. Who swings the cat."

"You're homesick." Aggie smiled.

"Maybe a little." The sights, the smells, the dirty sidewalks and exhausted doormen did move me. I took every porno flyer handed to me, just to help out the workers.

"Nudes. Nudes. Nudes," a tiny man kept repeating. I smacked him on the back to get him going again. "Totally, totally, totally," he switched. "Nudes totally."

The atmosphere had me thinking about Felly. How many Felulah Matins were spreading their lives open inside these clubs? How many visions were being missed? A fog fell over me. I leaned against a wall to catch myself. Aggie never noticed. She skittered away into the crowd of lust and tourists. My body heaved. There was no sound from my throat. Looking up, I saw the hustlers and hookers, pimps and playboys spinning before me. They smiled with tarnished gold teeth and shook fistfuls of money. Spinning. Spinning. Spinning. I held on. I needed to see Felly on this merry-go-round. I was certain she'd come into view, slide off the wheel and tell me again about her vision. About the snow. About the laughing.

"Free." Aggie's nails bit into me. "I thought I lost you. Come on. Are you all right?" she barely wondered as she dragged me down the desperate street.

"All right," I spat. "All right."

Three hours we stalked the boulevard. The people were friendly and very impressed with Aggie's tattoo, but no one was talking. Most had never seen a fleur-de-lis and even wanted to copy it for later sale. In each parlor, the owners, customers, all the help would crowd around us. They were

eager to know about America. Most had relatives somewhere
in the States and had just visited, or were planning to come
soon. "Maybe we see you there," they'd say, as if America
were just one small neighborhood. They were surprised Aggie
didn't know their friends and disappointed that she couldn't
speak Cantonese or Mandarin. Like I had been for years on
the streets, Aggie was now the carnival freak. A Chinese-
American with no ties to her race. They touched her as if
she'd break. Near the end, it seemed she would.

We were getting frustrated as we passed a bombed-out
building at the head of Jaffe Road. Bamboo scaffolding ran up
it like splints, and it looked ready to topple. We never would
have noticed it but for the Chinamen exiting onto the street.
He wore a dull grimace, smelled of rubbing alcohol, and he
was stroking his arm. After he rounded the corner, we stole
inside.

The door led to an open room that had been cremated.
Exposed beams stretched like withered matchsticks over our
heads, and we hurried deeper into the building. There were
exposed wires and puddles of water in dangerous patterns
along our way. Down a wide hallway we walked, chasing a
shaft of light. Dead rats kept watch. The walls wrinkled as we
scampered by. We were moving faster than we wanted to.
There was nothing we could do. I got to the door first and
pushed it open, a child on Halloween. A series of bare bulbs
scalded our eyes, but we pushed on. A tired radio played a
forgotten rock song. The walls were covered with pictures or
drawings or mystical cave etchings. In the glare, it was impossible to tell. I was stepping in a pool of black water when
our hostess appeared. She was no more than twenty, with
bone-white glasses holding back her black hair. She looked

like a snowcapped mountain. Her left leg was missing from the thigh down, and she hopped effortlessly into our presence.

"Welcome Lung Hing Parlor Tattoo. Help you, can?" she chirped. Her lips were large and red, with tooth marks of determination. The glasses avalanched out of her hair and crashed uneasily onto her flat nose. She didn't flinch.

"We didn't mean to barge in on you like this," Aggie pushed out.

And I was right behind her with "And we didn't mean to scare you." But of course it was we who were afraid. Nothing could scare this streak of light.

"Is okay." Her easy manner relaxed us a little. "Am to get tattoo for you? And both, I think."

"This is a tattoo parlor?" Aggie asked.

"Lung Hing Parlor Tattoo. We do for cheap. We do for you." Her smile made the bulb look dull.

"Are you the owner?"

"Father owner. Need tattoo? Want pretty tattoo?" She said tattoo like it was a cure. "Plenty tattoo in alls color and many animal." Her English was awkward but confident. "Speak Cantonese?" she asked Aggie, who shook her head. "Two tattoo. One of each." She meant one for each. "I give deal. Very cheap, no little pain, show all friends. Yes. Show all friends." Looking again, I saw that the pictures on the wall were all tattoo designs, and we had stumbled onto another chance.

"This is it for today," Aggie whispered to me.

"Not a bad way to end it. She's making me want to get one."

"Artist good. The best. Trust me."

"We're looking for a special tattoo," Aggie said.

"Can do. With picture, you hold picture, bring picture, can I do. Can make copy for anything. Good artist. Perfect. You see." Aggie looked around to make sure we were alone. Her skin shone like a mirror. She slid her blouse down off her shoulder, and exposed her red fleur-de-lis.

"Funny color," the girl said, laughing. She stood on her toes. Her calf was a shiny rock.

Aggie was confused. She didn't know how to break through. "Do you know?" She stopped. "What is your name?"

"Name? Name is Comic."

"Comic?" Aggie repeated.

"Is American name. From television. I am Comic." Her face was everything.

"I am Aggie. This is my friend, Free."

"Free. You are Free," she pronounced.

"Thank you," I said.

"We need to find a tattoo parlor that does . . . that has this design. Not to copy, but one that is sure. Someone who knows this exact flower. Maybe even done this exact flower. Red. This red flower. Do you understand? It is very important." Aggie spoke too loudly, as if Comic were deaf or foreign. We were the foreigners. We should have been whispering. "In Wan Chai, is there anyone . . . ?" Comic smiled for a long time, like she hadn't understood a word and was laughing at our sorry situation. She hopped back to her desk and fell down into a chair. It was a move she'd perfected. I spied a dragon tattoo so real it scared me. It had a bearded head and razor horns. Its scales shimmered, and its clawed feet clenched ferociously. There were others that reminded me we were in Hong Kong; Buddhas in various positions and of varying weight, temples, strange gods, but also the American touch. Harley-Davidsons shooting off great tongues of flame, Mickey Mouse, Bugs Bunny, the White House. Comic pressed a hand against the wall and one on her desk, and shimmied to a standing position.

"All on Jaffe Road same. All in Wan Chai same. No red flower. Try this address," she said, handing us a piece of paper. "Knock twice and twice also. Shun Peng. Shun Peng. Shun Peng." She kept repeating the name, and Aggie and I stood there motionless for a moment, entranced by this one-legged tattoo artist. "I understand," she added, "and luck good. Luck good. I know you understand. It is good. America."

"Thank you. Thank you, Comic," Aggie sang walking out the door. Comic waved like an orphan left behind. It was hard to leave. We snaked our way back out through the debris. The smell of burned carpet and melting glue clung to us.

"We should take her home with us," I added as we broke out into sunlight and inhaled as if for the very first time.

Aggie turned on me suddenly. "Don't feel sorry for her."

"I don't. I just know what it's like to have only one leg to stand on. I don't feel sorry for her."

"She has a light," Aggie admitted.

"She has a light like you, Agatha, and I'm definitely taking you home." I grabbed her, and kissed her on the neck. She folded into me, and a taxi screeched to a halt.

"We're far from home, Free." Home free, I thought. Home free.

Could've found her by the saltines, all bent in half. Where. That's where. The first hiding place. Covering tracks. The disappearing act. No good.

*Insects tell everyone everything. And the blood making its own baby pool.
To, maybe to start her over again. Dear, hated woman, all bent in half.
There. Over there, bent in half, by the saltines. Did I mention the saltines,
left over from his soup. It was so simple, like pulling a finger through
Daddy's shaving cream. Hell of a time cleaning it up. Didn't get it all,
did I? Damnit! Yeah. Jesus loves me, this I know, for the Bible shoots to
kill. Hah, that's the one. The one I was looking for. The one upon my
tongue. That's the one I can remember. The rest is a blur.*

Our cabdriver was either late for an appointment or having
a seizure. He had that vacant stare I'd seen so many times
before down around Camp and O'Keefe. The five-minutes-till-
nowhere stare. We torpedoed through Hong Kong's streets,
leaving breathless pedestrians and bus drivers in our wake.
We just missed an old lady at the corner of Des Vouex and
Jubilee. Aggie and I were sure she'd been a target. The cabby
was devastated over missing her. She'd have made a damn
good hood ornament. Then again, just blocks from our destination, a young woman had to do the two-step mambo to
save body and sole. We quickly paid and poured out of the
taxi.

"They don't like each other." Aggie coughed. I rubbed her
back and she slowly straightened.

"Let's take the bus next time."

"Let's walk." From where we got off, we traveled up Aberdeen Street, till we hit Hollywood Road. Then west, where the
hot promise of incense led us past the Man Mo Temple. We
walked down treacherous steps, then right onto Cat Street, a
tiny, gluttonous collection of shops and sidewalk merchants.
The street was elbow to elbow with locals selling battered

books, toothless combs, Catholic and Buddhist trinkets, Chinese sunglasses and a world's worth of unusable junk. One old-timer tried to sell me a watch that had the minute hand running faster than the second hand. I tried to explain to him that I didn't believe in time, but I couldn't get through. Peering over the shoulders of the miniature hucksters were fancy shops filled with jade and Chinese artwork. Life-size horses dipped in gold, a porcelain Buddha big as a man, with tiny babies tickling and pulling on him. He wore his smile like a wound. Aggie and I muscled our way up to Ladder Street, and we shivered through the crannies of the city. Finally, legs tired and noses full, we found ourselves at Dai Lan Chinese Medicine Shop. A unicorn stared down from the sign, his horn pointed at my heart. A breeze rocked him to life, and I stepped behind Aggie. The windows were filled with strange roots in the shape of women and with animal parts I'd never seen. It looked more like Ripley's Believe It or Not, back in the Vieux Carré, than a friendly pharmacy.

"She sent us to a medicine shop?" I asked. "For a tattoo?"

"Maybe the cabdriver . . ."

"No, this is the right address. She didn't speak English so great. It's a mistake." I wasn't eager to enter the house of cures. Its strange window display reminded me of the voodoo shops back home. I had made a vow a long time ago not to mess with the gris-gris.

"At the very least, we could ask for Shun Peng," Aggie said.

"I don't like the look of this place." I'd seen enough powdered bones and black magic for a lifetime.

"It's not witchcraft, Free. It's natural medicine. Probably good for you. Just teas and vitamins. To help the body stay in balance." I leaned close to the window and began reading the medicinal descriptions.

"Deer tail: Optimal for reinforcing vital kidney function, strengthening sinews and joints, treating the seminal emission and frequent urination, especially for the depletion of virility and impotence of men."

"Deer symbolize promotion. My mother told me that."

"Look, Ag, I never trust something that offers too much. And if the stuff's so effective, how come the deer wound up dead, with his ass in the window?"

"You're really scared. I didn't know you were so superstitious."

"I'm just reading. They really take this stuff? I think Detective Hai's been nibbling on a few too many deer tails. Here's a good recipe. Deer's tail wine." I'd tasted a lot of weird liquor in my time, but I'd never seen a piece of Bambi floating in my drink.

"It's Chinese traditional medicine. Don't talk too loud. My mother used to say that nature has ears. Keep it up, and some of that ginseng root might come to life."

"You're so eager to go in there, maybe we ought to pick up a package of Codonopsis Pilosula Root for you."

"What's it got, Doctor?"

"It increases saliva secretion and has a special effect on excessive thinking, worriment and psychiatric anxiety."

"That's more up your alley."

"They've got bat wings, eagle talons, chicken, crane . . ." My eyes strained to take in all the weirdness inside.

Aggie's forehead tightened with memory. "Bats are for longevity. No, no, bats are happiness, cranes are longevity. The rooster guards against evil. And the eagle . . . damnit! What's the eagle for?"

"Looks like you're the superstitious one, Agatha."

"Growing up," she said, breaking her train of thought, "growing up, my mother would tell me these wonderful Chinese myths, but of course I can't remember. I didn't want to remember. I blocked them all out." There was a long pause. "Answered prayer," she nearly yelled. "The eagle represents answered prayer. I can't believe that. All of a sudden I'm back in my bedroom, surrounded by stuffed animals and flowered sheets, listening to my mother tell me Chinese bedtime stories." Aggie savored the moment just long enough to get me to relax, then grabbed my arm and dragged me inside. The place was quiet as a mausoleum. Like the New Orleans cemeteries I'd spent so many nights around. Dancing with ghosts, and shadowboxing with St. Paul in all his marble stillness.

The glass counters were stocked with sample roots and remedies, the chrome shone bravely in the fluorescent light, the beige tile floor was spit-shined and scrubbed. It felt like the surgery wing at Charity Hospital. My head spun again, and I leaned against a display case to keep from falling. My hand left a sweat scar on the glass.

We walked like thieves toward a door near the back that was slightly open. I could just see into the room, and a short shadow did a steady dance on the wall. The paint was cracked and the floor grimy. It set the sparkle of the shop off even more. Aggie knocked and the shadow stopped. A tiny man with a hump the size of a football helmet sputtered to the door. He fired words at Aggie's head, and she ducked them shyly.

"I don't speak Cantonese. I'm sorry."

"ABC," he gritted. He lit a cigarette with an unseen match and jabbed the air. He seemed degraded to be talking to us. The sooner the conversation ended, the better. "ABC," he repeated. "American-Born Chinese. Don't have time for American-Born Chinese."

"We were sent here." Aggie didn't get pushed around or put down. "Comic sent us."

"The knock," I spurted. We'd forgotten the knock. "Twice, and then twice again." Aggie looked relieved. The man's hump swelled. I yanked the door shut on that crooked imp and knocked twice, waited and let Aggie knock a couple more times. Magically, the door opened, and our friend stood there, angry as ever. The cigarette had been inhaled in three puffs, and he exhaled like a factory.

"Comic?" he barked.

"We're looking for . . ."

"I know what you are looking for. Come back tomorrow." He slammed the door on my foot.

"It's just a simple . . ."

"Tomorrow." He kicked my shin and shut the door. A scab tore off, and my pants soaked up the blood.

We ended up wandering down along the harbor for the afternoon. It was gray, and years of trash lined the pavement. We walked past a fortress with secret markings and barbed-wire fences. It looked like the kind of prison no one ever got out of, even the guards. Trying to cut up into town, we were trapped by a crazy gathering of highways and streets. The only way to cross was to hop onto a ledge and dare the traffic, only feet away. With our courage out front, we made a run for it. A cabdriver veered toward us. He looked familiar. Once on top of the ledge, we could see what was hidden from the road. It was a small community of homeless. There were two groups of three huddled around repetitive fires. One group had a fast game of cards going on, and they were deaf to the screaming cars just beyond.

In the far corner of the paved area was a man covered in electrical tape. He had it around his wrists, his neck, all across his face. Scabs and sores peered out from behind peeling tape. He walked in circles, ever smaller, until he fell down and pulled out a fresh roll of the silver tape that set him apart. His armor. A knight without a sword, without a horse, without a prayer. Very carefully, he laid out three long strips, put away the roll and wrapped his left knee around the joint so he could not bend it. Then he stood and spun his circles again. The stiff leg kept him from losing his balance, and he went round and round, happy to have stopped his falling. I turned to tell Aggie about the beauty and the horror, but she had made it across the ledge to the next streetlight. A canyon tore open between us. We were miles apart. She waved at me from her distant country, and I waved to the spinning Tape Man alone in the corner, turning perfectly, like the earth.

"The more you do, the more trouble you have; the less you do, the less trouble you have. If you do nothing whatever, you will become a model citizen." Mei Ling quoted a Chinese proverb made popular during the Chinese Cultural Revolution of the sixties and seventies. "It is safer to only breathe in and not breathe out. Fu Ch'i. Control, doing nothing. Is safest."

"Then the homeless," I said, "are the best citizens in Hong Kong. Model citizens."

"They are lost because they act Chinese in a British city. There is not pity for the Chinese soul here. We play at being Chinese. We love the West. It is difficult to teach young children old myths, old ways. They know America. They want America. Soon they will get China. They need to understand the difference." A candle wrapped a yellow moon around Mei Ling's chin.

"Do you want China?" Aggie asked her aunt, stroking her black, black hair with a shaky hand.

"I do not know China. All I know is Hong Kong. Cheung Chau. Easy life, the walk to and from school. Faces still young enough to smile. This is an island. I live on an island. I think am safe. I do not have to want China. I do not think China wants me."

"But this China wants everything," Aggie said.

"We will see. Nineteen ninety-seven tell all the secrets."

"Not all of them. There will be surprises even after that. People are leaving, Mei Ling. Good people are running to America with pockets full of drugs, just to get out, to have a new life. Doesn't that scare you? I can feel the city laboring under the weight of all these fears."

"You have heard, even your mother, my sister, said, I am too old to be afraid. Too old. Well, I am too young to be afraid. I still believe in tomorrow."

"That's because all your tomorrows have been free."

I was lost in their conversation. I knew about waking up in chains. I had never known a free tomorrow until I woke up with Aggie. But even then, the voices were chasing me, promising to lock me back up, with locks I couldn't pick or shatter with a bullet or bald rage. And I didn't have until 1997. I had until the glass made its final slash across my humanity, leaving me wide-eyed and silent, gaping at nothing.

"I have nowhere to go."

"You could come and live with me in New Orleans," Aggie stressed. The veins in her neck bent blue.

"I have nowhere to go. Cheung Chau, Agatha, is my place.

Let China come. Let the smugglers go. Let the tide and moon and stars, let them all do what they must. I must stay. It is the only thing. When Chairman Mao died in September of 1976, I said, now China will at last be free. No. When England gave us back to China, everyone said we would surely lose our freedom. Yes? No? We will see. I cannot guess. Only live."

"You can act. Instead of react. You could do something."

"I am Mei Ling. That is enough to do." She blew out the candle. "Good night."

While Mei Ling had stayed calm as a heat wave, Aggie had gotten worked into a frenzy, ready to free the world, starting with her tight-calved aunt. An hour after we went to bed, when she was sure I was asleep, Aggie went for a walk. I followed her. Down to the beach she skidded, a flashlight to get her past the moss and lizards. I kept a safe distance, going barefoot to stay unheard. She made it to the edge of the water and sat on an upturned kayak. The moon muscled through a cloud bank and shone at the waterline. I could see Aggie breathing hard, sobbing by the water. For Mei Ling, for Hong Kong, for herself. I was getting the idea that she was losing herself, piece by piece. That she was forgetting who she was and what she believed. Probably because she didn't believe in anything. She never had. Life without faith, any faith at all, was deeply, darkly lonely. And Aggie, for all her protests, saw herself in Mei Ling that night. She heard herself in the resigned folds of each sentence. Aggie lived across the world, but the Chinese way of fitting in, doing by being, the inexorable walk to death, had gotten hold of her. The less you do, the less trouble you have. But at that moment, Aggie had everything to do.

It was me. I was forcing Aggie to do something. Care, fix,

save, protect, but not anonymously like a cop. Intimately, like a friend, a lover. Alone, I knew who I was. Aggie knew who she was. But together, we were nothing and everything, and in the end, we didn't know what would be left. I knew I was dying. It was plain as the sand between my toes. The future was my constant companion, and it was sure. But Aggie knew nothing, and ignorance was breaking her heart.

Late the next day, we returned to the spooky medicine shop, and Shun Peng answered the secret knock. He was no happier to see us, but an appointment was an appointment.

"Come here," he called, leading us into his dirty den. It looked like something out of the Desire projects. Empty soda cans, candy wrappers and cigarette cartons crowded the floor. Laceless sneakers, jackets without linings, an old pedal sewing machine.

Aggie asked, "Isn't this stuff off the course?"

"Chinese medicine is all bullshit. My father gave me antler and ginseng from age thirteen. Now I'm forty-four, with a Chinese hump on my Chinese back. It's all bullshit. Want a Hershey?" The bitter man whipped out two Hershey chocolate bars with almonds. There was no turning him down. He led us along behind the back of the store, through narrow, dripping halls. Exposed pipes drooled on our heads, and rust bled from every crack in the walls. "Comic is not her real name." His voice was nicotine thick.

"We didn't know."

"She's ashamed of her Chinese name. She's ashamed of being Chinese. Since Tiananmen Square, she changed her name, watches nothing but American and British television, tattoos her friends for free. She's my daughter. I guess you knew." We made it to a small annex at the end of the hall. Inside was an examining table, some tattoo needles, a bottle of alcohol and Kleenex. The floor was dotted with used cotton balls. "All out of cotton balls. We have to use tissue." His English was as strong as his back. He was still in a hurry, but friendlier.

"How did she lose her leg?" I gambled. "Your daughter." His mouth twisted like a boxer twice punched.

"She visit my sister in Beijing. She was done with school for summer, and she was just visiting. Just visiting." A draft snuck under the door and scattered cotton balls like tumbleweeds. "She went to student rally that day. It was her only day. She was sixteen."

"I'm sorry," Aggie said solidly.

"First rush of soldiers was absorbed by students. The people. They drew them in like water, took away guns. There was reason to stay in the square. It was a celebration." At the time, I didn't understand, but Aggie explained later the tragedy of the June 4, 1989, massacre on Tiananmen Square in Beijing. The Army had opened fire on unarmed innocents demanding democracy. Comic took three bullets in her thigh. The local doctors decided to amputate.

"Why send ABC, I do not know. But okay now. Who is first?" The story had made him sad, and he wanted to speed things up. Aggie eased her blouse down over her shoulder. "Why have you come back?" he said sharply.

"I've never been here before. Take a close look." He stared at the tattoo and shrugged.

"I don't remember you."

"I've never been here before," Aggie repeated.

"Cow's Demon and Snake Spirit," Shun Peng growled. His hump reared up as if to strike us. "Cow's Demon and Snake Spirit. You should know."

"What?" Aggie pressed. "We just want to ask a few questions."

"Cow's Demon and Snake Spirit. Walk like human, talk human, look like human, but I can see you as you truly are. You are devils. Cow and Snake." Suddenly he switched off the light and bolted out the door. The darkness pushed us into the wet hallway, and we struggled to keep up with the humpback, but he knew the layout and we were trapped mice. In the shadows, his hump jumped into sight, then disappeared, an escaping dolphin. We groped our way back to his room, but the door was locked. A shaft of light slid from beneath another door beside it. It was locked too. We heard a click, and the light went out. "Break it down," Aggie shouted. It took me four runs, but I busted through, back into the medicine shop. My head rattled. The lights were out, and in the dying daylight, the hanging herbs and animal parts came alive. They chewed at the locks, tapped on the glass, began their private after-hours march. I dragged Aggie out of the store.

"We've got to beat him to Comic."

"I want to check this place out," Aggie insisted. "This is our chance. He's gone, he doesn't know who we are. And we can find out who he is." I was too spooked to let her take me back inside.

"We don't know he's gone for sure. He could be hiding anywhere. And if we don't get to his daughter, we'll never figure this thing out. This store's not going anywhere. We can come back tonight." Aggie didn't like it, but I signaled a cab, and we headed off on another neck-breaking ride.

Down on Jaffe Road, the streets were beginning to clog with night crawlers. Nameless strangers ready to watch the sexless strippers peel off their skin. Neon and headlights cut into the descending darkness. At the Lung Hing Parlor, we broke through a weak lock and into the corpse of a building. The rats hadn't moved, and new ones seemed to be piling up. I picked the lock into the inner sanctum. The walls were bare. No tattoo designs, no needles or sterilizing equipment. Nothing.

"He closed her down."

"Maybe she went home early."

"Free, he closed her down. This is their fail-safe procedure. I've seen it a hundred times. Fold the tents and make like a ghost. We need to get back to his shop."

Out front, a door slammed. Footsteps, more than a pair, scuffed down the hallway toward where Aggie and I stood. There were whispers, and maybe a laugh. Another laugh. They were after me again. I grabbed Aggie, and we crashed out the metal back door. A light rain was falling, and deliveries were being made. A few strippers got out of limousines and entered their workplaces.

"What is it?"

"Didn't you hear the footsteps? They followed us here."

"Free, who are you talking about?"

"Let's go!"

We shoved our way into a cab, and headed for the medicine shop. "There was no one there," Aggie insisted. "We could have checked out the shop. Why do you keep yanking me out of places before I can check them out?"

"There were guns and men. I heard them laughing."

"Are these the same laughing men from back home? Do you get followed everywhere?"

"Lately it seems that way."

"It's just people, Free. You're not used to being around so many people. You need to calm down. No one is tailing us. No one even knows what we're up to."

"The way they pulled the plug, somebody's in the know."

"Just don't take me out of any more rooms by bodily force. I don't need your help. I've been doing this for a decade."

"You said you needed me," I responded.

"I do," Aggie tried to cover. "I do."

When we repeated the steps to the medicine shop, I felt a secret shame. It was tied to an invisible balloon in my heart, and it kept tugging and pulling till I nearly flew away. The shop was gone. It wasn't physically gone. The building was still there. The doors, the windows, the roof hadn't vanished. But the inside had been scraped clean. There was no sign of violence or a hasty retreat. The store had been sucked away. No herbs to snag me, no ancient deer tail to wiggle or antler to stab. It was a useless, empty building, a discarded crawfish, eaten and swallowed. If we had stayed to investigate, we would have disappeared too.

The door was open, so we walked in. I could tell by the way Aggie stared at the side of my head that she blamed me. So I didn't look at her. I hadn't hired any thugs to do this undoable thing. I was just afraid of the medicine. I'd always been afraid of drugs. It wasn't my fault. I'd seen its hideous dance. We tiptoed for no good reason. The glass and chrome still shined. It had been a hands-off job. Everything had evaporated. Into the man's filthy room we walked, and all the wrappers, garbage, cigarette butts were gone. It had a sick gleam to it, like a gold tooth in a corpse's mouth. Even the hidden tattoo room was history. One dried-up cotton ball proved we'd been there before. The pipes had stopped leaking.

"You did this. You wanted to go back to Wan Chai." Aggie's hands shook.

"How could I know? This is ghosts." She grabbed me by the shoulders and shook me.

"I know it's not your fault, but I have to blame someone. This isn't real."

I let Aggie get some air, and started doing some digging on my own. I tore up sections of floor, ripped out electrical wires and exposed beams. It was noisy, and it was fun. There were some old jars of decayed antler and unidentifiable strange roots hidden away. Yellowed newspaper, broken glass, a comb. The same junk that filled the walls of any abandoned house in New Orleans. Animal remains and historical remains. But nothing of any use. No phone numbers, addresses, information of any kind. All the clues we needed had been vacuumed out of existence. From beneath the floorboards, and from within the walls, I heard the laughing again. Gray-suited men chuckling in rapid fire, their joke rattling my bones. I called out to Aggie, but no sound came. Or she ignored me. Something clicked. A pistol hammer? A thought? A broken piece of fever? I panicked. Adrenaline walked the ladder of my spine, climbing up into my brain, bringing light to a musty attic. I stood on my hands. Took out a wall with a running start and a teeth-gritting tackle. I was roaring. I kicked out pipes, sending poisonous water everywhere, and thrilled to my insanity. I danced in the flood, splashing designs onto the wall, where they spelled out hope and despair, drying and dripping, drying and dripping. Aggie found me hunched over, ready to scoop a new handful onto a dry spot.

She caught my eye and let me spend my rage. I exited an hour later, dried blood stretched across my lip.

We ran a check with the hesitant assistance of Detective Hai. There was no Shun Peng listed, no Comic Peng, and the Dai Lan Medicine Shop was a myth as far as the Association of Hong Kong Businesses was concerned. He said he'd send a couple officers to check our story. But only when he had time. He was a busy man. There had been a near riot that morning out at the airport. Protesters shouting down workers who were part of the construction. China was taking a leading edge in the new facility, and Hong Kong could feel itself slipping further into the abyss. Comic's tattoo shop wasn't registered, and when we went by the next day, city workers were busy repairing the exterior of the building. Fire damage, they said. Asbestos in the air. No one allowed inside. They spoke through gauze masks like lunatic surgeons. Shun and his beautiful one-legged child had disappeared into the cracks.

Aggie was steaming, but I had a silent respect for Peng's tricks. I'd eluded certain capture many times. It was no easy blow, and pulling it off was the closest I'd ever come to success. It had to do with thinking underneath the surface, just below the skin. The cops did their work between the ears, but to survive, to get away with being alive outside the rules, you had to think with your bones, your muscles and blood. Count the heartbeats to the next fire escape, remember the walls that have doors, open the windows that wouldn't break. It was a delicate, dangerous game. I tried to think like the humpback. Where would he go? Why disappear so completely? How did he know what we were after? Because he had known. His face folded when Aggie said she'd gotten that mark somewhere else. He knew he'd been fingered, but better yet, he knew how to get away. I admired his mastery, his quickness and precision. Gone without a trace. Beautiful.

We were back to basics, and the long walk up Cheung Chau's hills. Aggie crept up the streets twenty feet behind me. When I waited to let her catch up, she stopped in her tracks. On Peak Road, we passed a funeral procession. The old men were dressed as if for Mardi Gras, with great sparkling hats and flowing robes. They pushed us away with their eyes. It was a private and public spectacle. One woman stood by a paper Mercedes, waist high, and a paper house just as big. Another palmed a thick wad of fake money. They took a torch to the house and car, tossing money in as it all burned. The shaky smoke rose up to mingle with the incense trail that led the way.

"Funeral," Aggie said, tugging at my shoulder. She had the fatigue of failure in her body.

"What's with the Mercedes?"

"They're sending things to the afterlife for the deceased. So he'll have a nice car, a nice house and plenty of hell money." The procession faded away, a lost parade float.

"Death doesn't seem like such a bad option."

Mei Ling was ready for us. Sweet-and-sour pork, dim sum, steamed rice and a bunch of dishes I couldn't identify.

"How was school?" I asked with a mouth full of pork.

"The children are teaching me a new song. An American song."

"I thought you were the teacher."

"Everyone," Mei Ling responded, "is a teacher." We hurried dinner while Mei Ling unsuccessfully tried to remember the song. "Are you . . ." she hummed. "Are you . . . yes, yes. Are you sleeping, are sleeping you, brother Jacques, brother Jack. Like that, you see."

"Frère Jacques," Aggie corrected. "It's a French children's song."

"Yes. French-American. Are you sleeping?"

That night we weren't sleeping.

"Are you still awake?" Aggie whispered from across the room. We had set up two sleeping areas to ease the tension.

"We are both wide awake."

"Can I?" she asked.

"Yes." Aggie slid over in the darkness and crawled under the covers. I wrapped around her like the wind.

"When I was a little girl, not so little, a teenager, I used to go by myself to the woods in Chicot Park, in Ville Platte, and spend all day Saturday and Sunday out there, by myself." I kissed her on a solitary ear, and she wriggled closer. "I had a sleeping bag and some fruit and some gum. I'd leave gum wrappers and chewed gum as signposts to get me back on Sundays, back to the car. I built fires, walked around all day staring at the ground, the way my feet hit the ground. All those sticks and fallen branches and the leaves were like maps to some faraway place way up in the sky. No alarm clock, just the sleeping sun and the crows to push me home."

"And you weren't afraid." I knew.

"No, I wasn't afraid." Her body was relieved, I understood. "And now I am. I'm surrounded by safety, and I'm terrified." I stared at an angel Mei Ling had hanging from an abandoned light fixture. It was too big, and it hung crooked, its head tilted down toward the ground. Its purple gown spread wide and its golden hair fell about its twisting shoulders. It looked like something I'd stolen in my youth. "I'm afraid I hate my job. I'm afraid I don't know what else to do. I'm afraid of you, of us. I'm just afraid." A slow breeze spun the angel around. Was it bringing a message from heaven? A fleur-de-lis? A gift?

"I don't remember not being afraid," I began. "It seems normal. I wouldn't know what to do if I felt safe. I don't ever want to feel safe." Aggie faced me and kissed me on the head. She snuck her fingers beneath my hair and found my scar. "It's still there," I said. "It will always be there."

"You fell out of a church."

"I didn't have a choice."

"I don't know what to see, and what to ignore. I don't know how to watch you playing in the dirty water, blood coming out of your mouth. You're like a dog, a wild dog, but also as gentle . . . as gentle. Just gentle. Do you know?"

"I don't know how to be anything. I'm not on top of things. I'm in front of them. And they're pushing from behind."

"Like Mei Ling?" she asked in the darkness.

"No. She chooses what she feels. She's very careful, and beautiful. All control. She showed you her strong legs. Then she showed you her soul."

"Have I seen your soul?"

"I want to run off the cliff tonight. Grab the hem of some cloud and drop into the ocean from a million feet up. It makes me tired. Like the laughing men in the gray suits. They make me tired. They make me feel guilty. Like I did something, and they know it. And they're not going to stop laughing until they make me pay for it."

"Pay for what?"

"They were there today in Wan Chai. I heard them. It isn't about imagination. It's about punishment. Punishment and the bad man."

"I'm getting really tired," Aggie stuttered. "What are we doing here?"

"I don't know. Just don't hold on to me, or I'll take you with me. You understand that I have to disappear."

"Tonight?"

"It will just happen. I can't say when."

I touched her swollen lips. "Where do you come from, Jefferson?" I held her, and her sobs shook into me, rattling my knees, twisting my ankles.

"Ever feel like you're going to die, Aggie? And then you don't?" No answer. "You're certain you're going to die. Right then. You know it's over. And you beg for forgiveness, and you make a million promises to a thousand saints. But then you don't die. You open your eyes, and the pain is gone, the fear is gone. And you're not dead at all. You're alive."

"All the time."

"Then what do you do?"

I woke up before everything. Even the air was still asleep. It was hard to breathe, and my hungry lungs forced the day to happen. Aggie had squirmed to the far side of the bedding and was squeezed tight into a ball. Tension striped her neck and bare shoulders. I peered in on Mei Ling, feeling guilty and curious. Back in New Orleans, I used to watch other street urchins sleep, throw nickels in their open mouths and see them spit out quarters. A person asleep was pure. No reactions, no hatred, no desire, just asleep. I covered Mei Ling with a fallen sheet, straightened her slippers and emptied a cup of cold tea out her window.

In the bathroom, I cooled the fist of a fever with an icy washcloth. Something big was pressing down. I slid out of the apartment and hurried to catch the morning's first ferry. There were no white faces in the predawn crowd. I was the only *gweilo,* a Cantonese expression for foreign devil, and I found a lonely seat on the windowless bottom deck. I thought I was going to check in on the medicine shop or the tattoo parlor. The spirit buildings that had shaken us like a cough. I thought I was figuring things out, clearing my head, getting away to see things better. But something else was in charge of me. I was being carried somewhere, and I couldn't ask questions, just wait for arrival.

Hong Kong felt like New Orleans that morning, because I was alone again. I'd been tied to Aggie's investigation since our arrival, and it had taken its toll. I knew she had been saving my life, but I was less and less sure I wanted it saved. It felt good, delicious, the open space of the ferry. Some people staring, others strapping on their masks for the day's fury. The water wrapped the boat in salty arms, and carried it to Hong Kong. I felt a little lost without my Agatha compass, but the direction and destination pointed themselves out. It was just next to the highway and the huge, prisonlike building. I listened intently to the path curving out in front of me.

I bucked the traffic and jumped onto a familiar ledge. The fires were out, and the locals were already gone. It was the homeless community I'd stumbled onto before, and I'd returned because I had to. There were no card games being played or demons being chased. It was as dead as a cemetery.

Small strips of scabby electrical tape lined a corner area. I
dug through bags of old bottles, cans, shredded clothing, un-
matched shoes, string, newspaper. Just as in New Orleans,
the Hong Kong homeless were great collectors. It didn't matter what it was, just that you found it, and it was yours.
Possession was important to people on the avenue. The things
would never be used, just hauled around, bedroom to bedroom, melting together in the bag underneath the soldering
sun. In the end, it might add up to something, all that garbage
pressed together. It might add up to a life.

I took off my shirt and stuffed it into one of the bags. The
gray day was already matching my fever, and sweat spread my
pores wide. There was a rumbling underneath a pile of rags. It
didn't seem possible, but from beneath an avalanche of
ripped cloth rose the Tape Man. He shook his covering like a
butterfly and stood too quickly, falling against the wall. We
stared at each other. I had stolen into his kingdom, but he let
me stay. His eyes were cracked black marble, and they
locked me in. Tape covered every inch of skin, some of it too
old to hang on, fluttering like dead moths as he stepped toward me. He was every doorway I'd ever slept in, every streetlight I'd shattered, every abandoned car I'd hid inside. He
was the cruelty of the world, held together by silver strands of
tape, of hope, that kept him from splitting open and spilling
into the gutter. Ten feet away, I could feel the odor. The
perfume of pavement and despair. I didn't hold my breath. He
sat down right next to me.

For a long time, we didn't speak, we just searched each
other's eyes for some connection. A return to a place we
shared, a memory, a dream, a lie, anything. And if we found
it, we would know freedom. We would explode with the truth
about breaking free, escaping, shedding teeth, flesh and mar-

row to finally fly. I stared. I stared. I stared until I saw the day
of his birth. I saw him red-faced and screaming, that first
moment, when he was completely naked and completely
whole. No tape, no collection of dirty antiques, no odor but
the sweet smell of new. He turned away. Traffic shot by,
soundless. He dug into his bag and pulled out a brand-new
roll of tape. The silver hurt my eyes, lighting up the cave of
our communion. With a steady hand, he handed me the roll,
and I spun it around my finger, peeled off a section and tore it
like flesh. I wrapped it around my shoe and tore off another
piece for my left shoe. For a moment, his eyes healed and
almost smiled. He took the tape, wrapped a fresh piece
around his already tape-heavy sneakers and walked away.
Back to his ragged tent he scuffed and fell off into himself
again. I sat for hours, shining the ribbons on my feet. The
tape held tight, squeezing the hooves long, pressing the rhino
out, promising me toes. The cardplayers and fire stokers returned from their A.M. beg, not taking notice of me. Stuffing
their bags with the latest find: a child's sock, a calculator, the
index page of a magazine. And Tape Man slept on, maybe
dreaming of his birth or a shirtless *gweilo* with silver shoes
and a familiar face.

Walking back up into town, I jumped the back of a streetcar and slid off at Central Market. The sick smell of meat
steamed from its doors. Death was here. I recognized its presence. An old man, with an anvil-flat head, buried an ax in an
ox skull till it smiled wide. Severed pig snouts smelled nothing. Antelope hooves hung like exclamation points over a
butcher's head. I thought of Billy and Cheng, even Felly, and
how easy it was to take a life. To commit a murder. Hurry up
and die, they seemed to be saying. There's no room in the inn.

I stumbled upon a fish market nearby, where the dying was

visible. Great silver fish were stolen from water tanks and slapped onto cutting boards. They eyed me sideways, unable to blink, to close their eyes to the killing, to swim away. Their tails beat out a frightened rhythm on the wood. A knife sliced the top half away, sending the eye into another pile. Fresh blood seeped into the package paper as the purchase was completed. A lady carried her dinner away, its heart still beating.

Mary had a little lamb, whose fleece was red as blood. Grab the gun, check the clip, the magazine, no pages only bullets, now grab the gun. Squeeze the . . . Don't wave it around, don't point it at . . . Grab the gun. Ready? Fire. Hell of a hole. Hell of a hole you put yourself in. Hah, hah, hah. Same laughter. Blew a goddamn hole through her, didn't you, you son of a bitch. Feels good. Bang. Lazy is what you are, laziness is the problem, but let me tell you, I've got the cure. Bang. All dead. Bang, bang, bang. She forgot to say please. You weren't kidding, were you? Hell of a hole, son. Helluva hole. No way to sew that up. Jesus hisself couldn't plug up that hole. Can see across town through that hole. Drive a fuckin' truck through that son of a . . . Hell of a hole. Helluva hole you put yourself in. Mary had a little . . . Bang. Hell of a hole.

Taking it from the heroin angle was a thought, but with the statistics Hai had mentioned, two thousand locals splitting a week, that meant a lot of drugs were going to a lot of places. Finding the red-eyes on their way to New Orleans seemed near impossible. Aggie and I retraced our steps on Jaffe Road, and all over the Wan Chai district, but the tattoo artists weren't talking. We looked at thousands of mug shots in search of Cheng or Billy, but nothing registered. No one knew of Felulah, Wong's or even New Orleans. The ports of choice were New York, Los Angeles and San Francisco. Cities with large Chinese populations where it was easy to blend in. We were beating our heads against a wall, something I couldn't afford to do. Without Comic and Shun Peng, we were dead in the water.

That night, we counted our money and headed for Hong Kong Island. Just above Queen's Road, we found a bar a young British cop had recommended. Post 97 it was called, in a swing at China, and it was the sort of place I'd never been inside. It was packed with easily dressed young men and women, just younger than I, but worlds apart. People who had never slept outside, under the black veil of night. They moved and spoke like liquid. Our waiter had the puffy white face of a loaf of bread.

"Do you feel Chinese here?" I wondered.

"I don't feel Chinese anywhere," Aggie said too quickly, running her hands through her hair and rubbing her nose. "I don't know what it's supposed to feel like." Other than Aggie's, there wasn't an Asian face in the crowd.

"It looks like it'll feel pretty dangerous to be a Hong Kong Chinese here after 1997."

"Free, I hope not. That would make too much sense. I hope you're wrong."

"Billy and Cheng were betting on it."

"Maybe they were just drug runners, thieves."

"They were too lousy to be thieves. Thieves don't leave bags full of heroin undelivered and letters unburned. I think they were just trying to get out. Get away. I can appreciate that. They just chose a stupid way. Maybe it's the only way

there is. There must be something coming that's worth escaping."

Aggie slammed the rest of her beer. "It's funny because
Tiananmen means Gate of Heavenly Peace. Really, I guess it
doesn't mean anything. In the end, before they left the
Square, the democracy protesters, the students, hung a giant
poster on the Great Hall of the People. It was a message to
one of the leaders, but really to China and its history. 'You
will never know peace,' it said. You will never know peace."

"What the hell is peace?"

"I don't know how China could have peace, with Deng
Xiaoping and his cronies, after the bloodbath. But they seem
to. Hiding up there in Zhongnanhai, sealed off from their
subjects, the rest of the world. People only keep things secret
when they're ashamed."

"Shame."

"You have something to hide." It sounded more like an
accusation than a guess.

"No. I just don't remember a lot. That's not shame, it's
amnesia."

"Won't remember, not don't," she stung back.

"What do you remember? Do you remember every fucking
thing that ever happened to you?" My profanity surprised us.
I wanted a gun.

"My father's China-born. In Chongqing. He brought my
mother to Louisiana the year I was born. He had one cousin
in the States, in Lafayette, Louisiana. He was escaping the
Communist life. It was 1960." Aggie stopped and ordered
another beer. "But he changed. Being far away from all the
shit, he turned hard-line, reciting Mao, telling me that work
was more important than school. I was only six when the

second Cultural Revolution hit. Back in China, family members were being beaten, tortured, imprisoned. My father backed the government. 'If poisonous weeds are not removed, scented flowers cannot grow.' That Maoist proverb was a favorite of my father's. From his soft couch in Lafayette, eating panéed pork and crawfish till he puffed up like an American Mao, he backed those bastards till the end." Detective Li trembled, and two tears escaped. She wiped them away fast. "I loved him as a little girl, and then he made me hate him. I hated him till the day he died. I was eighteen. He didn't want me to waste my time on intellectual pursuits. He called intellectuals the "stinking ninth category," beneath dirt, beneath hell if possible. The day he died I enrolled at UNO."

"And your mother?" I held her shaking hand. Her voice steadied.

"She died the next year. We never really talked about it. I think she was too ashamed to say she hated him, but after all those years, it killed her. Free, you have to understand, Chinese don't cry. She kept it inside till it drowned her heart. As you can probably figure out, I'm not a very worthy Chinese. That's when I dropped out of school. I returned to Lafayette to bury my mother, and I've never been back." I wanted to ask again why she was a cop. To me, cops were the government, the stupid fist of corruption and control. I never saw them help, except maybe a few times. They were the blue streak to avoid, riding around on their motorcycles with the star on the engine. It wasn't the star the Wise Men had followed to find Jesus. Nobody followed the NOPD's star. They ran from it. But the world was twisted and strange. There I was holding a cop's hand, drinking with a cop. I laughed out loud.

"I'm sorry. I was thinking of something else."

"It's okay. I wish we could go hear some zydeco."

"We're a long way from C. J. Chenier, Aggie."

On the street, we had to duck empty bottles being thrown out of windows. Since the massacre, breaking bottles had become a form of protest with the Chinese, because the word for "little bottle" was *xiaoping,* as in Deng Xiaoping. In that morning's paper, Deng had lit into Hong Kong again, with another tirade on the evils of capitalism and how things would change come 1997. If Deng wanted to see the evils of capitalism, all he had to do was spend a week on O'Keefe back in New Orleans. That was evil. Syringes stacked like thin soldiers, and bloodstained whiskey bottles, that was evil. Still, Deng was making his move, tightening the noose around Hong Kong's neck. The fever was starting to rage in the streets and apartments. Pulses were quickening, escape plans being hatched in basements and medicine shops.

We dodged shattered glass and hurried to a highway overpass. I was having flashbacks of swan-diving out of St. Patrick's. The rain of crystal splinters wrinkled my memory. I could feel the impact, the lightning-fast tearing of flesh, the snapping of bones and brain cells like kindling. I saw the pavement out of the corner of my eye, rushing up to kiss me.

Up on the crosswalk sat a young man, not yet twenty, with his face buried in his knees. He had the light brown hair of a Brit, an upturned cap with only a few coins inside in front of him and a sign propped on top of his shoes. It read: "Please help. Awaiting money from England. Have no food, clothing or shelter. Thank you."

He was shame. Hundreds hurried by him blindly, not even pausing to drop some pity in his hat. I stopped Aggie, and she began to dig in her purse. The closer I looked, the more I realized it was me, crumpled there, afraid to raise my head. I could see the horn pushing out from under thin hair. And the way he held his feet, cocked, ready to charge if challenged or frightened. I wanted to pick him up and carry him some-where. Maybe the sea, or the airport. A barstool, a strip joint, the morgue, anywhere he didn't have to hide his face like the bad man. Here was a beggar without the courage to beg. A dreamer without any knowledge of dreaming. A human with only a few twitches of humanity left. It wasn't money that would strip his shame. It was something unspeakable, flicker-ing in the mist. No one saw it, of course. No one felt it tapping on their souls to bring it to life. So it just hung there, like an executed man, and the lonely creature just sat there, and I just stared there, like I'd been stared at so many times before.

No food, clothing or shelter. Thank you. Thank you for what? For reading the sign? For feeling connected, warm, guilty, alone, the same?

As I looked again, I saw that everyone was wearing a sign around their neck. They bounced with the rapid pace of the Hong Kong walkers, but I could still make them out. No wife, no job, no future. Thank you. No faith, no chance, no hope. Thank you. No guilt, no forgiveness, no prayer. Thank you. No freedom, no passport, no escape. Thank you. Thank you, they all said, knowing no one would notice, but hoping against hope someone would. Maybe someone would throw some hope in their empty caps, some freedom, some faith. But no one did, and they trudged on, smileless. Aggie dropped a Hong Kong ten-dollar bill in the hat, but the wind blew it away, and the shamed man, with his head bowed, never knew what he lost.

Down on the street, we found an eight-dollar transistor radio at a roadside electronics store and hurried to a quiet section of waterfront. We dialed up the slowest Chinese song on the band and danced. Her bare back was cool against my hand, and our bodies agreed. We rocked and sank into each other. A docked sampan rattled approval against a post. My mind caught the voices like a chill. They teetered on the edge of me, and held on.

"I've never known what it is to be . . ." My words traveled round the rims of her ears and fell in. "I never want to know what it is to be without you."

"You won't have to."

"Am I in love, Aggie? I don't know what it feels like."

"I can't tell you. You're the only one who can know."

"Are you in love, Aggie? Do you love me, Detective Li?"

"I love you, Free. I'm in love with you." We kept dancing, tapping out the rhythm on the damp concrete. "There's no reason. And I don't want to be. But I am. I'm as crazy as you."

"I don't think so, but, Aggie . . ." Every sound in the city stopped. I was deaf, not dumb. "Aggie. I love you. Aggie, Aggie, Aggie."

Rubble. The aching aroma of burned memories. Mei Ling was standing outside what remained of her apartment. She was standing outside of nothing. Every bit of the building's structure was gone. The explosion tore the bark off trees up and down Peak Road. The local firemen had already done their best to douse the flames, but there wasn't anything left to save. Books, photographs, furniture, a lifetime, all ashes getting in our hair.

"Late," Mei Ling whispered. "I stayed late at school. Get-

ting ready for tomorrow. I don't know why. I never stay late."
She collapsed into Aggie's arms, sobs punishing her body.

Aggie and I knew who the bomb was meant for. Rage collided with confusion inside my head. My brain was a fireball. I could barely see past the flames. "Somebody's making a move," I said.

Aggie didn't want to admit the danger. "No one knows where we're staying."

"Not anymore."

We helped Mei Ling search through the wreckage, but there wasn't anything worth salvaging. She never stopped crying. Nothing dammed her tears. All that remained of her angel was an outline smashed into a far wall. The force of the blast must have hurled the small statue with such speed that it left one last imprint on this earth.

All of Aggie's and my belongings were eliminated too. It didn't bother me. I was used to not having things. It even seemed normal. But Aggie was furious. We were supposed to be dead. All three of us, and Aggie couldn't stand the fact that she'd almost gotten her aunt killed.

"Do you still want to stay here, Mei Ling?" Aggie nearly shouted. "This is what China did to you."

Mei Ling gathered herself in the carcass of the kitchen. "You know this is not China. This is Hong Kong. You have upset the balance. And they will try to make you pay. The less you do, the less trouble you have. You did not want to listen." Aggie had no response. She already blamed herself. Whether this was because of China or not, lives were at risk. We had to move.

"Can we stay on the island?" I asked.

"I have a friend living on Kwun Yam Wan Road. Near

Kwan Tai Temple. We can visit with her. Her husband is in Singapore for one month."

"Just tonight," Aggie said. "Then we'll have to lie low. You'll come with us."

"No," Mei Ling said sternly. "I will not be frightened away from my home. You go, but I will stay on Cheung Chau."

"I'm afraid for your safety."

"It is no longer your concern," Mei Ling finished. She bent down to pick up a slipper that had managed to escape harm. "It is no longer your concern."

With the bombing, things were heating up. There was no way of knowing who had planted it. But we knew why. We were getting close to something, to somebody. And we were becoming inconvenient. Aggie and I weren't able to speak that night. There was too much in the air, too much awaiting us tomorrow. There was the silent wish that it would all go away. That we'd wake up back in her Uptown apartment under cotton sheets and roll over into each other. It was my first taste of love, and I wanted to hang on to it, savor it, figure it out. There was no time.

Mei Ling's friend, Mechian Tseng, took us in without question. We had awakened her from a light sleep, she said, but she instantly had tea prepared and cookies for everyone. Mei Ling did most of the talking. I just smiled and ate, hoping for bed. Around one in the morning, we all drifted off to sleep. Mechian set up two small sleeping areas in the front room so Aggie and I could sleep in honor. We turned our backs on each other and closed our eyes.

I started to fold into myself. Just as Aggie's love was calling me out, something was calling me back in. It was stubborn, and getting louder, more certain. There finally seemed to be a message. I was remembering things. Bullets. Bullets. Bullets. Like firing a gun. Memories, fantasies, lives lived, lives taken, deeds done and left undone. It didn't seem to matter. The words were less scattered. Like buckshot healing together, forming a singular thought. I couldn't duck, I couldn't hide. I was caught. Even the people that had planted the bomb in Mei Ling's innocent apartment knew where I was. Everyone, everything knew where I was.

I thought if I could figure it out before it hit, I'd have a tiny chance of survival. To see it once in clear daylight, to hear the message, the screaming sentence, to read it before the book closed, that was my only chance. But the noise came when it chose, and pressed me with the riddle. Riddle, riddle, riddle with only the blurriest clues. I was just living the days until the blowout. And only good luck had spared me another. I didn't want Aggie to be around when it hit. This needed to happen alone, like a rhinoceros. I was the only one who deserved to suffer.

My scar became wildly tender, and there was some drainage at the very top. Jesus was cutting his way out. The sharp stick of glass kept me awake. In the dark, the strange surroundings of Mechian's apartment closed in on me. There were shapes and sizes I couldn't name. Horror danced in the corners and the closets. Without a sound, I found my way into the bathroom. I remembered sitting on Cheng's toilet back on Numa Street, laughing at the killer in the mirror. Shaved head, unshaven face, yellow teeth, a gorgeous maniac. By instinct, I reached for my gun. It wasn't there. I'd had to leave it in New Orleans. Customs.

I rubbed the dark circles under my eyes like lottery tickets. Back in the Big Easy, things were still hard. Aggie's frequent

calls home just told us that no other tattoo murders had gone
down. Why had the killing stopped?

I dressed, stole a beer from the fridge, ate a chocolate bar,
kiped Aggie's gun and crept out into the dark. I made my way
down to the beach and looked out over the water, scanning for
dancing demons or wrestling angels. For Mary to descend
with a fleur-de-lis to set Hong Kong free. To set the birds free.
To set me free. I cocked the pistol. It felt like a friend resting
its muzzle in my palm.

I spotted a shark. Or a whale or a rock or a Snake Spirit or
Cow Demon. Or a unicorn with a deer's tail, drinking wine
with an eagle who had lost his talons in a poker game. There
was a bat shooting craps with a rooster, and a dragon in white
was the pit boss. I unloaded the gun, killing them all. But
then they popped up again, arcade targets, and began wading
toward me. Their steps made no splash, but they closed in,
angry, iced-over eyes in pursuit. Were they wearing gray suits
and black-soled shoes? In the dark, I couldn't quite tell.

Click. Click. The gun was empty, and I scampered back up
off the beach, catching my knee on a rock, spilling blood like
a drink. My heart ricocheted off my organs, rearranging the
furniture, tripping over the intestines. I breathed my way
back to Mechian's doorway and crept inside as quietly as a
scared man could. Outside, hooves and wings scratched away.
Aggie was gone, looking for me, or maybe not. Maybe she was
out chasing demons and shooting at unicorns. Or maybe organizing them to come after me. But I had the gun. I could
hear Mei Ling and Mechian sleeping in the other room.

Ten minutes later Aggie came in. I was standing naked in
the tub.

"Did you hear the shots?" I wondered.

"No." Her tone was as flat as New Orleans.

"Were you worried? About your gun? Did you come looking for me?"

"No. I just went for a walk. I couldn't sleep."

"I didn't want to sleep. I can't afford to sleep," I said.

"Did you get anything? On your hunt."

"I think I caught the unicorn in the shoulder. You can only seem to get those bastards in the shoulder. The angle and everything. He seemed to be limping when he came up the beach. And there was blood. It wasn't easy finding my way back here. Did I tell you I hit the unicorn?"

"That's bad luck. Unicorns are good. You shouldn't shoot at unicorns."

"It was dark, Aggie, and they were all charging me. Bats, eagles, roosters. I'm not sure what I hit. Maybe I missed the unicorn." I paused, remembering all of it, remembering nothing. "No. I'm pretty sure I scored the unicorn."

"If you hit a cow or a snake, it's okay. I hope you didn't hit the unicorn. There was only one unicorn, wasn't there?" Maybe she had organized them. She seemed to be more on their side than mine. Warm blood bubbled out of my gash and spread like butter down my leg.

"I guess we'll find out in the morning," I said, picturing a white carcass on our doorstep. Aggie didn't smile. She went back to her makeshift bed. I stayed up all night, waiting for the unicorn to pick the lock with his horn. I stared the moon to bed, and the sun bled another morning.

That day at dusk, with mayhem gnawing on my cells, Aggie took me to the Peak Tram, a railcar to the top of Hong Kong.

She hadn't figured out a place for us to stay yet and needed time to think. Or was it something else? Something necessary. It seemed extremely important to her that we make the trip up the ribs of the island. Aggie shouldn't have taken me, but like children who look too long at the sun, she didn't know when to turn away. The pain in my head was so severe, I could barely breathe. My skull was caving in, face crumbling, in minutes the collapse would be complete. Disappear. Disappear.

The streetcar crept straight up the mountain, with the city falling off at either side. We seemed to be chewing our way through a jungle, and the buildings were our crooked witnesses. At the top, we got off, and had all of the island to gaze at. The blue mountains of the New Territories were just visible in the twilight fog, the last rim of safety before China. The signs and office buildings seemed less obscene from such a height. The bushy heads of a million trees dominated the upper hills. We sputtered around the souvenir shops, restaurant and information booth. Vomit blocked my throat, but I wouldn't let it escape. I left Aggie by a rack of discounted T-shirts and went to the telescope-filled balcony. Kids begged parents for coins to see Hong Kong reclining below us like some giant hooker. But I had a better vantage point in mind.

I saw a hawk, fresh snake in his talons, soar up and over the treetops, crew-cutting branches and leaves. I closed my eyes and entered the hawk's mind. I looked again, and I was free-falling, face first over the trees. My arms sped me downward, a fallen angel, as I kissed the boughs and soared over Hong Kong. A shoulder shrug to avoid a billboard, I tucked my knees darting by a hotel. The air caught fire in my lungs. I exploded in flight. Stretching wide, my face felt the tug of the snake in my mouth, and I spit it out, watching it fall sideways into the green abyss. The low clouds pressed down on my neck. I would crash. I would eat dirt, swallow the land and come to my rest. I had escaped.

"Free? Jefferson? Jefferson." Aggie's hand tore at my wing, pulling me down from where I had soared. I smashed into my body and fell onto the concrete. "Where did you go?"

"I was flying. I was inside. I was the hawk." There was blood in my mouth. Snake blood.

"There was gunfire. Didn't you hear it?" She pointed at a small blue house with beige shutters. It was a stone's throw away, hung like a picture in the woods. The second-story windows were freckled with bullet holes, and one shutter had been blown to pieces. Aggie and I were the only ones on the balcony, and she hustled me into the main building. "I called the police. I'm going to go check it out."

"You can't. I don't have my gun." Words fell funny off my beak. Aggie hurried off, shouting a warning back at me. I didn't hear a word. I slid down off the balcony with the ease of an orangutan. Sneaking through the bushes and trees, the branches snapping at my command. Insects hid, birds shut up, leaves hemmed me in, giving me cover. There were gum wrappers on the forest floor. They led to the house.

The house had the eerie silence of people forced to be quiet. Breathing, breathing, only breathing in and waiting. As I came to the side door, the sick wail of a siren spanked my ears. I crashed through and was in the basement. The room sweated under a single bulb. The floor was wet to my touch. I bounded to the base of the steps and looked up from my misty womb. Two large white men stood at the top of the stairway, their backs like castle doors. I took the last five steps in two strides, and hit the men blind. We all fell, and my head split wide open. A loose gun spun like a bottle near me. By the time the hoods got their sights, I had the lousy weapon pointed at their hearts. It felt good, familiar. I would have pulled the trigger. I tried to pull the trigger, but my feathers were slick from flight. My hand was too weak. My wing. My hand. If they'd known, they could have walked up to me and made me shoot myself but they didn't. While I desperately tried to squeeze the trigger, five uniforms and Aggie fumbled into the house. They cuffed the men and left me alone on Aggie's request. She was too shocked to speak to me, and I didn't move from my floored position, gun still cocked. She slid down the wall like blood and sat next to me. She saw the opening, the great canyon that was my skull.

"Now I know why you're shooting at unicorns."

"I like to shoot. I try to talk, but the words just spill out."

"You're coming apart, Free. All the stuffing's coming out."

"I flew, Aggie. I got on top of it all." It was something I'd been trying to do my entire life. "I was on top of it all." I fired the gun. The bullet burrowed six inches into a thin plaster wall, shredding a photograph of Richard Nixon with a panda. Aggie caught her breath, uncurled my fingers and took the gun. She ran out to the cops, yelling for an ambulance. The laughter and the blood came at once. It spilled out warm over my ear and down into my eye, down the cheek into my wide-open mouth. I howled with laughter. A gorgeous maniac.

"Who were the gorillas?" I asked my doctor. She looked just like Aggie, and thought I was delirious.

"You rest now, okay?"

"Can I see him?" I heard Aggie ask from the hallway. Next, she was at my bedside. "Jefferson, you're off the case."

"You're not supposed to call me that. Don't call me that."

"I'm sorry," she retreated.

"And I'm not off the case. I'm just warming up."

"Not only have you got enough glass in your head to build an aquarium, but you upended a score that had nothing to do with us. I've been yelling and screaming for four hours to keep them from laying obstruction of justice charges on you."

"I made the bust for those clowns."

"You don't wear a badge. You don't make busts. Especially on foreign soil. They're pissed, and so am I. You could have been killed."

"With a head like mine, what's the difference?" Aggie didn't have an answer. "Aggie, I'm losing some vision, I have constant headaches and both shoulders are going numb. I'm disappearing. I'd rather go out with a bang. If we'd been at Mei Ling's instead of out dancing, we would have gone out with a bang. That's the best solution. You still don't see it."

"You're going out on a plane. We're flying you back to New Orleans. There's a specialist at St. Jude's who's waiting to operate." Aggie shifted from leg to leg. Back and forth. Back and forth.

"St. Jude is the patron saint of lost causes, Aggie."

"I know."

"To be operated on, I have to sign. And I ain't signing."

"Free, you're dying." She said what she didn't want to say. It crushed her. I smiled.

"I've got a calling to answer. I'll stick around long enough to find out what it is. Now, who were the wide bodies I broke my face on?"

"Nobodies. Two slugs that work for a British numbers runner. It was an interior squabble. That was one of their safe houses, and apparently they were settling accounts. Somebody was unhappy with the calculations. It broke out in gunplay. This has absolutely nothing to do with us."

"They found another guy in the basement with a bullet in his head," I added.

"How did you know?"

"I tripped over him. I'm not going home."

"As soon as you're able to travel, you're getting on a plane. It's been cleared through NOPD. They're very grateful for all you've done."

"I'm not going home," I said steadily. "What's the name of this numbers runner?"

"Thatch. Earl, no, Early Thatch. He's small-time. Hai assured me. Let it go, Free. There is no connection. I should have stayed out of it. I was just going on instincts."

"Get my pants." Aggie found my pants neatly folded and washed along with shirt and shoes. "Look in the pockets."

"There's nothing in the pockets, Free. Everything's been washed. This is Saturday afternoon. Everything's different."

"My wallet and passport!" I hurried.

"I'm sure the nurse has them."

"Get them! Get everything now!"

"You better calm down, killer. Don't pop those stitches to delay the flight. You are going home. And I'll come soon after. I'm going to check a few small leads and then get out. The murders have stopped, and LeMaire can't justify the expense. It's over, Free. It's over." Aggie backed out of the room talking, but I knew it wasn't over. Maybe I was, but that was a different story. She returned with a small brown bag in her hand. She pulled out my wallet and passport, waving them at me like only a cocky cop could.

"Everything. Is that everything?"

"Just some loose change." She paused, fingering through the bag. "And a necklace." Her expression shifted. "You don't wear a necklace." Slowly, she pulled the necklace out.

"I can't go home, Agatha. We've got another saint to find." At the end, hanging like one more question mark, was a sterling-silver fleur-de-lis.

Despite the necklace, Aggie wasn't too excited about me sticking around. Words like "infection," "blood poisoning," "emergency surgery" and "permanent brain damage" were used to chase me home. But I'd lived with my jigsaw head long enough to know when to quit. Or so I convinced her. I still didn't know how fast the doors would close on me, but I wanted to be there when they did. Not under some surgeon's knife or the nerveless kiss of anesthesia. I spent another week in the hospital, swearing I'd be operated on as soon as we got home, together. I had gotten to like together and wasn't in a hurry to end it.

Aggie kept me updated with morning and evening visits. She was keeping her investigation into Early Thatch very quiet. Of course, Detective Hai wasn't eager to assist in any way, so she used her charm with some of the British officers to dig up the dirt on our mystery numbers runner.

Turned out that Thatch had been a local nuisance for more than ten years. He'd moved from Ipswich, England, to Hong Kong in his twenties and set up shop on the island. His luck as a legitimate businessman ended in the early eighties, and he took his ability with numbers crunching to the other side of the law. From investment banker to gambling chief inside six months. He had friends in the right places, who helped him stay afloat. He was a small-time horse-race fixer, buying off jockeys for payoffs as simple as European vacations. He also had a knack for keeping the odds on certain races from getting out of hand. Throw in the occasional rugby and soccer fixes, and Mr. Thatch was sitting on a pot of gold. Nobody seemed to mind as long as he kept to himself. The ease with which the blue-house murder was forgotten was clear proof of that.

"They call him a seven down at the precinct," Aggie said, pushing my wheelchair. I had just been released, and we were headed out of the hospital.

"What the hell's that?"

"Sort of a Chinese joke. During the Cultural Revolution, there were nine categories of enemies of the Revolutionaries. Number seven was a foreign agent. You get the feeling he's not a real favorite among the locals."

"Then why isn't there more of a crackdown on the murder? Come on, Aggie, something's missing."

"His paperwork lists him as Anglican, not Catholic."

"And what about the other suspects? Tattoos? Jewelry?"

"Not as far as I know, but they haven't let me question anyone, look at a lineup, anything. They are holding a suspect. Thatch has been trying to get the bail down all week. With some measure of success, unfortunately."

"Let's pay him a visit."

"Free, I tried, believe me, but he's safer in jail than on the streets. Hai won't let me touch the guy because it's not related to our investigation."

"Bullshit!" My head throbbed. "A fleur-de-lis makes a connection."

"I can't very well tell him you removed evidence from the scene of a murder. They still want to bring you up on charges. Trespassing, even assault with a deadly weapon. You fired the gun."

"There was no one in the room, Ag."

"It was still stupid. And the guy says he wouldn't shoot a co-worker, a buddy. They'd love to pin this on somebody, and the necklace might just give them an excuse. Free, you're too sick to get locked up."

"What's bail?"

"Two million, Hong Kong."

"That's a joke."

"I guess Mr. Thatch isn't as liquid as he'd like to be. He's playing the legal end, but I'm guessing he just can't come up with the two hundred fifty grand."

"That can't be much for a heroin smuggler to coin out."

"Either that or he's a bad gambler. Remember, his last two sends wound up dead. Then again, we don't even know if he's the guy."

"Aggie?!?!"

"Yeah, yeah, yeah. Shut up and heal."

"And what's Thatch's score sheet?"

"Small-time, wall to wall. No import-export fraud, or even any transactions, from what I could gather. I hate to say it, but for a crook, he looks squeaky clean."

The cab dropped us off at the Grand Hyatt, and I was slow to get out. "I don't feel much like eating, Aggie. My head's a little light."

"We're not eating. We're lying down. I booked us a room.

Whoever's gunning for us will never look here." From the
streets of New Orleans to the Grand Hyatt in Hong Kong. We
took the elevator to the twenty-second floor. The bells were
like birds, sweet and clear. The carpeting was so thick, my
wheelchair protested, but we made it to room 2218. A king-
size bed, beautiful pictures on the wall, a basket of fruit.
Even the oranges looked holy. The bathroom was almost too
bright, and Aggie bathed me in a tub big enough to live in. I
recalled stealing sink showers in the train station men's room
or nabbing a bird bath at a public water fountain. Staring into
fractured mirrors wondering who I was, who I'd ever be, why
God had taken the time to drop me off on earth. Now, beneath
the tender hands of a woman, I lay clean, scrubbed, touched,
almost forgiven. I lay in the water till my hands aged, dove
into a giant robe and eased into the bed of a king. Aggie fed
me an orange, slice by slice, and we kissed the sourness
away. As my eyes winked shut, she reached into the night-
table drawer, and pulled out the hotel Bible.

"I want to read you something my mother used to read to
me when I was scared. Can you concentrate? Are you too
tired to listen?" I nodded no, and Aggie began her sweet
song. The words slid under my bandage and tucked my
thoughts in for the night. "No longer will violence be heard in
your land, nor ruin or destruction within your borders, but
you will call your walls Salvation and your gates Praise. The
sun will no more be your light by day, nor will the brightness
of the moon shine on you, for the Lord will be your everlasting
light, and your God will be your glory. Your sun will never set
again, and your moon will wane no more; the Lord will be
your everlasting light, and your days of sorrow will end. Then
will all your people be righteous, and they will possess the

land forever. They are the shoot I have planted, the work of my hands, for the display of my splendor. The least of you will become a thousand, the smallest a mighty nation. I am the Lord; in its time I will do this swiftly. The Spirit of the Sovereign Lord is on me, because the Lord has anointed me to preach good news to the poor. He has sent me to bind up the brokenhearted, to proclaim freedom for the captives and release for the prisoners, to proclaim the year of the Jubilee."

I know that one. I know where it is. I just can't remember. I'm about to get it, about to remember. I know I can get it. I just need a minute. It's all I need. I need to get past this thing, if I can just get past this thing, then I can get past this thing, thing, thing, thing, thing . . . God damn it! A word hasn't been spoken. There is nothing inside. Not a word, a spoken word for eighteen years. A memory. A word. A lie. Tongue probably forgot how to talk. I can't wait, afford to wait. This is it. This. This is the push.

The sun was awake the next morning, setting the normal mist on fire. The harbor water even looked clean. Aggie brought me breakfast in bed, and we planned our attack.

"I have Thatch's home address from police records. He works at home. But we can't bug the place or get any kind of look inside."

"Stakeout," I managed between bites of omelet.

"Not in your condition."

"Aggie, all I can do is sit. I'm custom-built for the job." She didn't like it, but she was getting used to losing these arguments.

"I suppose I could use the company."

I sat up in bed. "It'll be great. Coffee and doughnuts, bad jokes. Right? You cops tell a lot of bad jokes to each other."

"I don't know what you're talking about."

"Sure. Every time I see two cops together, one's laughing, but with a sick expression on his face, like he can't help himself."

"That sick expression," Aggie leaned in, "is from dealing with punks like you." She kissed my nose. "Your nose healed pretty good. I like it a little crooked." I finished breakfast and wiped my mouth with the back of my hand.

"Time to get back to work. I'll go pick up some stuff and rent a car." She stood with purpose.

"Don't forget to call Captain LeMaire. Tell him we're taking a few extra days to see the sights. And don't be nervous. Cops are *very* understanding."

Alone in the room, it took me ten minutes to turn on the television. Lolly and Sup had a television, but it just turned on regular. This one came out of the wall and had extra gadgets. I tried every button, from every angle, without luck. Finally, I sat on the controls and the TV blinked to life. There were a few stations talking Chinese, loud. The actors were yelling at each other. It seemed important. There was a movie on Channel 7. Something with a shark and a lot of nervous actors. They were screaming in slow motion. Even the shark. One of the men wore glasses, but no matter how many times he got dragged under the water, they never got wet. I turned on the news. A woman with a startled look on her face filled the screen. Maybe she'd seen the shark. She kept saying how bad things were, but with a smile. She reminded me of the hookers on Basin Street, all that happy sadness in their eyes.

I switched off the set and paced. I still wasn't used to being inside. The walls were a beautiful prison. I pressed my hands mightily against the shatterproof windows. In the bathroom, I used the hotel toothbrush, toothpaste, soap, powder, Q-tips, I even took out a few cotton balls. I ran the shower, because I missed the sound of rain. Flushed the toilet, filled the sink, threw all the towels in the tub. I emptied the Kleenex box and stuffed my pockets. Shaved with the supplied razor and cream, which went on like soap and tonic water. My head jangled, so I nipped two mini-bottles of scotch from the bar and inhaled them. I turned the desk on its side, sending paper and pens flying. Put the chair on top of the bed and lay down on the couch. I woke up minutes before Aggie returned and straightened up.

"The place is a mess," she said anyway. "I had a hell of a time finding you doughnuts." She set down the bag she was carrying.

"I was only joking. You found me doughnuts?"

"That's why I'm so late. The stupid doughnuts. They're not even doughnuts, really. Just a British imitation, but close enough."

"I want to kiss you, Agatha Li." So I did. We did. For a long time.

Early Thatch lived way back at the top of Victoria Peak. His house on Mount Austin Road was more a castle. Separated by elaborate fences and a security system worthy of royalty. It loomed over the whole street.

"This guy must be important."

"The fellas in the department say it's all ego," Aggie answered. "He's small-time, but he's from old money."

"He'd like New Orleans."

"He probably does." The more I stared at the house, the more obvious it was that it would have fit in New Orleans. Large, white pillars, fancy railings, even a balcony and, downstairs, a small porch.

"He's a Southern gentleman."

"We'll see." Aggie had rented a dark blue Ford, with seats that lay back so I could rest. We brought extra pillows to ease my head. The first signs of Hong Kong heat steamed the windows.

"This is like making out in high school," Aggie remembered. "Alone in a car with a boy at night. Those high school boys never did know how to kiss."

"High school?" I said.

"Yes, on dates in high school. Didn't you ever go parking with a girl in high school?"

"I don't remember. Let me have another chocolate." Aggie handed it to me like an apology.

"I didn't mean . . ."

"I don't remember much of anything before New Orleans. I don't think I went to high school. Maybe I did. I don't remember."

"Are you afraid to remember, Free?" A passing car tried to drown her out.

"I just can't, that's all. There's nothing there. Coming to New Orleans was a big wall, and I can't see past it."

"Maybe you block it out. I try to block some bad memories out sometimes. It's normal."

"Normal." I laughed. "More likely it never happened at all. I was born at seventeen at the corner of Royal and Canal. That's where I was alive. As far as I'm concerned, that's where everything started."

"You don't remember your parents?" She was pressing. A doctor looking for glass to pick out, to make a pretty picture. But there was nothing beautiful in my past. There was nothing.

"Agatha, let's do our job."

The hours passed. I slept off and on, yet each time I woke up, there was Aggie, eyes locked on Thatch's house. As if she could see inside, eyeball his secrets. The next morning started quickly. Birds hammered out the blues above us, and Aggie punched my shoulder.

"Wake up, cowboy. Here comes our man." I scratched the sleep from my eyes in time to see a brown-haired man smooth by us in a silver Rolls-Royce. Aggie waited till he cleared sight, and started the car.

"What time is it?" I asked, not being able to focus.

"While you were snoozing, this house was on fire. At the crack of dawn, there were heads popping around in the upstairs windows, and goons everywhere, in and out of the front door. They were carrying boxes, but not heavy ones. I could see by the way they were jostling each other. It was an easy detail. Then it got real quiet for about an hour. Breakfast, I'm figuring."

"Go on," I prodded.

"Only one car leaves, that was the Rolls, and it's Thatch. I know from his police bio. His car is loaded with a shipment of some sort."

"The boss making a delivery?"

"Maybe it's an important one."

"Better be, because he woke me up from a beautiful dream."

"Tell me." Aggie's hands were loose on the wheel, and we

wound our way down the mountain. The piercing gleam of Thatch's bumper cut into my bones.

"I was on the streets, minding myself, sleeping off a particularly active night of something. It was a doorway, and I was warm. Oh yeah, it was raining." A cat zipped in front of us. Aggie swerved and got us back on track. The cat perched safely in a tree. "A nightstick banged just above my head, took a chunk out of the door, and my boots—I was wearing boots—popped off. My cigarettes all burned, and a sandwich I had in my pocket dried up and blew away. That part was really weird. Then I looked to see what bastard was sending me out into the rain." Thatch took a left onto Queen's Road Central. There were two cabs between us. "I looked up. Aggie, I looked up and it was you. Then I woke up."

"What about the sandwich?"

"The sandwich?"

"Yeah, what about the sandwich? Did I get you another sandwich?" Her voice was worried.

"I tell you this dream, and you ask about the sandwich."

"You have to eat. I worry about you eating enough."

"It's a dream, Aggie. You don't have to eat in dreams."

"I love you."

"Don't lose this guy. Stay with him."

"I love you," she announced, reaching over to kiss my cheek. She did it without losing sight of the road. It was one of the balancing tricks she did effortlessly. "I love you, Freeman." Thatch took another left onto Peel Street and shook his way further from Central District.

"This looks familiar," I said as we retraced our steps toward the medicine shop. "I hope I'm wrong." Even empty, the place gave me the willies. He parked illegally on Bridges

Street and got out of the car. When he reached Ladder Street
he took a right, looking back over his shoulder a final time.

"I'm going after him." Aggie popped her door open.

"Do you have your gun?" She touched it. "Okay, I'll watch
from the car." As Aggie disappeared, a group of four Chinese
men casually approached the Rolls-Royce. I ducked down
low. At first, they looked like car thieves, but when they
found the keys in the driver's seat, it was clear. They opened
the trunk and grabbed all the boxes. They moved quickly in
their dark Mao suits, like bats trying to get out of the light.
Shutting the trunk, they flew off. A minute later, one hustled
back. He'd forgotten to leave the keys.

It was twenty minutes before Aggie returned. It was just
past 7:30 A.M., and the city was already wide awake. Cars
could be heard busting to work down on Aberdeen Street, and
the shopkeepers were lugging their goods over to Hollywood
Road. An ancient woman with spiderweb hair carried two
overstuffed baskets of trinkets. She balanced them across her
shoulders with a bamboo pole. Her bones stuck out like
shelves to ease the job. Rounding the corner, Aggie almost
took her out, but the old-timer slid by the near collision with
grace.

"Anything?" She was out of breath.

"You were the one who was gone so long," I jabbed. "Were
you eating breakfast with the guy?"

"He went into the temple. I grabbed a few joss sticks from
outside and followed him in. He knelt the whole time. He
really seemed to be praying. A British Buddhist."

"You sound shocked."

"They don't mix religion with business. Business is their
religion."

"Don't get too excited. He was just killing time. He left the keys on the front seat, and four Mao choirboys cleaned out his trunk. This is a regular drop."

"Where did they take it?"

"On your tail. Right up Ladder Street, but after that . . ." Aggie chewed her lip like gum.

"There was some noise, in the back of the temple. Just behind the altar, but he didn't flinch."

Outside the temple, a bonfire raged in a small pit. Thatch was gone. A handful of early-rising tourists took flash pictures in the dark belly of the room. There were three altars, one to each side of the main Buddha. Several worn-out kneeling pads waited for knees of desire. I thought of Mobley and all the saints. A man stood behind a counter and sold incense and souvenirs. *"It is written, my house will be called a house of prayer, but you are making it a den of robbers."* I remembered Mobley quoting Jesus years before. But this wasn't Jesus' house, it was Buddha's, and the man was selling everything but T-shirts and pennants. Through an open window, two mute birds flew. They landed on the altar and pecked at an orange left for the temple god. The man behind the counter was too old to chase them. He lit a cigarette like a flare. The tourists took a picture and flashed the birds away. Outside, we could hear the noise of business: shuffling feet, banging metal, early-morning bargains being shouted out loud. More people rolled in to join us. Worship seemed the last thing possible. A woman and her young daughter took a container full of long wood sticks. They knelt before the central altar, rattling their sticks like bones until one shimmied out. They smiled at each other in the dark.

"It tells their future," Aggie whispered.

"Must be good news."

"They pray for money, and they keep shaking out the sticks until they get the one they want. It's always good news." Aggie snuck us out a side door. We stood in an alcove, hay and trash at our feet, sacred confetti. To our left was the temple, to our right a wall. It was diseased and bleeding blue, red and black paint.

"There's nothing here. They could have taken those boxes anywhere."

"It could be underground." We got on our hands and knees, feeling for a break in the floor, but there was nothing. If there was an underground room, there was another way in.

"It's probably inside the temple," I guessed, "but it's too dark to see anything in there."

"They could have come in behind the altars. There's got to be space back there." We circled the building several times, but found no entryway, no secret passage. "The Chinese are very good at disappearing."

"Thatch is down there, wherever it is. Because he didn't come back to the car, and he's not in the temple. It's happening right underneath our feet."

"We're so close," Aggie pushed. She knew we'd hit another dead end.

We got back to our car, and as expected, the Rolls was still sitting there. We both had tickets. "Keys are in the car," I hinted. "Maybe I should check it out."

"I don't know if we have time."

"There's only one way to find out." I flashed her a grin as bright as an electronic billboard.

"I'll cover you." Aggie dashed to the corner, gun at the ready, and gave me the signal. I felt reborn. Like my old days as a small-time thief. I rocketed through the Rolls's interior. Three cigars, a lighter with a fleur-de-lis on the ivory handle, a newly cleaned hairbrush, a checkbook, three pairs of polished shoes. They fit, so I took a pair. A box of tissues and a glove compartment that actually held gloves. And an empty Smith & Wesson. The trunk was a zero. Not a clue as to what it had held. Only a tire jack, gasoline can and a passport. I slammed it shut, waved Aggie off and walked back to our car. Then it hit me. The passport thought had been cut to ribbons by my glassy brain. I had to picture it all over again. Passport. Passport. That was strange, to see a passport in a trunk. In the trunk of a car. I sprinted back to the car and fumbled with the keys. Aggie had the panicked stance of someone caught red-handed. As I popped the trunk, Thatch rounded the corner. Aggie was behind her wheel and then beside me. She revved the engine.

I went cross-eyed. Leather soles slapped the concrete between the owner and me. Thatch bore down, as I blindly searched for the passport. I had it in my hand when he slammed the trunk on my wrist.

"I don't think that would be appropriate." He glared. His accent was so fancy I almost bowed. I decked him with one punch. My left-handed power surge left him on his knees.

"You'll ruin your suit," I said, kneeing him into the soggy gutter. I jumped in the car, and we took off. Thatch was too punch-drunk to follow us.

At first, I was too excited about my solid punch to remember I'd gotten the booty. I was crushing it when Aggie looked down and noticed.

"I cleaned his goddamn clock! That was incredible. Line

drive, late night, son of a bitch hammer fall! God, that felt good." I floated six inches outside my body.

Aggie yanked me back in. "What did you get?" she yelled. She barreled down the road like a Hong Kong cabby.

"There was nothing in the trunk, nothing in the car." My wrist throbbed.

"Nothing!?!"

"Nothing but this." I held up the passport and opened it. There was no picture, no writing, no international travel stamps. But the country was clear as stars on a flag. The United States of America.

Things were finally starting to come together. We still couldn't get the local cops involved. I'd broken into his car to get the passport, and the boxes might as well have never existed. But somewhere on that side street or under the pavement or hidden in that Buddhist temple, American citizens were being born.

"Shun Peng and Thatch must be working together," I said over a cup of coffee at Jimmy's Kitchen. "It's the only way he and Comic could disappear so fast. Thatch has bodies. He has a payroll. He has the bones to pull the vanishing off."

"That may just be because somebody's bankrolling him from back home. They bring the heroin, the N.O. connection gives out cash, Louisiana licenses, a place to live."

"And Early gets a percentage. He must be doing this all over the country. New Orleans isn't big enough for all these bodies."

"Two thousand a week, Free. He's got an easy market. Hong Kong nationals must be knocking down his door. And there's a fair share of Asians in New Orleans East. If a person really wants to, he can disappear anywhere."

"Guess what, baby? You're going undercover again."

"It won't work." She wanted it to but wasn't ready to commit. We weren't in our backyard anymore. The dangers were greater.

"My cover's blown," I explained. "I practically took the guy's head off. You are Chinese."

"I'm American."

"You know what I mean, Ag."

"Yes, I do, but I'm not Chinese. I don't speak the language. If one of his Hong Kong sidekicks decides to strike up a conversation, I'm finished."

"We'll work it so you're only with him. Alone. We'll isolate you. You'll demand to be a special case."

"And just how do we go about doing that?"

"We tail him, catch him alone, and you can play hide-and-seek. Sit down at his table, say you know his game and need help."

"Use my charm." Aggie grimaced.

"Exactly. Set up meetings, always around people. British places, not Chinese restaurants or anything."

"But if he's the one who planted the bomb, then he knows who we are. It doesn't matter how far undercover I go. Or you go."

"What's he going to do, off you in public? He won't have a choice if you make him deal with you. If he doesn't know you, then we can get inside. If he does know you, maybe we can draw his fire, or at least watch him sweat. People hate fearlessness. It scares them to death. If you act like you're unstoppable, then you are."

"It's hard to argue with firsthand experience," Aggie admitted.

"You're damn right. I'm sick of sitting this one out. My meter's running out, Ag. We've got to make a move. Either get Hai involved or play out this hand. I don't think we have a choice."

"I won't work with Detective Hai. I won't give him the pleasure of bossing me around."

"That's it, Aggie."

"Look, we don't want this guy. All we need is some information."

"And now we have a way to get it. Or at least try to get it. No shame dying if the dying's done face first. We find out who this fool is tapping in New Orleans, and we go home. You make an arrest, and I make a doctor's appointment. Kill or be killed. This way I'll be able to relax."

"You think he knows about the deaths in N.O.?"

"I bet he doesn't give a damn. He ships and collects. It's just business."

"Probably thinks he's doing them a favor," Aggie said, tugging on a roll. "Sending them to the land of opportunity, the land of freedom. Sending them to die."

"He does have nice taste in shoes, though." I swung my new wing tips into the aisle.

"Free, you are a thief."

"If the shoe fits."

We had to rent a new car. A beige Isuzu was the only thing left on the lot. We sat in that beat-up Japanese car for two days before Thatch left his house again. He was waiting for his face to heal. I'd hurt him good. We bought a pack of cards, and Aggie beat me at gin twenty-six times in a row. I could drink it, but I couldn't play it.

Then the screw tightened again. The brain shredding

heated up. I started to see and hear things way too clearly. All
the extra stripped away, leaving the core exposed. When Aggie spoke, her words were huge, and they filled the car till I
had to open a window. Leaves applauded our coming and
going. Cat meows and dog barks came through giant speakers
in my head. Colors were brighter. Red was fire, purple was
blood, black was death. I could see every notch in the radio
knobs. One on each had been left unfinished. The dashboard
was lousy with gashes and scars. I felt in tune with the air
conditioner. Watching the antenna go up and down was a
mystical experience. It rose and sank with such steadiness,
such promise, with only a little tremble on its way out of
sight, a nervous goodbye. I could hear Aggie bat her eyelashes, and the sound of her putting on makeup was like the
building of a house. Rumble, scratch, rub, paint, coat, tear
down, start again. The glove box, seat-belt buckle, hood and
trunk were all the same sound, only slightly changed. The
hood was my favorite. Even amplified, it still sounded a dull
thud. Like a body hitting the earth, dropped from someplace
safe and warm. It sounded like regret. I couldn't explain it to
Aggie, so I kept my mouth sealed. Speech was all scrape and
scream anyway. I didn't mind being mute. It was just past
noon on a Thursday when Mr. Early Thatch finally made his
move.

He was with a crony, but we followed him anyway. They
stopped to eat at the Marriott on Pacific Place. Thatch and
friend headed straight for the restaurant and a back table.
There was no way to keep an eye on him.

"I could take a waiter out with a quick jab and bring them
their drinks."

"Free."

We craned our necks, but no luck. "I can hear what they're

saying." I almost could. "If they'd stop clinking their glasses."

"Quit fooling around."

"May I help you?" the host asked us.

"Just looking. We're hotel guests," Aggie lied.

Shhh, I thought inside my head. Words, silverware, plates, door swings. It was an orchestra of pain.

"Well, enjoy your stay. Hope you choose to join us for a meal," he said, handing us menus. Thatch's friend got up. He headed for us. I ducked behind a dessert display, and Aggie made a beeline for Thatch. She told me later what took place. I ate a piece of cheesecake.

"I want to go America."

"Excuse me, but this seat is taken." Thatch didn't blush.

"I have big money. I know you do this. I heard some friend come to you."

"Madam, I have not the faintest . . ."

"Dao Tei Cheng. He go America. New Orleans. I know. I know Shun Peng about, and tattoo. Please send. I have much money."

Thatch shifted gears flawlessly. "Meet me at Mad Dog's pub tomorrow, near Post-97. Noon. We'll talk. Come alone." Aggie shot out of the chair, mission accomplished. I was waiting for her by the elevators.

"Did it stick? Did he recognize you?"

"I couldn't tell. We'll find out tomorrow at noon."

Something popped inside my head. "We need," I stuttered. "We need to . . ."

"Slow down, Free." Her face was a church.

"We need to get me out. Of here get we out of need for to get me into the where I need to get me out of I need . . ."

Aggie hurried me to the car, whispering into my ear that

she loved me over and over again. Loved me. Loved me. Just hold on.

The smell. The aroma. The odor. The stench. Something precious, something shattered, something burning, something battered. Perfume into blood. Yes. Yes. Finally goddamned yes. Sweet and sour. Like a barbecue. A cook-out. A shoot-out. And she was just dying. Dying to come over. Dying to come over and say something so . . . to come over and smell so familiar. Like family. Like someone everybody knows. She's not going to scream, though. Not this time. No, this time, she won't make a sound.

I screamed. We were on the Star Ferry, about to begin the ride to Kowloon. We hadn't left the dock yet, and the last passengers were straggling aboard. I'd said I needed to see the birds. The miraculous birds in their miraculous cages. I had begged Aggie to take me to the birds. To see them ricochet and wail, with broken beaks and splintered feathers. That would calm me down, I'd said. They would pull me together. But we never made it to the birds. We never made it out of the dock. We never made it because I screamed. The children on the ferry held their ears. They also smiled, eyes wide open. I was a carnival freak. Something to fear and take home. It wasn't a normal scream I screamed, high-pitched and afraid. It wasn't an angry scream, or a confused scream. It was a rhinoceros scream. It started in the thick of my neck and vomited up and out through my horn, just below the sloped, gray eyelids. It was the scream of seeing my own death, the end of me. Of being slit gill to everlasting gill. Of tasting the razor of good night. It was the scream of Cheng and Billy, who saw their own death coming on June 30, 1997, when the Chinese would take over all their dreams. And the screams they howled on the pool table and in the alleyway when the bullets took all the oxygen home in a jar. It sounded so familiar. Maybe it was Hong Kong's own scream, and that's why the children smiled. For though it hurt their ears, they knew it was a true scream, their scream, a sound they had not yet learned how to make. All the lights in the city dimmed at my horrible cry.

Aggie bowed my head, showed her badge, and silently walked me off the boat. The passengers crowded at the edge of the boat. For a wave, a tear, an autograph, something grotesque. I didn't have the strength to give them anything. Aggie got us back to the car, and back to the hotel. She undressed me, changed my bandage, cleaned out the dirty river in my head. She tucked me in and lay beside me.

"You're really dying, aren't you? Right in front of the whole world. You just couldn't wait."

"Yes."

"When will you die?"

"I don't know. Soon. I thought I was already dead. Many times. But now I know those were only practice. It's all been practice."

"I can't stop it," she said, answering her own question.

"You have stopped it. Over and over again."

"I won't send you home."

"Thanks, Aggie." The words toppled out.

"I won't send you to the hospital."

"Thank you." The ceiling fell down an inch from my face. "Agatha, I can do whatever I do. But one moment, I won't be able to do things anymore. I'll have finished my walk."

"Don't die alone, Free. Don't die alone."

"It's the only way I know how."

"Nobody knows how to die."

Aggie's adventure with Thatch at Mad Dog's was the next step. She waited by the employees' entrance until he entered. I was in the kitchen, flipping burgers. I was dizzy as a falling leaf, but I lied to Aggie so I could keep my cataract eye on her. At least it was something. I couldn't leave her out there all by herself. I was prepared to spill myself into one last flood of rage. Hoping it would be enough. We had the whole staff in on our little stakeout. They thought we were spies. It was beautiful. I used a spatula to keep my balance. The sausage on the grill sizzled like firecrackers. I was wildly aware.

Thatch came in wearing a classic gray suit. He took a corner booth, ordered a Bloody Mary and waited. He wasn't nervous. This deal would make him money, and that relaxed every muscle in his greedy body. Aggie scuffled over, dropping glances like bombs. She played the uptight bass. He didn't like it.

"My dear madam, one mustn't make a public display."

"I got tattoo," Aggie belted.

"You shouldn't have done that. We have our own man. It's quite a tricky design. Very regal. Holy, really." Aggie bared her shoulder to the most honorable Mr. Thatch, and he sucked air. "Good heavens, not here." But then he saw how exact Aggie's tattoo was. He was blown away. "Shun Peng didn't do this?"

"Shun Peng," Aggie repeated. She was in deep waters.

"My artist, Shun Peng, with the hump," said Thatch. His

lips were as gray as his suit. "Or Comic. Did they do this tattoo?"

"Dai Lan Medicine Shop Dai Lan," Aggie lied.

"That particular site is out of business, my dear." Suspicion curdled at the edge of his mouth.

"Long time ago, 1990, January." Aggie was scrambling. "Before Cheng, but I get frightened. No ready for travel. I am nervous now again."

"Calm down, peach blossom, calm down. Daddy's here."

"I am frightened too much. I must go to Cheng. To America. I have money. Many money. China is coming. China is coming."

Thatch's eyes lit green. He was a pinball machine on tilt. And he didn't seem to know who Agatha was. "Here's how our little ride works. You transport our precious package to New Orleans. Now, you're sure you want to follow Cheng to New Orleans? It's not an easy town for little things. I could send you somewhere less exciting. Vancouver, San Francisco, Tucson. Tucson's become quite a popular little getaway, if you know what I mean." He laughed at himself.

"The Big Easiest," Aggie announced. "Only city in the world. New Orleans. Queen of the South, the Heart of Dixie, the city that . . ."

"It is a gem along the Mississippi, is it not, my flower? Now, they'll take care of all your financial needs, housing, all the sordid details." His laugh was capped white, and short, like he'd been hit in the stomach. He leaned in, taking Aggie's hands. "My dear, dear girl, you have absolutely nothing to worry about."

"I worry Dao Tei no write. I worry."

"You let me worry about our friend Mr. Cheng. I'm sure

he's quite caught up in his brilliant new life in America. Now, about the money. Such a terribly naf subject." Aggie took her hands away.

"Money no problem. I have many money."

"Two hundred fifty thousand dollars. American." I dropped a medium-rare baconburger on the kitchen floor. A waiter washed it off and served it.

"That's more than Cheng pay," Aggie gambled.

"You understand, the Gulf War played a dirty trick on all our purses. The price stands." And so did Thatch. Aggie was losing him.

"Who I see in New Orleans? Who get package?"

"Oh, my nervous hummingbird, all of that will be settled once we have your investment safe in hand." He coolly patted her on the shoulder and strode out the door. Aggie put her head down as I brought her a burger.

"Well-done, ma'am?"

"Not a chance."

There was no way in Hong Kong to come up with that kind of money. We had no other choice, so we sucked up our pride and went to Detective Hai.

"Detective Hai."

"Hello, Detective Li, and sir, I can't quite recall . . ."

"John Wayne," I said, shaking his hand.

"We nailed Early Thatch," Aggie started. "Or rather we have him nailed, we just need the hammer." Hai wriggled in his chair.

"John Wayne it is. I don't suppose you realize how many jurisdictional regulations you must have broken." Aggie caught her temper a whisker from Hai's throat. We all took a deep breath.

"Detective, we have broken no regulations. We followed leads your investigation chose to ignore. Our inquiries relate directly to an ongoing murder investigation in New Orleans, of which Mr. Thatch has now become a chief suspect. Or at least a vital link in the chain. I have no reason to believe that we should not be able to cooperate fully, and run our separate cases on parallel lines."

"Don't lecture me, Miss America. I am not in the mood for lectures. I am never in the mood for lectures. Especially when they have no basis in fact or logic."

"Do you have to practice to be this much of an asshole, or is it genetic?" Hai's eyes flashed like Roman candles. "Look, all friendliness aside, Detective Hai, I have a drop set up with Early Thatch for two hundred fifty thousand American dollars in exchange for an American passport and a shitload of smack. Unless I'm mistaken, that's still against the law here in Hong Kong. This seems like the perfect opportunity for me to help you get scum off the streets, and you to help me get home sooner. Which I assume would make you very happy. Now, will you help me make this bust, or do I go to the American and British consulates and ride all over your regulated ass?" The hair on the back of my neck stood up and saluted.

"The money, that kind of money, is not easy," Hai mumbled, looking for an out.

"Screw the money. Just give me a suitcase full of towels. All I want is the drop. I've got four murders on my hands back home, and this pompous Brit could very well be responsible. Or at least be able to point me in the right direction. Not to mention the heroin local project kids are shooting into their veins. Unlike here, horse is not a recreational drug in

New Orleans. Give me the threat over his head so I can get some answers and go home, get out of your hair. You can do what you want with Thatch, just let me wave the stick at him."

Hai scraped his rubber soles across the floor, as if to shake a piece of gum. A tiny tremor ran through his chin. "I will tell you a story."

"I don't want to hear a story," Aggie spat. "I want an answer. I want some goddamn support. I want you to do your job."

"I will tell you a story. There was a boy, and he was born in the country. Outside his window was a peach tree. It was an ugly peach tree. It grew small, tasteless fruit, and its branches were weak. Each winter, it seemed sure to die, but each spring, it somehow struggled back to its job of growing these peaches no one wanted to eat." Aggie was going crazy, barely able to contain her fury. She felt manipulated and ignored. But the story had a hold of me. Each word falling out of Hai's small mouth, wrapping another link around my attention. "The little boy loved this tree like a trusted friend, but the little boy had a brother who hated the tree. 'It is ugly,' the brother would shout. 'We are not a poor family, yet we have the poorest tree in all the countryside.' One night, while the little boy was sleeping, his brother went outside and chopped down the peach tree. In the morning, the boy looked out his window, and all that was left was a stump and one ugly peach. That winter was very harsh, and the boy's brother became very ill, and very hungry, but there was nothing to eat in the house. The little boy brought his brother the ugly peach from the ugly peach tree, saying, 'Eat the peach, and you will live.' But the brother refused to eat it. Then on one very cold night, the brother breathed his last, and died. There was a funeral, and the brother was buried. On his brother's chest, the little boy lay the ugly peach." Aggie cleared her throat. It sounded like a car crash. "On the first day of spring, the little boy looked out his window, and the peach tree had returned, with boughs full of fruit. It was still ugly, and its peaches were still ugly, but it had returned to its place outside the window. It had returned to the little boy." Hai was silent. Phones rang all up and down the precinct.

"What the hell does that have to do with anything, Detective? What the hell did you just waste our time for with that utterly meaningless story?"

"The story means many things, Miss Li, but your response means only one thing. You are neither a woman nor a Chinese."

With a sick grimace of pride, Hai picked up the phone and began organizing the bust of Early Thatch. There was no more conversation, no more stories, only business. Though I would have listened to Hai all day and night. Whatever it was he'd tried to say, there was one thing he communicated loud and clear. It was time for us to leave Hong Kong. The code was getting thicker, and we couldn't read the signs. Still, Aggie was determined, and I knew the longer I stayed out of St. Jude's Hospital, the longer I'd stay alive.

Hai assembled a team that would go undercover as Peak Tram operators. The blue house where I'd done my kamikaze mission was still under police seizure. It would serve as a rendezvous point and the center of communications. It was close enough to the Thatch mansion, where the drop would go down, to make a perfect temporary headquarters. Once the Hong Kong police kicked into action, they knew their stuff.

Two ugly suitcases were filled with matched-weight play
money and real dollars on top. More than twenty-five thousand G's anyway. It made me want to buy a wallet.

Aggie made her last contact with Thatch at Grappa's, an
Italian restaurant inside a crowded mall. I was in the kitchen
again.

"You're a lovely young lady. Perhaps we could take in the
cinema this evening. As a type of keepsake." His educated
manner was so fake she had to fight back laughter. He had
dark brown hair and round features. His face looked like a
ball that had been kicked too often, with sudden, uncon-
nected splotches and crooked ears. He appeared to be listening intently and ignoring her at the same time.

"Thank you, no, Mr. Thatch." Aggie threw him a grin like a
fishing line. "Why flower? Tattoo flower." Early seemed relieved someone finally asked.

"There is a woman. A heavenly creature who believes in
the power of symbols. She has educated me in so many areas.
The wonder of it all."

"Magic?" Aggie asked.

"Not magic, but an aura even more powerful." Thatch
opened his hands, and Aggie could see for the first time what
filled the center of his palms. Fleurs-de-lis. Red. "The fleur-
de-lis is a gift from heaven," he continued. "It is a special
blessing from the Virgin Mary, brought by an angel to those
who bear its mark. I carry that power in the palms of my
hands. It protects me. It watches over my every breath. I am
blessed, and so art thou, my brave child." He touched her
cheek and stroked her shoulder. The one bearing the tattoo.
Agatha didn't pull away.

"And red?"

"Red is blood. Everything that is of the blood, that most

precious humor, is everlasting. We are protected. It is part of the promise. We cannot perish. You are completely safe." Thatch was transformed, glowing, lit from behind. His features swam about in the pool of his face. He hovered an inch off his chair. "Touch my hands. Feel the power. Feel the protection." Aggie placed her hands in his and sat up, ramrod straight, like she'd been electrocuted. After a long moment, Thatch let go, and Aggie slumped back down. "It is not a myth. Some play at symbols, trifle with their beauty and power, but these bent petals, this blood-red promise is from above, and it is alive."

"Who is woman?" Aggie said, still feeling electric.

Thatch sank back into himself, his lips tightening like two fan belts. "It is the symbol. Remember, that will be your safeguard. On your journey and forever."

"And the woman?" she pressed. Thatch was silent, a different man. Part of him was missing, and it shimmered in the air between him and Aggie. He asked for the check and bowed his head, exhausted.

"I have go now, mister. Thank you for pizza."

"My child, the pleasure has been distinctly and entirely mine. Until Tuesday, when the clock thunders nine." He rose and kissed her hand.

"Ten thousand volts. That's what it looked like from the kitchen, Aggie."

"It was just a reaction. I didn't expect him to take my hands like that. Nothing happened."

"You gave him your hands. I watched it happen. Something passed through you."

"Nothing happened. Believe me, I was the one touching his clammy skin."

We were sitting in the Botanical Gardens again, this time

by the jaguar's cage, waiting for nine o'clock on the telltale Tuesday night. The sun didn't exactly set in Hong Kong so much as it slinked away. The heavy darkness moved in relentlessly. "I prefer the nights here," she said. "They're not so long as the days. I guess I prefer the nights everywhere." The jaguar paced his cage, staring over our heads to the city below. He would have blended in down among the corporate lions, tigers and bears. All he needed was a chance, an interview, a first job. I wanted to pick the lock and let the jag do some wandering. He flashed a jagged smile and curled into sleep on his ledge. Not tonight, he said. I don't have the strength.

"You know he'll count the money."

"As soon as he takes the suitcase." Aggie stood and paced like the wild cat. Her jaw was flexed. "As soon as I have the passport and/or the heroin in my hand, Hai's boys will close ranks."

"There will be shooting." I felt certain.

"No, there won't."

"Yes. There will." Aggie sat on my lap. She was small, a child hurt at play. "But I'll be there."

"You're not leaving the blue house. That's been agreed on."

"Yes," I said.

"You don't have a gun, so don't get any funny ideas. You may know where you're headed, but I'm not ready just yet. Kill or be killed, that was just a line. No bullshit, Free. Do you hear me? This needs to be short and sweet. Remember, we don't want this guy. He's just a step on the ladder."

"Remember."

There was an endless pause. Aggie seemed to be searching for words just in front of her lips. She started to speak several times, but always fell off. She was planets away. I could barely hear her when she whispered, "Free?"

"Yes, Agatha."

"I can't be . . . There can't be any more. Us. I mean, I think we're done." The jaguar smiled a killer's smile.

"We never were." The words came out of me without feeling. For some reason they seemed absolutely correct. I couldn't agree with them, only recite them.

"But we were, Free. We said love. We felt love. But, there just can't be . . . love."

"Because I'm dying," I said dully.

"There is no reason."

"Okay."

"No, it's not okay. It's not fucking okay. I'm going to miss you. Whatever that means to you, I will always miss you. I will always remember you." She never looked at me, tears raining down unwiped.

"We're all alone, I guess. You had me fooled for a while. Thank you." I was numb. It was like waking up under a car or eating week-old muffins, peeling off the mold. It was the street. I was back again. No more together. No more home. No more we. I was back again. It was only the street.

"I'm sorry."

"I'm sorry for dying."

"Yeah. I'm sorry for dying too. I thought I could only do this alone. All these years. Then I found out I could do it with someone. With you. With you. But even that is too hard. I can't do it at all. I'm putting it away. Free. I'm letting it all go." She sounded like someone I'd known long ago. Someone I couldn't quite see, couldn't quite remember. Aggie's face flickered, faded, disappeared. I opened my eyes and she was gone.

At 8:30, everything was set. I was in the blue house, in the company of more cops than would have shown up at a riot in New Orleans. I felt caught, at last. Ready to confess. They all looked so stiff, in their dark uniforms with shiny silver pins. A strong wind would tumble them like tall blue dominoes. I opened a window.

The communications gear was tied in to a van that had contact with Aggie. She was parked in a parking lot awaiting instructions. They bounced Cantonese off each other's ears. They seemed to be making fun of something. I bummed a cigarette from an officer. I hadn't smoked much since Aggie, and the first drag calmed me down. I drew the smoke deep into my lungs and let it play there, echoing off the walls, creeping back up the rope of my throat and out. It burned just right.

The loud click of mah-jongg turned my head. Two cops doused the minutes with the game that sounded like drunk horses on cobblestone. They rocked their heads back like Pez dispensers, serving up pieces of laughter.

At a quarter till, Detective Hai showed up to check on everything. He eyed the telescope and camera equipment. It was all in order. We had a pretty clear shot of the Thatch porch and entryway, and a little bit of upstairs. Once Aggie was inside, she would be on her own, and that was where she would be in the most trouble. She was wearing a wire, but the dampness and altitude had been screwing with it all day. It was the third unit Hai brought in, and it still would be a risk.

The tiny detective didn't like having me around. He must have thought I'd escaped from the Revolutionary War, with my bandaged head and glazed stare. It made him nervous to look me in the eyes. I looked too crazy to be afraid.

"Hello." Hai paused. "John Wayne."

"It's the only way we know how to do things. The right way."

"Don't be so sure until your lady comes out of that house alive." There was a smile hiding somewhere on his face.

"Aggie's come out of a lot tougher situations than this. She had to deal with you, didn't she?" Hai checked all the gadgets one more time, and headed to his position in the van. His last orders in Cantonese rang off the walls.

At five of, I walked down to the basement. I saw where they'd dusted for fingerprints on the door handle. The white spray left my prints in clear view. They spiraled and spun, spelling out my name. My muddy shoe tracks remained, and the chalk mark of the man they'd shot. It stretched out at the base of the steps, a flattened ghost slithering to safety. He'd never made it. The stenciled corpse was about my size, a little heavier, and I lay down inside the lines. The cold cement floor iced my cheeks, like the formaldehyde cool of Billy's back and the cool softness of Cheng's bed. I lay down in all that coolness, all that death. Soon, all that would remain of me would be an outline, the legacy of a madman.

A mad scuffle of cop shoes above brought me back to life. I got upstairs. It was crazed.

"What?! What's the shake?"

"She inside," one corporal yelled. "She go inside." That's all, I thought. A cop spoke frantically on the radio.

"Do you have her wire?" I asked calmly.

"She is dead." His face was solid. "Wire is dead." I backed
away from the console, away from the telescope, camera and
window. I put myself to the wall. All the bulls were facing
away. The store of guns for a possible push stood at attention
by the door. In a blur, I had a rifle and a foot out the door. No
one saw, followed or even cared. I crept along the side of the
blue house and up the hill through the underbrush. The trees
looked different from the ground. I wasn't kissing them with
the hawk, I was wrestling them with the lizards. The forest
groaned. The incline to Mount Austin Road was slippery. It
took a series of vines, rocks and dug footholds to reach the
top. From flat on my stomach, I could see Thatch's house. The
earth was cool, and it tugged on me. It took a few minutes to
get within striking distance. There needed to be a sub-level
door, one that led to a cellar or storage, in order for me to get
inside clean. A random burst could end Aggie's life. I needed
patience. I wished Mobley were at my side, leading the
charge.

I knew the cops hadn't made a rush yet, as I bellied up
closer. There was no one in the window. Two thugs sat on the
back porch. They were lazy, but carrying metal. A side door
sat just below the dining-room window, like the servant's entrance in an Uptown New Orleans home. It was shut. I
hotfooted past a narrow group of trees, then went full out for
the door. I let the stone wall break my fall, and something in
my head popped. The door was double-locked. It took a sudden, silent blow to the handle to get me into the pitch-black
room. The third wall I tried held a switch, and it lit the place
up like an underground ballroom. The floors were polished
hardwood, and three chandeliers hung from the ceiling. There
weren't any tables or chairs, and the room ran the length of

the house. One of Thatch's doughboys investigated and
caught the butt of my rifle with his stomach. I couldn't hit
anybody in the head with a gun. It took a final right cross
between the eyes to lay him down. Now I had two guns. It
wasn't until I headed upstairs that I heard the bad news.

"Lady, you need to explain to Mr. Thatch why you would
insult him by entering his house wearing a wire and carrying
only twenty-five thousand dollars. Which, I'm afraid, we'll be
keeping as a consulting fee." The voice belonged to a Thatch
worker. Aggie was silent. From my spot at the top of the steps,
I tried to guess how many there were. "Your words come too
slowly." I heard the sharp smack of hand on flesh. "Up with it
now, missy. No point in wasting everyone's time." A chair
scraped, gashing the floor.

I could hear everything. There were eight nostrils. I listened to them breathe and came up shooting. I wasn't shooting at anyone or anything, just creating a distraction, setting
the room on fire. The bullets exploded, shattering windows,
lamps, fancy furniture. Thatch hit the ground first, his two
bad boys reaching for their guns. I was on them like a scar. I
dropped one, threw a gun to Aggie, and we pinned down the
other without a struggle. He threw away his .45 as the two
rooftop extras joined us. They quit without a fight. It was too
easy. Thatch still lay motionless on the floor. Aggie, with a
welt rising on her eye, nudged him in the ribs.

"Your payroll just waved the white flag, Mr. Thatch. You
can get up. You'll have plenty of time to sleep in jail."

"I think I tossed my back." Even muffled, he sounded
important.

"You'll get to see a specialist as soon as you've been
booked."

"Nice place, Early," I said as he unfolded to a standing position. His circular face had more red splotches than before. As if I'd shot tomatoes, not lead. "Ever think about selling?"

"I've never been shot at before. Certainly not in my own dwelling. And who do you two renegades think you are? I've never seen you before. This is unheard of. I pay my taxes. I want this taken care of immediately. Of course, I'll expect full reimbursement." He spoke with the confidence of a man who knew he'd get off. On the streets I'd always heard the rich crooks went free because of cash. Now I was seeing it first-hand. We got everyone to sit in a circle on the floor, surrounded by broken glass. It was Aggie's way of humiliating a bigmouth.

"Things are going to go a little differently this time," she stated. She circled them like the snake-eating hawk. She could take them in her angry jaws any second.

"You are not even Chinese."

"Oh, yes, I am," Aggie bragged.

"ABCs are not welcome in this maison. I run a service business, and foreigners, aliens, have no place here. And my God, why must we sit on the floor? Where's your sense of decency? I want to see . . ."

"Detective Hai?" I finished for him. My words pushed his head down like a punished child. "Like Aggie said, things are going to swing a little differently."

A group of uniforms busted in, guns at the ready. They came looking for a shoot-out and got a card game. They looked at each other, not sure whether to laugh, fire their weapons or go home. Detective Hai, no taller than a parking meter, parted the sea of blue. His eyes met Thatch's and looked away.

"I guess you two know each other," I said.

In the station the next morning, Thatch had traded his linen suit for prison gray. I called him by his number just to piss him off. His hair dangled over his eyes like loose wiring. Aggie paced the interrogation room, and Hai drank a soda through a straw in the corner. I couldn't tell who was the guiltiest. Aggie was the only innocent one in the room.

"You mean to tell me," Thatch blubbered, "that he's not even a cop, and she has no jurisdiction!?!?"

"Hey, 2455694, get over it." I felt amusing, maybe for the first time.

"The point is, Mr. Thatch, that we want New Orleans. It's even beneficial to you. How long will the faithful come to you if they hear their brothers and sisters are getting spiked on the other end?"

"I am a businessman, and America is a prodigious country, fortunately. I shall do business until business dries up." Aggie grabbed the back of his hair and yanked his head back. His Adam's apple peered out like a turtle's head, and sucked back in.

"Business is officially over," Aggie spit into his teeth. She was close enough to kiss him. He needed a kiss. "I am in a position to make a lot of noise. I'm not some Hoko cop you can squeeze or rent. I'm an American citizen and peace officer, traveling with another American citizen. We have certain unalienable rights."

"Oh, spare me the nationalistic parade." Thatch shook free. "We made America and we made Hong Kong. You have no idea what these people are facing in '97. I'm doing them a favor." His face cleared as he basked in his glory.

"I can tie you to heroin trafficking, bribing a police officer, falsifying documents and accessory to murder. You'll be the center of an international conspiracy, and your make-believe kingdom will fall right on its royal ass. Those are the rules. Where's your precious fleur-de-lis power now?" Hai slurped the last drops of his soda. "You can play my game and swing a deal with Hai boy once I'm gone, or you can string yourself up for the world to see. Think about it, King Early. Let me know what you decide."

"Are you finished, Miss Li?" Hai said, dropping his empty soda can in the trash can. "Are you quite finished?"

"For now, but don't think for one . . ."

"Oh, I wouldn't dare think that you'd let me have a minute's rest until justice raises its glorious head. Miss Li, I beg you not to underestimate me again." Everybody dug in. Thatch looked lost. "When you first came into my office, I thought that you would be a nuisance, but that, like most Americans, you would shoot off your mouth, do no harm, pack up your ego and go home. But you overstayed your welcome, didn't you? You bullied, you invaded privacy, and your crazy friend almost killed a man." I rubbed my head. "That would have been an international incident, Miss Li. We did wish, and how we did, that you would go home quickly, quietly, but it failed to work out in such a fashion." Hai beeped for a sergeant to come into the office, as he continued. "Let me tell you a story."

"You're a boring son of a bitch, Hai," Aggie said.

"Once there was a little girl. A Chinese little girl, who hated being Chinese, so she tried very hard to be what she was not. She learned to cry and to believe in nothing. She learned to use her muscles and her guns to speak for her, and she forgot, in all that noise, how to listen. She had a bad habit of chopping down peach trees, which any good Chinese knows represent longevity. This little Chinese girl liked death more than life, and fire more than soil." Hai caught his breath, lit up a Kent, and the sergeant entered. He carried Aggie's suitcase. Aggie's knees buckled, and she leaned on my shoulder. "Thank you, Sergeant. That will be all." The sergeant left, and the suitcase stared at us from the table.

"That winter was very harsh, and the Chinese girl became very ill, although she was not aware of her illness. She refused to listen to the doctor, until the doctor had no choice but to give her the only known cure." Hai unzipped Aggie's suitcase slowly, and we already knew the answer. It was packed with ice-white heroin. Aggie was speechless. Hai unzipped every compartment, and small packets of horse tumbled out. It was enough to keep New Orleans smiling for a month. "Your gun," Hai mumbled, and Aggie set it down on the table, backing away. Thatch glowed with approval.

"I can beat this. I've got you on unlawful entry, petty theft and a few more I'll be able to think of. You had no basis for a search and seizure of my hotel room. We all know this is a poker game. Now you've called my bluff, but I'm not ready to fold, Detective." Aggie refused to die.

"I don't suppose that having the signed reports of a hotel detective who sighted behavior often associated with smuggling, as well as three police force veterans with flawless records who discovered the illegal drugs about to be smuggled out of the country, would make any difference."

"No." She was teetering.

"I was afraid that would be your stubborn response. You are not Chinese in the least. You don't accept even the most obvious of situations. You don't like my stories or my suggestions."

"Call me old-fashioned, but I don't consider framing and blackmail to be suggestions."

"You don't understand, Miss Li. This isn't about you. This isn't about New Orleans. This is about the ugly peach tree. What we are doing here is institutionalized. It is not Mr. Thatch robbing the corner grocery. It is for the survival of the Chinese people. When England sold us back to China and then wanted to charge us for our freedom, we had no choice. Smuggling may be ugly, but it still bears fruit, and it keeps people alive."

"People are dying in New Orleans. They're getting kidnapped in New York and San Francisco in exchange for all their money and their dreams. They're getting murdered for envelopes full of cash. Good people. Law-abiding Hong Kong Chinese being hung out and slaughtered. You don't see them once they get off the plane. You don't see them getting busted for possession. You don't see the project kids shooting bag after bag, or professionals smoking smack cigarettes until their families fail, and people get killed. This is the next cocaine, you selfish bastard. Heroin is becoming nostalgic. You're not setting Hong Kong Chinese free, you're enslaving thousands you never see. People you don't give a damn about."

"How you love to cut down the tree." Hai smiled. It was a smile of total control. My eyeballs were dry from not blinking. Aggie had nowhere to go. Even Thatch was gaping, and he was in on it.

"Do you wear a tattoo?" I managed.

"Thatch believes in it because of the senses. I don't need a symbol of my power. I see it all around me. Every day." Hai opened a drawer, pulled out a long, thin case and a pair of old leather gloves. They were flaking and scarred. He put them on. "Ch'ing Ching, Miss Li. Control of emotions. Stay focused, don't become blinded by peripheral vision. Ch'ing Ching. It can save the soul."

The door opened again, and Comic and Shun Peng were led in. Comic had her weight on her father's shoulder as they hurried inside. A sergeant brought in two extra chairs and lined them up next to Thatch. All three looked straight ahead. Comic smiled sickly. Hai had the sergeant close the door and handcuff all of us to our chairs. All except Aggie. The sarge was in his late twenties, and he had a slashing scowl and bright yellow skin.

"Do you know that the Great Wall of China is not really a wall at all? Just a pile of stones and rock covered over. It has no foundation. For things to work, to last, to outlive the enemy, they must have a strong foundation."

"Who," Aggie asked, "is the enemy?"

"It wasn't until Deng killed democracy on June 4, 1989, that I had an enemy. Now my enemies are those that stand in the way of my focus. I lost a brother and a sister that day. China lost Hong Kong. China lost the rest of the world. China lost itself."

"There's no other way to do it," I thought out loud. "Free. Just get free at all costs."

Hai opened the case and solemnly repeated after me. "At all costs." Out came a silencer, which he quickly attached to Aggie's revolver. "Each of these bullets will exit your gun. Each murder will be yours. The fingerprints, the motive, an American cop caught while trying to smuggle heroin. We'll drive everyone back up to Mr. Thatch's lovely house, and it will all be so clear to the detectives in charge. Of course, I'll

be overseeing the entire investigation to ensure proper han-
dling. These international indiscretions can be so messy. This
way, our department will be able to explain everything in
detail to the gentlemen from the American embassy. Who
knows, Miss Li, you might even get caught in the cross fire."
Thatch's face broke out in hives, and he inched his chair
forward, to distance himself from the condemned. Hai's
pointed gun stopped his progress.

"I've been more than equitable with you, Detective Hai.
I've kept everything clean and tidy. You've gotten more than a
fair share of revenues. You need me."

"You were sloppy, Thatch. Your orders were to check with
me on every individual transfer of personnel. Your greed, your
selfishness cost me much grief, time and money. We were
trying to have these two people killed, and you almost smuggled her out of the country. You didn't check with me because
you wanted to cut me out of this little side deal. Well, I will
not be overridden. I will not be ignored or denied the respect
I am due. You, Mr. Thatch, are responsible for the demise of
this wing of the operation. I find that most disheartening. The
only way to begin again, is to make a clean start. If poisonous
weeds are not removed, nothing good can grow."

Hai put a bullet through Thatch's open mouth, killing his
last sentence on the tip of his tongue. Blood flew everywhere,
and Comic wailed madly. Everything froze. It didn't stop, but
it moved so slowly, I saw every second limp before my eyes. I
shook Thatch's British blood from my eyes in time to see Hai
point the gun at the hysterical Comic. Her head bobbed as
she wept, making her a difficult target. The sergeant had a
pistol pointed at Aggie's chest.

My feet hardened and split. My legs went wide as pillars,

and a shiny horn impaled the air. I thundered, chair and all, into the belly of the beast, spilling Hai in the corner, forcing the bullet over Comic's head. I trampled his hands, knocking the gun away, and rolled him brutally in front of me, where he caught the sergeant's panicked gunfire in the heart. Aggie retrieved her gun and put the sarge down. The room was mute. Aggie collected the keys and freed our hands, but not our circumstances. We were four people with new lives, but three corpses spelled out new death on the chilling floor. I could hear the blood spread like malice.

"They'll be waiting for us," Aggie spat. The pulse in her neck kicked like a fetus. I tucked my horn away and looked up and down the room. "Shun Peng, can you get us out of here?"

He wasn't sure he wanted to, but he looked at his daughter, alive, and made his decision. "Something. Some way. We find it."

Aggie leaned over the deceased Detective Hai and spoke into his ear. "Let me tell you a story. A little Chinese-American girl saw an ugly Chinese smuggler outside her window. So she cut him down. And he died. And he stayed dead. End of story."

With no reason for courage, Shun Peng led us out of the interrogation room into a roomful of cops. Certainly, many of the stares we avoided came from men directly involved with the smuggling trade. They gawked, most of them dropping their work. Telephones rang on and a few chairs scraped, but it was eerily silent. They made no move for us. Perhaps they were waiting for an order from their supreme leader. Or afraid to blow their cover in front of clean cops. But Hai was spilled out on a back-room floor. He wouldn't be leading any charge for injustice. Shun Peng walked with confidence, scattering cops like cats in an alleyway.

"There is a truck waiting," Shun Peng said to a British officer. "Where?"

The young Brit was flustered. There was blood all across the front of my shirt and some flecked along Comic's cheekbone. It looked like paint. "Truck?"

"Yes. Truck. Ai ya, it is urgent. Detective Hai ordered it to make delivery to Mount Austin Road. This is delivery," he said, pointing at us.

"Yes." The cop bought time by checking some unnecessary papers.

"Now!" Peng shouted. We were led to a loading area, where a large truck was waiting. The driver put out a cigarette and looked at us with complete boredom. "You take us to Mount Austin," Peng repeated.

"Yep," answered the stocky English cop who'd be doing the driving. "But I was told to expect bodies. I've got drop cloths, squeegies. I'm bloody prepared."

"Change of plans." I grinned.

"Where's Hai? He'll have to sign off on these changes." A bullet ripped a small hole in the truck. Then a thunderstorm of bullets, and we sprinted around the other side of the truck. "What the hell's going on?" the driver screamed. His fellow cop was slumped over in front of him, his mouth slung open.

"We're going for a little ride," Aggie started. She pressed her gun into his temple. A bead of sweat evaporated as it hit the muzzle. "You can take us or you can go all the way home. It's up to you."

"I fancy a good drive." He opened up the back for us, and we crammed in. Plastic body tarps and cleaning solution took up most of the space. We sat uneasily on what should have been our final resting place.

"Go!" The driver screeched out from the loading area and into the sticky night air. Aggie kept a gun on the driver like a tattoo, and Shun Peng calmed Comic with gentle caresses.

"Bullets," Comic whispered. Her leg ached where it used to be.

Aggie turned up the police radio. Words rang out in Cantonese and English. They were on our tail. "You're going to get us to Mount Austin. To the home of the late Early Thatch, or I'll personally end your career," Aggie blurted out. The driver nodded nervously. From the back of the truck, I could see Aggie transforming. I'd seen rage in a cop's face before, but this was different. It was humiliation, fear, adrenaline, death, muscle. Her face was about to crack wide open. She gritted her teeth until they fused. A circular purple vein glowed on her forehead, a sunken halo. Sirens wailed behind us, and our truck slowed on the hilly roads. "Faster!"

"Miss, I've got the bloody thing pinned." But he didn't.

And when Aggie realized she was being lied to again, she shot him in the foot and pushed him out of the speeding vehicle. All I heard was a thump and a groan. Aggie took the wheel. "Free, there's a squad car coming up on your side. Get his tires." I poked my head out the window to get a view, and the car was on me. I dove back inside as lead embedded into the dashboard. Snake crawling, I inched back into position. With a killer's accuracy, I popped two tires and sent our police escort spinning into a bank of trees. "Hell of a shot."

"I never told you how good I was. With a gun."

"No, Free, you never did. Peng, can you get us up to Thatch's? I need a chance to think." Shun took the wheel, and Aggie, Comic and I sat, heads bowed, planning anything we could. "It was Hai's game." Aggie grimaced. "He ran Thatch like a clock."

"But why New Orleans?"

"It's everywhere. Don't you get it? We haven't stopped anything. This has been going on full-time since '88. San Fran, L.A., New York, obvious places. And it's not just Hai. It's going to get worse. We're dead. We're going to die in Hong Kong."

"On behind!" Shun Peng shouted. Aggie got low, blew open the back door and eliminated a cop car that was right on our ass. Two others swerved into place. The tire burning lit up inside my ears. Metal curved around ancient trees that had never seen violence. Sparks bit at the ground.

"Yes, Agatha, we are going to die in Hong Kong," I said.

Peng took a wicked turn up an overgrown embankment, sending us sprawling into the corners. Comic landed on my lap, laughing. "Father no drive. Father no license."

"When we get to house," Peng yelled over the sounds of snapping branches, "I am talking only. No one else." Bullets sprayed the truck again, from both sides. They seemed to be ricocheting off Peng's hump. Aggie and I covered Comic with a tarp, and took aim on our pursuers. Like all the demons that had ever chased me, the Hong Kong cops bore down, closed in, smiled with yellow teeth. But this time, I had the bullets to fight back. I unloaded clip after clip, for all the nightmares I'd had, asleep and awake. Nothing could sway my accuracy. I left piles of government rubber and chrome steaming in the jungle. Five hundred yards from Thatch's house, we were alone.

"They'll send reinforcements," Aggie barked. "You're sure you know what you're doing?"

"I talk only," said Shun Peng. "Only."

"I don't want to die, Free." Aggie's face was red and white, angry and terrified. Her lips quaked, eyes darted. "I'm going to miss you." We could see Thatch's men lining up along the outskirts of the fortress. Their guns were steady in the wavering night. "I need to know something," she said, looking down. Her forehead arrowed, she held both my hands. She didn't spell it out, but it was clear what she needed to know. It was the same thing I'd wanted to know since the killing began. I was wondering if I should tell her, if I could tell her, if I even knew the answer.

"You were already after me, weren't you, Aggie?"

Shun Peng came to a sudden halt. Night birds hissed at our arrival. "Stay here." As he got out, Comic pressed her face to the windshield, covering her father with good intentions.

"This wasn't an accident," I continued. "It was all spelled out. The five qualities of a mountain peak."

"No."

"Are you sure?" The crunch of feet neared the truck. It could have been cops with our final bullets or Thatch's men carrying Shun Peng's head on a stick. They got louder and louder. I covered my ears. "Are you certain, Agatha? You do know who I am."

"No," she said, and kissed my forehead.

"Is Father," Comic breathed.

Peng looked into the back of the truck. "They're ready to listen. Follow me."

Aggie and I slid out of the pockmarked vehicle and followed Peng and Comic toward the house. Fifteen feet ahead, two of Thatch's bodyguards led the way. Their rifles were exclamation points of silver and wood. "This is the end," I whispered. "Just tell me the truth."

"There was a file. There is a file on Jefferson Alexander Freeman." Aggie coughed. "I don't know what to say."

"Just a file?" She didn't answer. "You don't understand the bad man." I looked into the black sky. My spine quivered like a whip. Fire burned in the palms of my hands, and my skin lay down in surrender. "I am the bad man. I'm the one no one touched, nobody looked at, unless to stare." Electricity shot through my gums, rattling my teeth. "No one talked to me, trusted me. I could clear an entire grocery store just by walking in. On the streetcar, passengers got off at the wrong stop, just to be away from me. Do you have any idea what that feels like?"

"Yes."

"There was already a file on me, wasn't there? The first day I met you. Before I even came into the precinct."

"Yes."

"For the investigation of the murders of Cheng, Billy and Felulah."

"Yes."

"I love you, Aggie."

Headlights, sirens and bullets chased us inside. Outside, an army of cops surrounded Thatch's house. A group of fifteen men stood in a circle. They were praying or humming. Each of their left hands bore a fleur-de-lis. We could hear the police scattering outside the walls. Peng had to move fast. "Thatch is dead." They cocked their guns. "Detective Hai shot him in the head." He flaked blood off his daughter's face. "This is the blood of your Mr. Thatch."

"Hai was our liaison," a blond gunman sputtered. "He was the centerpiece."

"Greed," Shun Peng shot back. "He murdered Thatch, but

we escape. Police come to eliminate operation. It has become an embarrassment. They will take you to jail. It is over. Only way to survive is get message to the gift giver." We could hear guns cocking, and Cantonese orders howled outside. Throats tightened. The walls shrugged.

"There's no bloody time!" a panicky Thatch soldier said. We were a second away from running screaming into the night. The invitation of death seemed calmer, sweeter than the anguish of the moment.

Peng bridged the gap with his hump of wisdom. "We can call for help. Not in Hong Kong, but tonight we send message. We can save. We can survive. These two are hope." Peng pointed at Aggie and me. The two fools that had crashed their party, destroyed their future and stolen their hopes, were being sold to them as saviors. I almost laughed, but Aggie squeezed my arm to get me to play along. The others were less convinced.

"Bullshit! These two American assholes pulled the whole castle down. I say, let them die with us."

"Remember," Peng shot back. "You are British. You only die once. I will be back. You are the one should be afraid." The first exchange of gunfire spanked the building. "The men on roof can protect until surrender. You can surrender. Only for now."

"They'll kill us."

"They could let us go," another henchman said. "They're as crooked as we are."

"You must believe. Surrender, and you have power. We get Americans to New Orleans. Home and safe. They can bring message to Mary of the Sky." For the first time, we heard the New Orleans connection called by name. Thatch's boys argued among themselves, but the shots were rocketing, and time was up.

"Bloody hell, all right. But they take the normal passage and the normal package. A sign of goodwill, and something they won't be able to skip out on. Take them to the closet."

We were rushed to a back room, where racks and racks of pants, jackets, shoes, overcoats and luggage were lined up wall to wall. Each was specially created to handle the smuggling operation. Small bags of heroin were strung together and sewn into the lining of the pants, jackets, luggage; even the soles of our new shoes contained smack.

It was obvious that Thatch had been running the game for a long time. The smack was totally undetectable, and there were more stylish clothes in every size and color than I'd seen since I'd broken into Dillard's in '87. I even recognized a jacket I'd seen in Billy's apartment. We ran into the kitchen, wearing hundreds of thousands of dollars' worth of drugs. My skin began to itch. A man entered with a quiet look on his face. "I've gone away," he said, and flopped into the sink, a bullet hole ripped through his back. I thought about Billy and how the bullet had stolen his tattoo. How cool his flesh was in the lab, how dead he was. I closed the man's eyes.

"We'll have to take the chopper. The gate's completely sealed off." A tiny, freckled thug grabbed Aggie's wrist and led us toward a back door. I turned to thank Shun Peng and Comic. I knew they wouldn't survive the onslaught. They would find no forgiveness, but they had forgiven us. Only God knew why. The lights had been turned off, but, in the illumination of a sick moon, I saw Shun Peng curled by the refrigerator. He raised a fist in salute, in anger. I smiled, and tear-gas canisters closed the curtain, as I chased after Aggie.

Aggie and the thug were taking the last bits of camouflage from a helicopter. Trees and branches stuck stubbornly to the blades. We climbed in, and it coughed to life. "I'm going by memory, chaps. No lights allowed. We should be to the airport inside twenty minutes. You'll be riding cargo to Tokyo, but there will be tickets waiting for you there. To get you home. To save our bloody arses." We rose out of a shock of trees and skittered away from the sinking ship. The chopper moved sluggishly, bobbing and weaving in the blackness. Our escape could have ended on any of a thousand trees. I felt like the hawk again, but blind, hungry, thirsty, not prepared to live, ready to crash, to die. "A bloke will meet you. Clive. He'll be unloading baggage in your section of the hold. He'll have the tickets. Two tickets to Dallas, Texas, U.S. of bloody A."

"Three ticket, please." Out from under a pile of tools and tarp popped Comic, bright as ever. My smile was so wide, it fell out of the helicopter. Aggie embraced her.

"What the hell?" the tiny pilot shouted.

"Extra ticket for go to America. I am Comic. I am to go. Father let me for to go."

The pilot wasn't buying what she was selling. "I don't care if you're Princess fucking Di, two tickets is two tickets. The airport is as far as you go."

Aggie cocked her gun and rubbed it against the pilot's neck like a dog's nose. "Why don't you see if you can get us another reservation." He grabbed the radio controls and made it happen.

"Your dad's a sly dog," I said.

"Sly dog," Comic repeated.

"Why didn't he come with us? We could have made it work."

"You not know Father," she said, a tear and smile coming at once. And she was right. I didn't know Shun Peng, the man who'd saved our lives so far. Or Hai or Mei Ling or any of the Chinese I had met. They refused to be known. Their actions and their words had a way of contradicting each other wildly and yet not at all. They existed as part of a large group, a single mind, yet were individuals to the end. Brave, a little crazy, beautiful in so many ways. Selfish and giving, deadly and alive, so completely themselves.

All the action made my head spin like the rotor blades above us. On the streets it had been simple. Me. Only me. It was dirty, but everything was so clear. There was absolutely no one to take care of, no needs to meet. When I stepped out into the world, when I left the dirt behind, life became much muddier, much thicker, crazier still. Crazier than having a conversation with a streetlamp at 5 A.M. over who shot Kennedy or who spilled coffee on the new Persian rug. Or cat, or dog, or anything at all. In all the frenzy, life and death seemed to meld into one. Maybe I was already dead, and this was proof that the struggle never ended. The dark muscled into the copter as the airport came into view. Aggie wouldn't look at me, shame striping her lips and jaw. "It's okay, Aggie. People lie all the time. It's a way of life." The pause was not long enough.

"I don't."

"Yes, you do. Everybody does. I do. I have. I will."

"For to America," Comic said with a child's wisdom. This was a celebration for her. She couldn't understand our obvious grief. She couldn't see the great gulf ripping between Aggie and me. She couldn't see that we weren't escaping but just being caught in another set of chains.

"You can ask me, Aggie. You can ask me if I did it. If I was so afraid of friendship that I took a stripper's life. If I was so cool for money that I iced two strangers for the cash under their mattresses. You can ask me. I'll tell you. I'm not afraid to tell you."

She squared to me and gave me her two black eyes, drilling a hole through the back of my head, pouring out remorse and confusion like summer lemonade. "I could ask you . . ."

"But you don't want to know?" I tried to finish for her.

"No, Free. I could ask you, but I don't think you know." The chopper dipped down toward the airport.

"Denby is your man on the tarmac. He'll get you to the JAL plane and secure your position. It's not a comfortable ride, but, hell, three hours in the pit for a lifetime of freedom isn't a nasty trade. Don't forget us," the pilot ended, an airport light leaving a white gash across his face. "Dear Lord, don't forget us."

"Don't worry," Aggie said icily. "We won't."

Without incident, we found our way to Denby. He was a chubby Englishman with swinging skin under his eyes, a place to rest his glasses. He bitched about Comic's surprise arrival, all the inconvenience, and how she would be a liability if something broke down, but her one-legged enthusiasm had her moving faster than the fat man, and by the time we reached the plane, he had started to fall in love with her. Just like we all had.

The Japan Airlines flight to Tokyo wasn't scheduled to depart for three hours, so Denby had plenty of time to sneak us into the secret compartment in the cargo hold. He removed a series of panels to unveil a bigger than expected area against the left wall of the plane. "It's big enough for three if you don't bandy about terribly much. I'll have to belt you in about ten minutes. That makes nearly six hours and a half before Eric unbolts you in Tokyo, after the plane's been completely unloaded. He'll have three tickets and photoless passports, all American. In Tokyo customs you are to get in line number twenty-three only. Line twenty-three. A Mr. Kamai will be checking passports. He is expecting you. From there you will fly to Dallas. See a Miss Ellenstrom, line four in Dallas customs. Have you got all that? A messenger is delivering three tickets to New Orleans to the Delta counter. Lovely city, that. They will be under the name Barry Burns, the name on the gentleman's passport. Any questions?"

"Yeah. Do we get any peanuts on this flight?" At midnight, the chunky Brit bolted us in. It was black as hell. Comic fell immediately to sleep. Aggie breathed loudly. I shut my eyes, bit my tongue and held on for dear life.

"Good movie," I joked halfway to Tokyo.

"Movie?" Comic perked up.

"I thought you were asleep."

"Was. I love movie. American movie. Gibson Mel. Tom Costner."

"America's not as hot as you think it is, Comic."

"Shut up, Free," Aggie cut in.

"I just don't want her to be disappointed."

"I don't think she's capable of disappointment."

"No movie?" Comic exhaled.

"No movie. Sorry."

"Okay. But yes America?"

"Yes, Comic," Aggie whispered like a bedtime storyteller. "America."

It was just as Denby told us in Tokyo. Eric let us out for air and calmly walked us in through an employees' access area.

We followed him to customs line number twenty-three, and an unemotional Mr. Kamai let us pass without sirens, guns or even a cold stare. He was just another cog in the massive machine of smuggling. He looked like a decent man. Probably kept his wife and kids fed on drug money. Another man living outside the lines but wearing the face of the good man. Thatch and Mary of the Sky, whoever she was, had a beautiful system. Comic kissed Eric on the cheek, and he fell in love too. He brought us coffee and the long-awaited peanuts. It was the best meal I'd had in years. We had an hour before our flight would take Comic to her final dream. I guarded her from every invisible danger. She deserved this flight. Whether it meant freedom or not, it sure looked like freedom to this young girl. Trapped in her body, in her homeland, but not trapped inside. Her spirit, something inside could never be locked up. She had floated to freedom by sheer force. The gravity of her soul.

But my soul was losing gravity fast. Anger shattered defenses I was too tired to put up. I felt a different person emerging behind my skin. Something was about to blow. I tried, but I couldn't hold on. "Mary of the Sky," I said out loud. "The Virgin Mary? Mary, Mary, quite contrary? Curds and whey? More like smack. How about Mary had a little lamb?" I was trying to prod Aggie into a little discussion or even to see a flicker of recognition in Comic's face. But it was clear from the start that Shun Peng had kept his daughter in the dark. She was truly an innocent accomplice. Doing tattoos, sending the demanding customers to her father's medicine shop, where they received their body's death seal. And now both Comic and Agatha Li stared at me blankly. "No more swapping hunches, Ag? No more stakeouts, doughnuts, coffee, Wong's costume balls? You do have a lovely tattoo to show to our fellow passengers, don't you? Tattoos are very big in Dallas this year. You'll be a favorite eight steps off the airplane. Hey, ABC, do you remember me?"

"Not now, Free."

"When?"

"That's not a question."

"The hell it isn't. Listen to how I raise my voice at the end of it. When? I know a question when I hear one. In fact, I know the sound of questions much better than the sound of answers. So I'm asking you. I'm looking for answers. Why can't you love me? Mary of the Sky. Do you know her?"

"Do you?" she asked back, catching my eyes.

"No. I don't know anyone."

"Neither do I."

"Maybe she'll pick us up at the airport and tell us who she is. That would help out. That would change things." My voice was getting louder and louder. A few passengers looked up from their newspapers and magazines. I could see I only had one foot on the wire. "But if you don't want to tell me the secrets of your mind, I can respect that. I mean, hell. There's nothing between us. Never was. Who the fuck am I?!!? Just some vagrant with a head full of glass and a pocketful of bullshit and promises."

"Free, pull it together!"

"Pull what together? I don't have anything left." Comic stared at me like a sister watching a brother get punished for something he didn't do. "I mean, you're the one with all the files and all the information, Miss General Deterrent, Miss Backwards Bookwalker." Glass bebopped frantically across my brain cells.

Aggie stood with the strength of ten men and yanked me down into a seat. She shouted in a whisper. "Shut the hell up!

I don't care about me or you, but we have a job to get Comic out of here. So damnit, pull it together now! Don't be so goddamn selfish!" Veins stood out like railroad tracks on her neck.

"Just tell me who Mary of the Sky is, Aggie. I know you know. You set me up."

"You're crazy, Jefferson. You're really beginning to lose it. Come on. We're almost home."

"Home. What is home? I remember the last place I called home. The one on Bourbon. You know the one. 327 Bourbon. You've been there. Haven't you, lover?" Aggie looked up as I stopped. "You know, the old car cover, third-floor apartment with city view. Remember? I was living there just before I met you, Detective Li. Just before Felly went home. Isn't that a coincidence?"

"I don't remember," she said with a bowed head.

"Of course you don't. You didn't know me or what I looked like or where I lived or what I did to relax. You didn't even know any of my favorite restaurants or movies or books. You didn't know me at all. You didn't know me from Adam. You didn't know me from Mary of the Sky. You told me you didn't lie. You see, Detective Li? Everyone lies."

"Stop it. Stop it." Aggie raised her voice, and a few waiting passengers looked one last time, too sleepy and bored to protest. "I don't know who she is. Or who he is. I don't know anything."

"But you do. You know more than I do. I should have shot you in the bedroom. Saved all the trouble." We didn't know how to react. That was a memory only I had. "I guess we'll see who picks us up at the airport. Or who picks you up, and who picks me up."

Comic touched my knee. "Tiananmen," she said flatly.

"Tanks, big loud, and tanks with bullets and soldiers." She swallowed. "We stopped many soldier. Too many. More soldier come. Too much soldier. War running to us. Do you understand? My friends carry away me on bike. Much hurt people on bike, ride to hospital. Escape. You know? Escape for to hospital?"

"Yes." I desperately tried to holster my anger. Comic's face looked so familiar. I'd seen that face in doorways and at the train station. In barrooms and bail-bond offices. I'd seen that face in the mirror. It was a face that had seen the horror and somehow survived. It wasn't a fair survival, a deserved or earned survival, just a small survival. And her face could do anything, suffer any blow, endure all the rain and razors the day could drop.

"Today, I get out of Tiananmen. The bike stop. The blood stop. Today I have leg again."

I watched her run with both legs a million miles away. I was glad for her. Not for me. "When do I get my leg back?" I rubbed my head and walked away.

We boarded the JAL flight to Dallas like real tourists. But people avoided me as if I once again wore the brown uniform of the homeless. My explosion in the terminal sent out a message. Two people changed their seats after seeing they'd drawn one close to the madman. The stewardesses got Comic crutches, and she fell asleep on Aggie's shoulder before we took off.

Aggie leaned over to me. "We'll have to leave her in Dallas. Do you know anyone in Dallas?"

"Good one, Officer." I laughed.

"I had a cousin living outside the city. But I think he moved. We may have to take her to the American consulate."

"They won't take her."

"She's not holding. Well, at least after we get her out of these clothes. There's no risk. Political asylum. They grant it all the time."

"Aggie, they'll send her back on the next plane. She's got fake papers, no money and nothing back in Hong Kong. You know what probably happened to Shun Peng."

"Political asylum. She was injured in an act of political terrorism. Doesn't that count for something?"

"I don't trust anyone who works in a building."

"That doesn't leave us much. If we take her home, she could get bumped too."

"What the hell do you think is going on back in Hong Kong? Use your head." The noose around my anger was loosening. It was starting to wriggle free again.

"I don't give a damn about Thatch's boys and the Keystone Kops. We won't be seeing them again."

"But, Agatha, they got us out alive." Aggie didn't answer. With as little commotion as possible, I strongly guided her to the back of the plane. When no one was looking, I pulled her into one of the tiny bathroom cabins and shut the door. The lock sounded like a bullet. Our faces were inches apart, legs firm against each other. We were hemmed in by my rage. My horn glistened in the yellow light. "I can see Thatch's doughboys smoking cigarettes at the police station while the cops try to figure out if there's an honest officer in the bunch. How many in NOPD, Detective? How many are taking a skim here or there? The heroin trade, the hooking, shakedowns. How many are dirty? It must be tough being an honest cop, not knowing which partners to trust. To tell the people you care about what's really going on. It must get so you don't know the difference between reality and make-believe."

"If we could have this conversation on the wing, I'd be so much happier."

"You weren't straight with me! You took advantage."

"Neither were you," she said weakly.

"But only you knew the whole score. You must have been laughing behind my back from the start."

"I never laughed."

"I would have. Look how pathetic. A street crawler, sleeping under a car cover, eating three-day-old french fries like manna from heaven. What a goddamn joke. Were you so desperate for clues that you kissed a derelict, a nobody, a zero? Is that part of your job description, or did you just take it on to pick up a medal of valor? What did you think you'd find behind these scarred lips, a prince?"

"Free."

"Yeah. What a fucking joke. Free."

"I was alone. I didn't know what I was doing. I didn't have anyone to take care of. I never have. And you needed fixing. Your head, your feet, top to bottom. I was . . . You're right. It's my fault. I wasn't honest with you. You were under investigation. You still are. Your coming into the station threw everything off kilter. No one knew how to handle it. So the captain told me to keep my distance but to work with you. I put the tail on you, Free. It was me. But after a while, you seemed so sincere, so docile. Not like a suspect at all. Not like a . . ."

"Killer," I ended for her.

"So Captain LeMaire decided to let things go."

"But he had us tailed too."

"You knew?"

"It's just how these things work. Go ahead. I don't want to ruin your momentum." I leaned closer to her, resting my left hand on the cool of the sink. She tried to squirm for some space, but there was none. I was a giant. I was the biggest man alive.

"Not all the time. I got him to lighten up after I started trusting you. He didn't come to the Mobleys' that Sunday. He didn't follow us home."

"Too bad. No surveillance photos of the big kiss."

"Jefferson."

"Stop calling me that. How in hell did you get them to okay me coming to Hong Kong with you? That's crazier than I am."

She tried again to maneuver some breathing room. Outside the door, a hand tested the lock. "They don't know. They don't know anything. As far as they're concerned, I'm on a fact-finding mission. I told them you skipped town, and the killing stopped, so they're satisfied. The minute we hit New Orleans, you'll be booked. They have your picture at the airport, train station, the bus depot, rental car counters. It's over."

"It was the cops on the tennis court. Those assholes in the gray suits. It wasn't a hallucination. Those were your buddies shooting out my lights."

"They weren't my buddies. I cared about you. That's why I took you to Hong Kong. Maybe I thought I could get you to stay."

"This is hilarious. You can't arrest me, because you don't know where the hell I am." I laughed at the insanity of it all. The plane lurched on into the pitch. "Well, if I'm supposed to feel sorry for you, I do. If that feels any better."

"Free, don't come home."

"Okay, Aggie, I'll get me a nice little apartment in Dallas, and Comic and I will build a nice little family. I'll teach them about survival and Comic can show them how to dodge a bullet. You'll send money, won't you, so the little Freemans can eat, and you can send a card at the holidays. The children will be so pleased to hear from you. Or maybe you'll even visit. Slip away from some cop party, and Comic will fix up the guest bedroom with everything you need. A wire tap, some surveillance equipment, a gun rack."

"I need to get out of here. I'm suffocating."

"Is it the truth that is stealing your breath, Detective, or something else?"

"Come on, Free. I'm serious."

"Dead serious."

"I want you to come home, but you can't. There will be too many questions. You have no hope in New Orleans."

"Nothing new there. Don't worry, Ag, I'm a good liar. Not as good as you, but pretty damn effective."

"You didn't do it, did you? You never pulled the trigger."

"Is that all you want to know? I guess that is the sixty-four-thousand-dollar question. Has Detective Agatha Li fallen in love and out of love with a murderer? You said you loved me, Aggie. No one ever told me that. No one. No one ever loved me before you. Before you pretended to love me. Now, who's the killer?"

She was mute, till she caught her breath. "I brought you to Hong Kong for me. Not for you, because I felt sorry, or for the investigation. I brought you because I needed you. I was alone, and you crashed into my life, and I didn't want anything else to matter. Just two people. Not a cop and a suspect.

Not a cop and her assistant. Just two people. Can you understand that?"

"I only understand one person. I've never been good at
pairs."

"I screwed it up. I don't know how to get out. I didn't plan
on falling in love with you. But I guess I wanted to. I've never
been in love. I've never been anything."

"No way out, sweetheart. This is it. It's always corners and
ceilings. It all comes crashing down. It's just a matter of
when."

"If I knew who Mary of the Sky was, maybe we could get
you clear." She waited but asked the wrong question. "Who is
she, Free?" The airplane buckled and threw us out the door.

*Mareseatoats and doeseatoats, and littlelambofGod, who takes away the
sins of the world, have mercy on us. Lamb of God, who takes away the sins
of the world, have mercy on lambseativy. And grant us thy peace. She was
asking for it, begging for it. And a man's gotta do what a man's gotta do.
Give us this day our daily dead, and forgive us our trespasses, as we try to
forgive those who have trespassed on our property. But it isn't easy, Christ,
you know it ain't easy. Guilt. Is a four-letter word. And punishment. So is
life, love, dead, free. Free? Now is the time. All you have to do is
remember. Re-member. All you have to do is . . . remember who. Who.
Who pulled the trigger. Pull the trigger. That's all you have to do.*

We landed in Dallas exhausted. Miss Ellenstrom, an obese
woman with hair dyed the color of a Georgia peach, looked us
up and down, eyed our fake passports and passed us through
like old friends. Aggie tried to explain to Comic about the

dangers in New Orleans, but she didn't understand. "America," she said over and over, a mantra. "America. America. America."

Aggie finally gave in and took her under her wing. I grabbed my ticket at the Delta counter, kissed Comic goodbye and disappeared into the wall of strangers arriving and departing. It was easy to ignore Aggie. I slid off into oblivion. "Where is Free to go?" I heard Comic ask.

"He's going home," Aggie answered.

I missed my plane on purpose. There I sat at the wrong gate, covered in drugs, smiling at every third passerby. There was no way for me to disrobe. All I had were the clothes and horse on my back. After I watched my plane leave the gate, I hurried to the podium. "Is that flight 206? Say it isn't flight 206." It was a killer impression of an insurance salesman. I was back in my element. Lying. It felt delicious.

"I'm afraid it is, sir. Were you scheduled for that flight?" The ticket agent's teeth glimmered in the fluorescent light.

"I need to get to New Orleans as soon as possible. Can you help a tired salesman get home to the family?"

"Well, Mr. . . ."

"Freeman. I mean, Burns. Barry Burns," I said, thrusting my ticket and passport in her face.

"I don't need your passport, Mr. Burns. But if you're willing to go standby, we have a flight 214 leaving in about ninety minutes for the Crescent City." She said Crescent City like she was biting down on a sour piece of candy.

"I've spent a lifetime on standby," I kidded. "I've just come from Japan."

"Tokyo?"

"Sort of."

"Tokyo is so lovely this time of year."

"I couldn't agree more, but I just needed to get out in a hurry. You know the feeling?"

"Who doesn't. Were you in Tokyo for business or pleasure?"

"More of an escape, really."

No one was waiting for me when I got off the plane in New Orleans. I tried to stay calm, but every blue uniform and shiny button or badge sent my heart sprinting. Aggie had kept her mouth shut. As far as LeMaire and company knew, I was still on the lam, so I had some time to get my footing. I kept my head low and stayed with the crowds. I took a bus to town and got off near the Salvation Army shelter. At last, I could get the itch off my skin. I stuffed the drug-lined outfit in a Dumpster, knowing some garbageman was going to have a tough decision to make.

After a little searching, I found an abandoned house on Napoleon, a block from the bar Aggie had mentioned once, Tipitina's. I broke in, chased the rats with a scream and a broom handle and dragged a filthy mattress from the living room upstairs to the third floor. Home, sweet home. The floorboard had been torn up by the window, and I could see down into the bathroom below. There was no running water, and the late-spring heat raised a stench few men could bear. It was a far cry from the Grand Hyatt, but it felt a lot more familiar, and even more comfortable. There was no one to talk to or hassle with. Just me and the heat. There were empty beer cans, Dixie bottles, pacifiers, a few plastic syringe covers and endless strings of Mardi Gras beads. They hung from light switches, broken lamps, closet doors, anywhere something could be hung. They hung like executed men, and in the strange breeze, they clicked like skeletons. The fatigue of escape, plus a biting jet lag, laid me flat on my back within minutes. As I drifted off to sleep, it was as if nothing had ever changed. I was back living in a bombed-out dwelling, counting my days by footsteps and breaths. The circle was closing, but I still had some business to take care of. I needed a gun.

I woke up at three o'clock the next afternoon and went straight to Aggie's. As I thought, she was at work, and after a long look and listen, I guessed she'd taken Comic with her. I waited till the street was dead quiet and punched out a window. A small line of blood trickled down my knuckles. It felt good. Once inside, I was a hurricane, toppling dressers, ripping up sheets, wishing there were pictures to tear off the walls. I found journals, letters, photos of Aggie at cop softball games, cop beer bashes, cop charity events. And in every picture, she looked lost, cut off. As if she'd been added to the photograph after it was taken. I didn't touch a thing in the guest bedroom, where Comic was staying. There was an American flag sticking out of the headboard. Comic had found a home. In Aggie's small office, I turned the desk upside down, emptying drawers and files, covering the floor with inches of paper.

There weren't any notes or files on me. I assumed the good stuff was under lock and key down at the precinct. But my ransacking finally gave me a chance. Beside the trashed typewriter lay the ink ribbon. It looked thin and useless on the floor, but it bore the indentations of letters. I quickly went to a sunlit window, and began stretching out the entire ribbon roll. It had an imprint of everything Aggie had typed on it over the weeks before we'd gone to Hong Kong. Somewhere in the middle, I found something. It was an address in New Orleans East with the following note: "Delegate House: Check against new info."

I took the gun from Aggie's night table and made sure it was loaded. In the kitchen, the bottle of whiskey she had put on the highest shelf when I was crippled still held its place. Only now, I could reach it. I poured myself a tall glass and let it barrel down. This had been a house of promise, a house of trust. A place of healed feet and perfect hips. Now it was littered with anger and paperwork. I put my foot through the television we'd never watched, knocked over the refrigerator and smashed the whiskey bottle on the coffee table. Picking up the broken glass, I found another piece of paper. It read: "Suspect 6'2", beard, shaved head. Current residence 327 Bourbon. May be armed. Considered dangerous. Proceed with caution." The words were typed, but they drew a perfect picture of me. It had started before I even knew it. The cops had cleaned out my car-cover dwelling. I had been watched and watched and watched. But not there. Standing in Aggie's apartment, no one was watching. No one knew where I was. No one knew what I would do next. No one.

In the bathroom, with a pair of scissors and Aggie's razor blades, I gave them back their suspect. I shaved my head down to the stubble they'd first come looking for. A smile curdled at the corner of my mouth, and I laughed again. A gorgeous maniac. A scar ran like a tributary from the top of my skull to my ear. It was fat with regret, and teeming with glass shards that couldn't be removed. Small speed bumps in my head. I had spun back upon myself and was ready to meet my end, to kiss the finish, to dive face first into my grave. I was ready.

I took the bus to the address in New Orleans East. It was

just past Gannon Canal on Reelfoot, the smell of Lake Pontchartrain only feet away. Nothing was recognizable. This was
as big a trip for me as going to Hong Kong. Asian faces
dominated the landscape. Old American cars crowded each
other for parking on shredded streets. The house on Reelfoot
was typical New Orleans. A sinking porch, peeling paint, a
door as crooked as a cop's conscience. With the gun, it didn't
seem to matter much what happened once I got inside. I
could go down in a hail of bullets. I didn't care. At least I'd go
down firing. There was a driveway, but no garage and no cars.
The mailbox had been painted shut. It was almost seven
o'clock, and long shadows draped the house. The roof shook
with the fading light.

The front door opened. I dove behind a line of brown
bushes, and out came an Asian man, Chinese, in his early
fifties. He was thinner than a grain of rice, wearing a too big
Tulane sweatshirt and a Desert Storm commemorative baseball cap. He emptied a pot of water into the thirsty dirt and
vanished inside. With five long strides I was on the door. I
didn't bother knocking. I kicked the weak-kneed lock and
doorknob off, and entered another world. Crammed into this
tiny house were at least a dozen Chinese people. Two small
children by the window, a wiry young man with what appeared to be his pregnant bride, the older man I'd seen outside and others. Their faces blurred into one in the cigarette
haze. Only two lights were on. The television, with the sound
down, and a Coors Light Silver Bullet lamp with a bulb bright
enough to burn my eyes. No one moved. They didn't seem
surprised to see a stranger burst in with a gun. But they didn't
say hello, offer me a beer, share part of their mystery meal
either. Someone cleared their throat. It was me. The air stunk
of cabbage and fear.

"I'm with the department," I started. "Just checking in to make sure there's no trouble." They didn't speak, just stared. I felt ugly again. Alone. I rubbed my unevenly clipped head. I cocked the gun's hammer. "I want some answers here. Who speaks English?"

"You not from police," the thin man said evenly.

"I am."

"Go away. We have peace. We wait. We have nothing you want. Nothing to steal."

"Wait for what?" I wondered. "What are you all waiting for?"

"Don't you know, Mr. Police?"

"Goddamnit, tell me," I howled, blowing a hole through the Silver Bullet lamp. More broken glass.

He decided to answer. "Be sent back to Hong Kong. We are only here on vacation." His sarcasm had years of frustration at its heels.

"You're waiting to be deported?"

"We no talk, they no deport. So we no talk."

"You came here from Thatch." A few cigarettes were dropped. "I know. I saw him get killed. He sent you here to be free. You smuggled dope. In the lining of your jackets and pants and shoes. I know everything."

They almost seemed relieved to be found out. "You work for Mr. Thatch? You come save us?" a woman hoped.

"I work for myself. The cops are holding you here until you ratted on Thatch, aren't they? Or on Mary of the Sky."

"Mary of the Sky," the pregnant girl repeated.

"We don't know Mary of the Sky."

"It doesn't matter now. Thatch is dead. It's over. You'll be deported. Unless they picked you up with the drugs."

"No," the man said. "The police raid houses, check for

papers. But we have no drugs. The gift giver already take our drugs. But protection? They promised protection, housing, money. We got some money. And houses like this house. A prison. But protection? Never. No protection for the unwanted."

"What the hell are you sneaking heroin into America for?" I asked, already knowing the answer.

"Freedom, sir. China is coming. Then I am leaving. That is all I need to know. This you cannot understand. This China, you can never understand. We are not criminal. Professional. Laborer, businessman, have job and home. This China you cannot understand."

"But you're not going to be free now. It was all for nothing because this gift giver sold your asses down the Mississippi." I waited, taking them all in like captives. "Who is Mary of the Sky?" No one answered. "I could kill all of you right now."

"Then you would lose your freedom."

"I have no freedom. I've never been free. It's a myth anyway. We're never free. You can run or hide away for years, but freedom doesn't exist. Somebody made it up in a fairy tale. And the sooner you realize that . . ."

"It is better to die."

"Exactly," I agreed.

"So shoot us," he said, taking off his Desert Storm cap. He was ready to be shot. "Shoot us if we are already dead."

I lined his head up in the gunsight. My finger massaged the trigger. He didn't flinch. "Who is Mary of the Sky?" Nothing.

"Do you believe in freedom?" he asked me steadily. "Do you believe in anything?"

My squinting eye opened. "No."

"Then you will never be free."

I locked him in again, then aimed at one of the women.

"Who is Mary of the Sky?" I repeated through ferocious teeth. The woman trembled and aged before my eyes.

"Do you believe in freedom?" he repeated.

"No." I turned the gun on the little boy, but quickly returned it to the thin man, the wise man, standing so tall, waiting for Christmas, waiting for a miracle. "Sir?" I spoke unevenly. "Knowing Mary of the Sky almost gave you your freedom. But she cut your throat. She stole your freedom."

"But still, you do not believe," he mocked.

"Whatever it is, she took it from you. Out of the mouths of your children and your wife. What do you owe her?"

"Nothing. But you must believe, or it is not worth my breath. Her punishment or your death. It is not worth such a cost. I cannot pretend."

"I'm going to blow your head off, man. Answer the goddamn question!"

"Shoot or do not shoot. Do not argue with yourself."

"I've killed before."

"I do not doubt that, sir. And maybe you will kill again. That is not my decision. That can only be yours. Leaving Hong Kong was my decision. This is the penalty."

"I'm not here to punish you. I just want to know something that can help me figure it all out." Something was severing. "You understand? Help me know who I am."

"Only if you believe."

"I believe," I lied.

"You do not."

"Goddamnit, pretend I believe. Help me out here. Pretend I believe." We waited. A cigarette was lit. A last cigarette? We waited. At my wit's end, he whispered a name, and I put down the gun.

My tears came fast, and the illegals circled and absorbed

me. They fed me rice like medicine and spoke of China, of Hong Kong, of escape. "You know many are here in New Orleans okay," the wiry boy spat between mouthfuls of Dixie. "We know from them. They write. They introduce Thatch and Miss Arnaud." Mary of the Sky was Miss Arnaud, the merciless madam, Felly's ex-boss and Thatch's link to New Orleans.

"And she'd meet you?"

"Met only once. Smile. Pretty. Too pretty. Felly is helping lady. Show us place for live and new ID. And money. American money." Felly hadn't been going out with counterfeiters. She'd been hustling immigrants for Miss Arnaud. She hadn't been on her back those last two years, but she was still hooking for Arnaud. Death was her only way out.

"Did you know Dao Tei Cheng?" They didn't, or Billy by description. With so many Hong Kong Chinese, this was a giant operation, sending the scared all across America.

"Felly like. We like Miss Felly."

I remembered something. "How much damage can China do in '97? Is it worth giving up your life to get away?"

The wise man took a swig from a warm bottle of Dixie and sized me up. He wanted to make sure I was worthy of his insight. "My brother die in a Shanghai prison during the Cultural Revolution in 1969. Intellectual, professor. Wore glasses. They torture him, but he not confess. Nothing to confess. His heart gave out before his spirit. They would not send body to Hong Kong. I would not go to Shanghai for funeral. Then I am dead again." He swallowed a fortune cookie without chewing. "My son thought I am coward for letting brother die, for missing funeral. My son not speak to me. I see running from China the brave thing I can do. Now, when I am return to Hong Kong, my son will be waiting at airport. Then we make new plan to come to America. I am Chinese. Proud of Chinese. Deng Xiaoping is Cow Demon. I see him, we see him for his true way. I hope government will in future again be Chinese. But today I choose freedom."

"And Hong Kong?" I asked. "What will happen to the island?"

"Will fall into ocean. Shark will swallow city. Everyone drown."

Everyone drown. I drank another beer and made it to the door. I wanted them all to stay, but what could I offer them? I was wanted by the law, and even when no one knew me, all I had was the street. No St. Charles mansion with room for all the lost and escaping. No bed, no chance, no gift, no frankincense and myrrh. Mobley quoted Jesus to me when I was twenty-one. On my twenty-first birthday. "In my house there are many rooms. I go there to prepare a place for you. If it were not so, would I tell you?" But Jesus wasn't the landlord in New Orleans. Nobody's house was open, no matter how many empty bedrooms there were. For to open your house was to open your soul, and there wasn't enough room inside. Aggie gave herself to me and got split wide open. A great canyon gaping from her mouth to her extra rib.

New Orleans didn't have room for the Chinese gamblers. Hong Kong said it didn't have room for China's sweaty fist, and China didn't have room for freedom, for Comic's courage in Tiananmen Square, for professors in Shanghai, for any idea with curves. No one had room. There was no room in the inn. Not one more child could be spanked into life. Not even Jesus. There wasn't even room in the manger anymore. Cops had it staked out to see if Joseph was smuggling dope into

Bethlehem on his donkey. Even the Wise Men were wearing wires. Just in case the baby babbled something they could use against him in a court of law. Everyone was under suspicion. Everyone was an informant. Everyone had a gun.

I was alone again. As alone as the bum I was when I slept in Cheng's bed after his murder. Alone as the bearded maniac running from Billy's apartment till my feet bled like hooves or my hooves bled like feet. Alone as the frozen fool stuck in Felly's dressing room after identifying her body. Aggie had come and gone like a long, fevered night. It had seemed like a night of rest, forgiveness, feasting, but even that had come smashing down on me. I was being watched. I was the hunted, and now the hunt was about to end. The rhino pawed the porch of the hell-bent house in New Orleans. He sharpened his horn on a fence post and shivered invisibly. The NOPD, Aggie, Miss Arnaud, the voices, had all chased me to this end. Something was about to die.

The next night, with a wild moon burning a hole in me, I walked my streets for the last time. I went back to the doorsteps, rotted porches, abandoned tree houses, stolen cars, all the places I'd laid my head. It was sad, saying goodbye to the secrecy of it, the solitude, the protection. I'd been rained on, frozen out, kicked by cops, laughed at by kids, ignored by good people, but I'd always felt safe. I had come out of my hooves to try and change something. In me or in the city. I still didn't know. It all started that night I fell out of St. Patrick's. That's when the voices started, when I knew I had a calling. Dauphine and Peter Street, Burgundy and St. Louis, the Voodoo Museum where I'd stand outside eating chicken for laughs. Barracks, Esplanade, Ursulines. Dark alleys and destroyed parking lots, hotel roofs and empty trash bins, the streets of New Orleans had been a home to me. It was over.

The tilted sidewalks tried to stop me, but I went on. Back to Bourbon Street, where Wong's stood in all its ragged glory. I pushed through the door, a cowboy returned. The place was darker than I'd remembered it. Three customers talked among themselves at a corner table while Mae did her solitary strip. She waved to me without missing a step. Dent wasn't behind the bar. I reached over and poured a tall whiskey. It went down hot and sweet. I shot a game of pool on the new table. My eyes were good, and I ran two racks plus five before missing. I wanted another JD, but it was a long walk back to the bar. The floor had been cleaned. Ten-year-old beer glue scraped away by strong hands. I could feel things closing in. The jukebox walked over to me, and the pool table stood on two legs. They were being friendly. The Budweiser lamp rocked, a cradle of light, and there was crying. A woman, a baby, an old, old man. I went back to the main room. The customers were gone, and Mae sat Indian-style at the edge of the stage, her scarf covering her. She arranged and re-arranged three dollar bills, her morning take. Out back, a beer truck backed in too far, taking out a caged service lamp.

"Sorry," the teenage driver winced.

"You'll have to pay for it," I joked. "Either that, or give me a free case." He smiled, glad to be off the hook, and I waded back inside with all that cargo, backing into Felly's old dressing room.

"You're not supposed to bring it in here, asshole," she said. "Hey, wait a minute. I know you. You're that cop." It was Katie Kelly, beautiful as ever. "You get busted down to private, or what?"

"Want a beer?" We toasted and drank. Her hair was fire-engine red. I wanted to light a fire, just to watch her put it out. "Do you hear sirens?"

"You don't look so good, copper. You look sort of angry. You know, mad." Katie was from up North, and her accent had settled halfway between Brooklyn and Baton Rouge. Everything about her said sex, and she enjoyed speaking. "Something happen to you out there in the trenches? You look like you could use a little rest. And for sure, a new hairstylist. My friend Johnell, well she could clean you all up this afternoon. Only take a phone call. Sure would make me feel better."

"Women like to take care," I said.

"Yeah. Usually gets me in trouble. But what fun is life without a little trouble? A scuffle feels good now and again."

"This is Felulah's old dressing room." Katie seemed out of place, a thief caught in the act. "She used to have pillows and candles. Unlit candles. She was afraid to light them."

"They might burn down," Katie finished for me. "I miss Felly."

"But her leaving helped you out. You've made a step up."

"Don't play games, sweetheart. You bulls are famous for these innocent questions."

"I'm not investigating anything. I know why I'm here. I'm not looking."

"Good. Anyway, it's too early to be interrogated. Why don't you shut the door. Want some tea?" Katie had a brand-new burner, and she made us Danish tea. "My brother sent it. He's traveling in Europe. He's the lucky one in the family." She poured the tea with a delicate wrist. "You're right, about this being a step up. I was looking to make a change, and I knew there was an opening."

"From on your back to on your feet. Congratulations."

"Thanks. You'll have to catch my act. It'll rip your pants off at the knees." The tea was too hot, but my tongue was numb. "Really, won't you just let me call Johnell for an appointment?"

"Ever go crazy?" I asked. "Ever died?"

"My old man, my ex-husband, back home, he went crazy. Threw the stereo at my head. Seven hundred bucks that stereo cost. My line of work isn't easy. You just can't throw money around like that."

"Did they shoot him?"

"My husband? Of course not. Shoot him. You're a funny one, Sarge."

"Sometimes in the zoo," I said, gulping the last of my tea, "an animal goes crazy. From being trapped. I saw it happen. It was years ago, or maybe days, but this rhinoceros was by himself in a cage. There was room, it was made up to look like the desert or jungle, but it was hot. August, I think. Or not. But humid. I'm just remembering this now." Katie peeked at her watch. She'd be getting naked for strangers soon. "And he was covered with flies, and they talked to him. Voices. They buzzed and circled and landed and laughed. Because he couldn't take off. He couldn't fly. There was nowhere he could go. He was trapped. They were on his head, back, legs, horn, eyes. He shook his tail like a hurricane, but nothing changed. They just told him he couldn't escape. Do you understand escape?"

"I have to change." She started to undress.

"Then he went crazy. He let out this horrible scream, a sound animals can't make. He ran into trees, rocks, water, trees again. Blood started coming out of his horn. He was trying to knock off his horn. He didn't want to be a rhinoceros anymore."

"Did he die?" Katie asked, standing only in her G-string.

"They killed him. They had to kill him."

"Why?"

"He didn't want to be a rhinoceros anymore. But that's why people came to see him. To stare at the rhinoceros swatting flies. So they killed him. They had to."

"That's a sad story, copper." Katie sat on her vanity and cried a few tears. "I don't know why it's so sad."

"There's no one out there for you to dance in front of."

"There will be. I have my regulars. You know, a girl can develop a following." Katie stood fast and hugged me. It steadied her, and she shook out the door. "I'm going to miss you, Blue." She must have known I was leaving.

I walked around Felly's old dressing room for a while, in circles, shaking my tail like a hurricane. I rubbed against the corduroy wallpaper. It sounded like a bandage being removed. The mirror fell down and cracked. I threw my teacup through the air-conditioning vent, shattering it on a far, invisible wall. In the hallway, I bumped into Mae. She was carrying a half-eaten turkey po'boy. She had mayonnaise on her cheek, and her mouth was too full to talk. She bobbed her head, the shabby doll, and disappeared behind her beaded curtain. The sounds of unending hunger could be heard.

A new janitor swept the hallway. He had long, stringy hair, black spaghetti, and a bandana wrapped around his neck. He carried the mop like a fiddle, almost giving me a mouthful of suds. He tried to whistle. He couldn't.

The poolroom had a few players missing shots and their wives, who were back at the hotel. Onstage, Katie moved up the silver pole, a praying mantis, gaining legs as she climbed. Her tongue shook with shame, her body in full attack, mind in hiding. I jumped a barstool, and waited for Dent to notice. Dent was growing a mustache. He tapped out two drafts for a man and his wife. The woman was taking notes on Katie's moves. The husband was thinking of the future and grinning.

"You know a street rat called Free?" I asked Dent.

"Never seen him," he answered. Then he saw me. He looked happy and lost. "I'm not going to believe this," he said, rubbing my patchwork head of hair. "It's been a helluva long time. Didn't think we'd be seeing you again, to be truthful."

"I've been away."

"No shit. What're you drinking?" His hands buzzed above the bottles, bees over a garden.

"Usual."

"Ain't nothing usual when you been away so long. Thought you was dead," he hummed, pouring the whiskey and water. He'd gotten sloppy. The drink overflowed and flooded the bar. "Thought your head cracked open like one of those coconuts. Thought you was dead."

"Almost. Not yet."

"Yeah, not yet." He laughed yellow.

"I've been away. I had to go away, because some of the things I did. Had to see if they'd go away. If I left them here. But they didn't."

"Where did you go, Free?"

"Just outside New Orleans. Not far."

"West Bank? Chalmette? Get you one of those Chalmatians. There's some sweet pickings. Dumb as a stick, but great on their backs."

"I didn't know you ever set foot outside of Wong's."

"Man has to love, spend his money on something special. On a purebred Chalmatian." My return had Dent talking. He was even surprised, the words coming in great floods, splashing all over us. "We miss Felly."

"Miss Katie seems to draw a crowd."

"But Felulah was special." Dent rested his tired elbows on the bar. "She had something."

"A light," I said. Dent pushed off to serve someone else. I spun to watch Katie. There were more than ten men at the foot of the stage. That was a busy night for Wong's. The men were conventioneers in from nowhere. They wore nametags instead of expressions and drank without looking, spilling rum on their ties. Katie was lost up on the pole. She was on another stage, where the audience stood to applaud, not to piss. Beer mirrors and bad lighting stole my vision again. I turned back around to meet Dent's face. He was the past. He was the future.

"Dent?"

"Hmmm."

"I killed Felulah." The loose skin on his face sucked back onto bone. He scanned to see if anyone had been listening and got an inch from my face. "I killed her, Dent. She was my only friend. And I killed the two Chinamen and the British bastard." He didn't speak. He slowly walked me into Katie's dressing room and sat me down.

"I don't believe you," he said, shutting the door secretly. "You're a crazy son of a bitch telling the world who you killed."

"It doesn't matter if you believe me. I did it. I shot Cheng twice, in the poolroom. I saw the new table. It's nice."

"Forget the table." Dent checked the mirror to make sure he was still there, and combed his mustache with long fingernails.

"I shot him, then slept in his house. The bed was stiff. I like hard mattresses. Just like the street." The words marched out, a news report. "Billy, I spiked outside in the alley. He was easier. No witnesses to worry about. Then Felly. She just knew too much. And this evil, resulting from friendships. You know the rest."

"No, I don't know the rest. You're out of your mind."

"Yes." Dent warmed to the idea. He'd always thought I was crazy, and people love being proved right. "Do the cops have any suspects?" I asked.

"They come in, ask questions. There ain't been no trouble since that boy bought six in the chest from the cop, and that was weeks ago. Just before you left." I could see him trying to figure it out, using tiny muscles long left sleeping. His forehead protested with purple veins. "I'll get a headache. I hate these goddamn headaches."

"I didn't want to. I'm sorry about your head. I just had to tell someone. Dent, you're it. I ain't got no one else. I need help. I'm going to the cops."

"No! No. That's a bad idea. There'll be cops crawling all over the place. You'll get us in trouble. What with the last shooting, we can't keep five customers happy."

"Unless Katie's on," I said, touching her discarded dress.

"Unless Katie's on. We do miss Felly. You didn't do it, did you, Free? I know you didn't do it."

"Four people. Cheng, Billy, Felulah Matin and the Brit. I'm sorry about Felly. I'm sorry. About Felly I really am sorry. She meant something."

FREE

"Why, Free? Why did you do such a goddamn thing?"

"I got voices, Dent, and they work twenty-four hours. Sometimes I can't shut them up. Sometimes they tell me to do things, certain things. They're taking me to the end."

"Doctors didn't fix your head."

"No. Voices, man. I can hear them now. Can you hear them?"

Dent left. I held Katie's dress in my lap. The room rolled and rocked like a dropped toy. I fell out of the chair three times. The glass pieces lined up for an important move. They'd cut a line right down the side, head to shoe, unzipping me, spilling me out on the hard ground. I'd hoped the finish would be more clear, a straight line, easy to follow. But it was jagged as my scars. Aggie's sleeping, I thought. Aggie is whole. Aggie sleeps. At least I hadn't killed Aggie. Confessing didn't feel good either. I was exhausted and dry. Saliva refused to come. The corners of my mouth sealed shut, while chapped lips scissored open. No.

She walked out her back door. BANG. Not yet. Remember it in order. Smell the barbecue. Inhale. Inhale. Perfume and pearls on a Saturday. Unnecessary. Uninvited. BANG. Daddy, Daddy. Just like you taught. BANG. For mother and country. BANG. For practice and fun. BANG. Blew a fucking zero the size of a baseball through her neck. Still. Stand still. Then fall. BANG.

Warm hands. Extra hands. Back it up. Remember it in order! Out the back door. Perfume. Perfume. The gun is heavy. Heavy with bullets. Too heavy for . . . Bullets. Bullets. Like firing a gun. Remember in order. Pearls. Daddy. Voice. Daddy. Hands. Warm hands. Extra hands. Aim. BANG. Extra hands. Steady aim. Perfect aim. Extra aim. Bang. Son, whatever happens, go out with a BANG.

I went to the kitchen to get more weapons. I put on an apron and stuffed the pockets with knives, forks, matches, towels. I grabbed the baseball bat Dent used to chase drunks. The wood cooled sweaty palms. I found Mae in the hallway.

"Mae, you should leave."

"I know this sounds crazy, with that zigzag haircut back and all," she said. "But I still think you're cute."

"Mae, please leave the building. Go get a cup of coffee at Cafe Du Monde. They have good coffee."

"Are you flirting with me?"

"Get the hell out!" I raised the bat like an ax and sent her tearing out the back door. I entered the main room and shot out one of the spotlights. The drunk businessmen rolled their heads toward me, unaware of the danger. Katie stopped on the pole. Only the music beat on. "Closing time, fellas. Last call."

"It's only nine o'clock," a fat one muttered. "The night is young and so am I. Tonight I'll dine on muffin pie." This cracked up his colleagues till I fired two more rounds into the speakers, sniping the sound system dead. They waddled out like they had horseshoes in their pants. Some forgot to leave their drinks behind.

"Go on inside, Katie. Better yet, go home. I can't be responsible tonight."

"Rhinoceros," she said sadly.

"Good night."

"Good night, Sarge."

The end. The end. I could taste it thick on my tongue. It was flat, like a hospital and cold. There was no smell in the air, and the right side of my face crumbled. In the Bud mirror reflection I was half a man. My mouth yanked up on one side, collapsed on the other, a seesaw smile. The right eye could just see past the dropped lid. With the room empty, I locked the door and went to work. I could still speak, but not for long.

"Hear ye, hear ye, hear ye. Now gathers the honorable court of Orleans Parish." I didn't know what I was saying. "The Right Honorable Jefferson Alexander Freeman presiding." The bat swung, shattering two stage mirrors. An attention getter. "Hear ye, hear ye, hear ye!" A running jump took out the other five spotlights and I waited.

Dent came in first. He wasn't sure what he was doing in such a crazy world, where a self-proclaimed judge in an apron, with a baseball bat as gavel, could get any attention.

"You should be lying down."

"I want to be punished," I shouted.

He noticed my crooked face and reached out a hand. "For what?"

"For killing. For murdering my only friend." I charged him, a rhinoceros in full bloom. He ran, and I thundered behind the bar. One by one, I broke every bottle across the top of the bar. The liquor ran thick, and I set it on fire. Dent disappeared and returned with a woman. I'd never seen her before, but I recognized her instantly. The heat from the bar had her floating a foot off the ground. She shimmered in the flame like a saint. A holy woman. Like Mary come down with a gift from heaven. She was tall, maybe once beautiful, and electricity bristled at the tips of her fingers. She was heat and light, ice and the abyss. Her eyes were above her eyebrows, or so it looked through the alcoholic flame. As she spoke, she took patient, long strides. "I am . . ."

"You are the Cow Demon," I said. "Mary of the Sky."

"Nice to have you back in New Orleans. Dent, get the fire extinguisher. And call the captain."

"Dent, I wouldn't do that." Dent froze. I was twenty feet from him, but he'd seen me charge. He'd seen the flash of the great, crooked horn, the pounding of the hooves. He didn't move. "You're too old to run away from this bat and these knives." I waved the silverware at him.

"You want to burn the place down, is that it? You've been coming here for a year and a half. Free drinks, free peep show, I let you talk to my girls, and I let you . . ."

"What do you intend to do, Mary? Will you forgive us or will you make us pay for our sins?"

"Do you believe in the power of the gift?"

"Did Felulah?" I asked. I wasn't sure where I was.

"Not enough. If you believe in the power of the gift, then you can live forever."

"What sign will you show me?"

"The sign is that you are here to claim your punishment. You know who I am. You've been drawn to me since the beginning. Only now, you have found your way home."

I rubbed my head like a crystal ball, begging for answers. "Are you inside my head?"

"Only you know what is inside your head. But I am inside part of you. That is why you ventured here."

"Get out of my head! Goddamnit, get out of my head! For Christ's sake, get out of my head!!!" I screamed and spun around faster and faster, then stopped on a dime.

"Let him go," she said, wavering in the flame. Her head curved into the shape of a lily, and her extended arms were bent lance heads. She spoke to me in unknown words. I locked my ears tight.

"You are the lie," I realized.

"Camille Arnaud is the name. I am the owner of this hovel s'appelle Wong's." She slid onto one of the tables and crossed her legs like closing a book. Her head was human, her long fingers painted red at the tips. Arnaud. "Arnaud, my simple friend, great-granddaughter of New Orleans' notorious Lila Arnaud, madam of the most famous, classiest bordello this town ever knew. In old Storyville, at the corner of Basin and Iberville. You've heard the stories. Hookers dressed as queens, johns living out royal fantasies. It was beautiful. I was born two generations too late and got stuck with this rather unfortunate locale. Still, it is a loss leader. My accountant tells me it's financially sound to stay in business. And I do have to support the house on St. Charles. And the one in Lafayette, and the one in Virginia, and the one . . . you get the picture." The fire on the bar cooled. I fed the flame.

"You've been watching me," I said.

"You poor fool, it's a shame that Catholic fall you took didn't kill you. They say there's still glass in your unsavory little head. It is such a terrible shame, your sickness, because you wind up snooping around in other people's business. And that's all it is. Business. Why does everyone have to take things so personally?"

"Murder is personal."

"Not where I come from. Then poor, sweet Felly. She brought it on herself. I had no choice. She was just too fragile a flower for our tropical climate. And it really did tidy up the picture. The fact that you two were so close and that you were so awfully deranged. It makes much more sense that you did her in than those Chinese trophies. Yes, adding Felulah Matin to the list made perfect sense. And I do love triangles."

"I killed Felly," I agreed.

"Oh, please. Quit rummaging through my accomplishments. I have a reputation to uphold. It is convenient that you killed Felly, but that doesn't make it true. Although I doubt the truth will be holding much weight with this case." Camille lit a cigarette on the flaming bar. "Really, I just don't understand you coming to Dent with this wild confession. Do you actually think you did this? Are you that burned out between those ears? Some men make it so easy on a woman." She twisted my nose. I couldn't move. She climbed up onstage, broken glass crunching with each graceful step. She grabbed the pole like a pro. "Honestly, the saddest attempt of all was getting your little Asian angel to wear that wretched tattoo." I lay down the bat. "A police officer with a fleur-de-lis on her pretty little shoulder. Especially when she doesn't begin to understand the power."

"Mary of the Sky."

"A gift from heaven, from the Virgin herself. A sign, you understand, that she's watching over us, protecting us."

"No matter what we do?"

"The power of the myth comes in the exercise of its validity. I believe, so I have the power. Mary visited Clovis fifteen centuries ago. It was time for a new Mary to flex her muscles."

"Aggie."

"Ah, yes. Detective Agatha Li. A poor excuse for a cop. She used to ride my horse when she was in Vice. All attitude and bluff. Bringing my girls in on imaginary charges. All she needed was a little loving. I could have arranged that."

"You know everything."

"It was pure vaudeville, her in that ridiculous dress, which, by the way, she doesn't have the figure for, and that blond wig. I just wanted it to go on forever."

"And the shooting, with the blond girl?"

"A delicate and lovely piece of theater if I do say so myself. I just told one of my poor workers to stage a shooting. Did you honestly think anyone could shoot so poorly? The blond screamer is one of my very own. Veronique. I'd recommend her if you weren't going off to jail. Although she does participate in conjugal visits. I just wanted to see how absolutely devoted you children were to pursuing this investigation. Poor Malcolm found out the hard way about police commitment. After that, we just needed to get Agatha off to Hong Kong, and you off to Angola. But as you realize, it didn't spin out quite that way. Still, I find it so ravishingly amusing." She laughed and leaned lustily against the pole. "Don't you see, Free, some people know, and some are known."

The new janitor walked in with a fire extinguisher. He snowed the bar cold. "Captain's on his way, Miss A.," he said. He walked toward me, ready to erase my face with the butt end of the fire extinguisher, but I pulled out my gun and he froze.

"You runaways just don't know when to quit." Camille laughed. "How many sweet little bullets you have hiding in there? Three at most. Well, then get it over with. Shoot us and go home. Or rather, go homeless." Another laugh.

"I want a few things explained."

"In your condition, honey, you'd need falling down explained."

"If I didn't kill Felly, then who did?" I still didn't know.

"Let's save that till all the players are in place. Why don't we talk about the glory days. Storyville, when Sportin' Houses dotted this landscape like great fruit trees, full of the sweetest nectar. Do you know," she said, scratching ashes off the bar, "that at its height, Storyville had two hundred thirty Sportin' Houses, thirty houses of assignation and more than two thousand ladies of the evening? A gentleman could spread himself around every night for five years and never taste the same fruit twice. Isn't that sheer divinity?" She reveled in her craft, a proud madam, a hollow tramp.

"Did you ever hook, Miss A.?"

"I've never taken an inch from any man. Took his money, but never his passion. The passionate don't think clearly, do they, my friend? You don't think too clearly." The trigger wiggled behind my sweat-drenched finger. I blinked. There were four of her, eight of her. She was everywhere, spinning in kaleidoscope, mocking in stereo. "There used to be forty blocks of sin connected thanks to Alderman Sidney Story. Now I have to sin all over town just to keep the tax man at bay. It's a pity, really, and it forced me to go overseas to pursue my ever-expanding economic dreams."

"Hong Kong," I said without emotion.

"Sweetie, you ain't so pitiful as you look. Yes, yes, my beloved Hong Kong. Shame what the Chinese are doing to it. Did you enjoy your stay in the 'Fragrant Harbor'?"

"No one knew I went."

"I hate to shatter any more illusions, but I know more about you than you do yourself."

"I killed these people," I insisted.

"Okay, all right, if it's that important. You are going to take the fall for them, so I guess I should let you feel some sort of responsibility. I'll let my ego go in this instance. I hope you're grateful." A door slammed and quick footsteps hit the hallway. "Captain, our captain, what splendid timing." Out of the bowels of the hall came Captain LeMaire, Aggie's superior officer, and the man running the entire smuggling/murders investigation. He saw my gun, and his lungs sank, breath hurrying out of his nose. As he reached for his, I aimed at his heart. His hair was the color of cotton, and his jacket didn't close over a globe of a stomach. The sleeves were too short. He was wearing cuff links and no belt.

"No, sir!" I shouted.

"Camille, what's the line?" LeMaire asked.

"Boys, boys, let's not have a spate of violence here. I already have to get a new bar. I don't feel like paying someone to scrape blood off the floor."

"Put your hands where I can see them, Captain. We're still playing hide-and-seek." LeMaire eased up next to Miss A., hands in plain sight.

"I was just explaining to our fall boy about the wonder of old New Orleans. I think he's beginning to see how beautiful corruption can be here in our fair town. Although I suppose you'd have a fair idea of the corrupt life, wouldn't you, Mr. Freeman?" Camille grinned. She was a cat halfway done with a bird.

"Damn right he knows about corruption. He's been thieving since he moved his ass here from Charlotte." The word "Charlotte" hit me like a freight train. A freight train I'd ridden out of town. I almost dropped the gun. "Juvi record as long as my leg, ain't that right, boy? Assault, grand theft auto, breaking and entering. Hell, you broke your parole so much, it couldn't be fixed. And let us not forget the little case of Miss Helen Armbruster. I believe it was a .38 missile you buried in her tender little neck. There simply is no justice. Person kills another person, punishment is due, even if the boy doing the killing's only twelve years old. Leave 'em out in the sun, and look what happens to them. They rot, and spread their stench into every corner of a city." I couldn't answer. I wouldn't answer. He was ticking off a past I'd spent a lifetime forgetting. I felt Jesus and Mary, ripe under my skin. LeMaire stood there fat and sweating, nervous as hell, my memory wearing a badge. "It'll all make sense in the bio. Homeless alcoholic kills illegal aliens for drugs and money. Also offs stripper in sudden burst of rage. Violent past, troubled youth finally catches up with derelict. The paper eats that shit up with chopsticks." He faced Camille, ready to kiss her. "Does he know what's going on yet? Has the poor son of a bitch figured it out? I guess not, by the stupid look on his face."

"You did the hits," I said. "You ran the smuggling. You ran Hai."

"That son of a bitch must be a lousy shot," LeMaire barked. "Because you and your black-haired lover were sup-posed to be Hong Kong dog meat. I'm always cleaning up somebody else's mess."

Miss Arnaud came close enough to spit on me. Her face blossomed out around the gun muzzle, as I stared her down. "You were the perfect suspect, honey. You'd been drinking on credit for too long, and I always collect my debts. Nothing is for free, young man. You should know that."

"I do."

"Painfully sweet Agatha Li kept intercepting my clients at the airport and storing them in safe houses, hoping for infor-mation. Thank goodness the Chinese are such an intractable group of individuals."

"You don't have to tell him this," LeMaire said. Dent and the janitor still hadn't moved, not willing to trust me with a loaded pistol.

"It is so much fun, Captain. I enjoy the thrill. And a dying man does have a right to a last meal."

I pulled my left hand away from the gun and drilled Miss A. with a driving punch to the forehead. It sent her tumbling like a shot fugitive. LeMaire pulled his revolver, but I was on him, and we dared each other to fire. "All right, all right," he said, knees bent, back straight. He toed the floor like an anxious horse.

"You are real. Mary of the Sky, you are real. I felt your bones. There is no power here." I had touched the spirit of deception and knocked her on her ass. I felt a tiny slit of freedom.

On her butt by the stage, Camille laughed. "I've never been punched by a man before. Strange. Very strange. You have to understand, Freeman, that it's all been economics. Financial opportunities were drying up here on the Gulf, so when China shot all those little protesters in '89, it was my Southern responsibility to tie my conscience to my pocketbook and make a little money. Isn't it ironic that one person's oppression is another's financial freedom? I find it exhilarating. But all good things come to a point where one must cut her losses, and you are a loss. A total loss. As is Detective Li, whose zeal has been most disturbing."

"And you made the hits, didn't you, Captain? Because Billy and Cheng were going to talk. They cut a deal with you. Immunity, political asylum, and then you iced them."

"Not personally." His guilt waved a flag over his head. "When Hai contacted us in a panic from Hong Kong, we realized that the two misfits together were more than we bargained for, and you were, until today. Until you were so sure you killed these saps, these ridiculous souls."

"Until the power drew him home. This is your home, isn't it, Jefferson Alexander?" Miss A. grinned. "You have come home to the end." There was a pause long enough. The only sound was the dying smolder of the burning bar. Swallowing took all my strength.

"I am the bad man," I said.

"No shit. And you're going to Angola for it," barked Le-Maire.

"I am the bad man. I am the bad man," I repeated. "I am the bad man."

"Drop the gun." I did, and Dent quickly grabbed it. Le-Maire got me face down on the floor, his knee knifing through my back.

"The bad man," I continued, "must be punished. For living outside the lines. For breaking the rules."

"The crazy man, you mean." LeMaire laughed as he cuffed me and yanked me to my feet. "You broke your own nose on the fucking bathroom wall. We know that too. Camille has a security camera in there. You ran into the goddamn wall."

"The bad man must pay for his sins."

"Who taught you this line? Learn that load of crap back in Charlotte? Did you learn that shit at home?"

"I don't remember."

"Jefferson Alexander Freeman, you are under arrest for the murders of Felulah Matin, Dao Tei Cheng and Kung Lao Chen. You have the right to remain silent. You have the right to an attorney. If you cannot . . ."

"Don't hurt Aggie," I interrupted.

"Hell, she thinks you did it. Poor bitch actually grew to like you. See what a bath and a shave can do? Kind of breaks my heart."

Bullets pummeled the front door lock from outside. Le-Maire grabbed me around the neck and stood behind me. Janitor and Dent took cover behind the bar, but Miss A. stood regally at the foot of the stage, a welt rising on her forehead. The door burst open. It was Aggie and Sergeant Derry.

"You scared the shit out of us, Detective. Just cool it." LeMaire tried to play it cool, but I could feel his grip trembling. "Everything's under control. We have a witnessed confession."

"Free," Aggie said. "I told you not to come home." I didn't respond. "Captain, I'm here to question Miss Arnaud."

"That's a hell of a way to arrive for questioning."

"Actually, sir, to arrest Miss Camille Arnaud for suspicion of smuggling and murder one. Isn't that right, Mary of the Sky?"

"Give me a fucking break, Li. That smuggling bit is old news. You've been wasting department time and funds keeping those illegals shacked up by the lake, and they haven't done one pound of good. We never got a drug bust, a deportation, not one shred of evidence that the killings were connected to smuggling. We know who offed these assholes. This bald maniac right here. Now, I got a confession to murder, three counts, and this case is closed."

"Do we have a confession, Free?"

"I don't know, Aggie. You tell me."

"Sir, I have an exact ID on Miss Arnaud corroborated on both ends. When I found my apartment ransacked, I knew Free was back."

"We can add B and E to the party, if you have the smarts to press charges," LeMaire bluffed.

"Then I checked in with the New Orleans East detainees, and they relayed what they had told Free. He didn't come here to confess. Even if he thinks he did, he came here to end it. To be forgiven for what happened to his friend Felulah."

"I don't give a good goddamn why he came here. All I care about is upholding the law, and this dirtbag broke it. I have a confession, probable cause, and you yourself know that this gentleman was the primary suspect in this case since day one. Camille has suffered enough, with the destruction of her bar by this idiot. This conversation is over."

"Camille?" Aggie repeated with doubt in her voice. "Sir, I'm booking Miss Arnaud on suspicion to smuggle narcotics and conspiracy to commit murder."

A fuse of rage caught fire in LeMaire's spine and exploded in his head. "Enough. Derry, I want you to cuff Officer Li!"

"Sir?" Derry said.

"Now!!"

"Don't do it, Kevin. I need you." Aggie was in trouble again. We all were. LeMaire tightened his grip on my neck. Guns glistened with sweat.

"This is a direct order, Sergeant Derry. I'll have you up on insubordination charges."

"Sir, request description of charge being filed against Officer Li."

"I don't have to describe a damn thing to you."

"Sir, request repeated."

"Your partner, Sergeant, is in cahoots with this psychopath, who killed three people for no apparent reason. A thrill killer. Isn't that right, you filthy son of a bitch?!?"

"Sir?"

"They're lovers, Derry. She sleeps with this trash. She's in love with him. That's why she concocted this story about Miss Arnaud. She wants to distract us from the real killer. But he's so fucking stupid, he beat her to it by confessing. Maybe he's got some voodoo hex on her. She took him to Hong Kong when he was a wanted criminal. Two days after we were about to nail his ass. We had a squad on him on Loyola's campus, and he got away. Then Detective Li covered for him until she could get him out of the country. She was going to try to leave him over there, but he was too stupid or crazy to listen. So she helped smuggle him back into this country. She lied to fellow officers, and falsified reports to protect his whereabouts. She has committed a felony, accessory to murder after the fact, and I order you to arrest her now!"

Derry went for his cuffs, and Aggie backed away, her gun cocked and ready. "Is it true, Aggie?" Derry asked quietly.

"Arrest her now!"

"Don't do it, Kevin. I just need a minute to see it fit." Aggie caught my eye, and my vision came together. "Free, listen to me."

"Take her revolver, Sergeant."

"Free, the captain is part of this, isn't he?"

LeMaire squeezed so tight, I could hardly breathe, but I shot out a single word. "Yes."

Derry paused and looked to the captain. "Don't listen to this killer. He just confessed. They're reaching, Derry. They're panicking because it's over. Their fairy tale just ended."

Aggie saw the guilt in LeMaire's face, and relief soaked her to the bone. For the first time, we both knew I was innocent. "You set him up," Aggie shouted. "You knew he'd take the fall, you set me loose on him. He was perfect. No home, no friends, nothing to protect him. You set him up. You set me up."

"You don't know what the hell you're talking about."

"You had me tail this man, smoke him out, but then he

came in to help. He wasn't a killer. He was the key to the case. But that wasn't part of your plan. You needed him, and he was getting away."

LeMaire wasn't defending himself. His shouting and ranting only shut him off more. There was nothing left for him to say. Miss A. was strangely silent. Dent and Janitor were just waiting for the ax to drop.

LeMaire's silence convinced Derry enough to put away the cuffs and reach for his revolver. "Don't even think about it," LeMaire grumbled. The walls were closing in on him, options were few. "Put your gun on the bar, Detective Li."

"You are right, Captain. The game is over. But you're the one putting down the gun. You don't have anything." LeMaire started backing us toward the hallway, gun at my temple, as Aggie and Derry moved in. "We have witnesses willing to identify Miss Arnaud, and possibly you. All you have is a retractable confession. Free, did you murder these people?"

"No," I said, and it felt finally right, finally good, at last a true confession. LeMaire tore a gash in the back of my head with the sharp butt of his gun, pushed me toward Aggie and took off down the hall. Aggie bolted out after him, and I stood to face Camille as Derry released my cuffs.

"You certainly know how to complicate things," she said.

"I don't believe in you, Miss A. I don't believe in Mary of the Sky. I don't believe in the power or the gift. No one does. No one believes." And with that, I decked her with another left hook. Dent and Janitor were next, but forgiveness had given me new strength. I sawed through Dent like wet cardboard, while Derry did the rest. Punches, kicks, broken chairs, a series of blows and ducks that brought blood and bruises to the living. In the end, Dent lay groggy in his favorite place, behind the bar. Janitor was bleeding by the jukebox as it howled out Screamin' Jay Hawkins' "I Put a Spell on You." And Camille was finished, her petals torn, her lance head bent. I didn't see it, but I knew then that Aggie's tattoo had just disappeared.

Aggie pounded back into the bar. They cuffed all three to the stripper's pole and called for assistance. A motorcycle cop was there inside a minute, and we hustled out front, into Aggie's squad car. We were out of the Quarter and onto Highway 10 before I could exhale. Aggie sat in the back seat with me, dabbing blood from my head, as Derry tore into the flesh of the night. "You're always bleeding, Free."

"It's the one thing I do well. Thanks for setting me free tonight, Aggie. It's good for a man to know what he's done and hasn't done." She kissed my cheek. Her lips left an oval of warmth that eased the pain.

"Suspect headed for New Orleans East, Reelfoot off Curran. Copy?" Derry announced into the police radio. "Suspect is Caucasian male, early fifties, driving an NOPD squad car. He's one of our own. Copy?"

"Copy. Repeat description."

"One of our own. Armed and dangerous. It's Captain Le-Maire. Backup requested. Out."

"LeMaire knows the address, but he's never been there," Aggie said. "That's our best chance."

"Those people are going to die, Aggie."

The night was as dark as the eve of our Hong Kong escape, but this time we were doing the chasing. When we crossed Chef Menteur Highway, Derry had us going one hundred ten mph. Cars scattered like cockroaches at our cherry tops, and we all pictured LeMaire standing in that dank living room, picking off freedom seekers with police-issue bullets.

We got off the highway and knocked over trash cans and bicycles on our spiraling way to the Chinese safe house. When we pulled up into the driveway, it was too late. LeMaire stood on the porch, his head slung low, and his pistol dangling from a loose grip. He didn't turn around at our screeching arrival. He was completely still, the patrol lights reflecting off the barrel of his gun. I was waiting for blood to come flooding from under the door onto the porch.

The house's front door opened. Out stepped the wise man, thinner than hours before. He wavered like gasoline fumes in the doorway. He held a six-pack of Dixie beer like a suitcase, packed and ready to go. LeMaire looked up at his shining face. The man's hair was crooked from sleeping, but there was a light in his eyes. Aggie and Derry had their guns zeroed in on the captain's back. My mind somersaulted. I winced. My knees buckled. Freedom. The thin man handed LeMaire the six-pack and slowly went back inside, content to let the locals sort out the tangles. For a moment, he seemed to be smiling at me. Freedom. He shut the door.

LeMaire turned around, sat on the porch, set down his gun and opened a Dixie. His mind had flown away. He looked like me. He had the glazed face of an ancient mausoleum saint. We crept close enough to hear him, but he spoke with his eyes gazing straight ahead. "I came here. I sped here to kill these people. I hit a cat on the way. I killed it. I came here to kill them. All eleven of them. But when he opened the door, I didn't know what to do. I've never killed anyone before. I've had people pull the trigger, but I've never done the finish. That son of a bitch asked me if I wanted to come in. He was going to wake up the whole family and make tea." LeMaire paused, but Aggie and her partner stayed homed in, watching his gun, studying his manner. "I didn't want any tea. All I could think was how thirsty I was. I was so fucking thirsty. Thirstier than I've ever been in my life. To the bone. So I said no, thanks. But I asked him for a beer. I came to kill them. We can go in a minute. I just want to quench this awful thirst."

It took all night to process LeMaire. Shock and fear were the obvious emotions at the precinct. As it had been in Hong Kong, many officers were squirming. They were a part of the scandal. It was only a matter of time before they were found out. There were looks of resentment thrown at Aggie and Derry for bringing down a captain, no matter how dirty. Most of the cops would have loved to simply toss my ass in jail and forget the rest. LeMaire told of an elaborate system of checks and balances that had palms greased from City Hall to the local hardware store. It was a series of dark tunnels and shadowy lies that had set up more than seventy-five Hong Kong Chinese in New Orleans in less than three years. And it was already epidemic across the South and the nation. LeMaire had been on Miss A.'s payroll for more than twenty years to ensure a smooth prostitution business. The smuggling became the new moneymaker after England walked out on Hong Kong and then China brought down the hammer. The captain reported that since 1980 the Asian population in the United States had increased by 107 percent, and it was sure to continue to grow. It didn't matter that Thatch was dead, or Hai, or that the New Orleans side had been arrested. It would go on. I understood that corruption rose to its level of need. And it was always hungry. It always would be.

Miss A., Dent and Janitor had nothing to say. They'd all seen prison bars before and were adjusting well to their stay. Lawyers would descend to chew at the bars until they could lead their clients home. It was all so efficient. Doughnuts, coffee, small laughs and firm handshakes. Computers buzzed into the early morning. It was miles away from Felulah's dressing room, where I had made my first friend. So far away from Aggie's feet washing, Hong Kong's helicopter escape. I felt like I was in a glass case, able to watch the cops in action but unable to communicate the losses. All the losses. Aggie was lost in an interview with an exhausted Dent when I headed for the door. But when my hand hit the knob, hers covered mine.

"Got a minute, cowboy?" We walked down the hall. Into LeMaire's office we turned, and Aggie shut the door. She needed a minute to break out of her investigative mode, but then her black eyes flashed like underwater spotlights. She was the same woman I'd asked for help in Antoine's two months before. The same woman whose hip curved beneath my hand. The same woman who once loved me under a Pacific moon.

"Now you know," I said. LeMaire's lamp bounced a circle of light off his desk that reflected up onto us. Aggie glowed.

"You too."

"Agatha, I killed someone."

"LeMaire mentioned something," she said flatly.

"He's the one who reminded me. Well, not really. It's been on my mind, I just didn't know it by name."

"I'm a friend," she reassured me, "not a cop."

Tears tapped from the inside. "I was twelve, and my father was teaching me how to shoot a pistol. Every Saturday we practiced. Since I was seven years old. Anyway, we were shooting. I was shooting live rounds." I leaned against the doorway.

"You don't have to do this."

"It was at a barbecue, July, a Saturday, and the neighbor, Miss Armbruster, Helen Armbruster, was all dressed up. She was young. And she was wearing pearls. I remember the pearls that were so shiny in the Saturday sun. And she smelled like . . . like something familiar. I didn't know what it was at first, but then I finally got it. She smelled like Daddy." The word "Daddy" fell out of my mouth like a piece of shrapnel, tearing the inside of my cheek. "There was one bullet left in the chamber, and he had me aim at Helen, who was walking over to explain something. There was something she was ready to say. I was pretending to shoot her in my mind. I hated her. I didn't know why, but I did. That's what I thought. And I had perfect aim." Aggie put her hand in the middle of my chest, anchoring me just in time. "But there were extra hands. Daddy's hands. He slipped his hands over mine, over the gun, and he pulled back the trigger. Helen just stopped. She didn't fall right away, or spin around. She just stopped and looked at me. There was a hole in her neck that I could see from across the yard. I remember feeling proud. It was just like target practice. Perfect." Aggie tried to swallow and failed. "Daddy always told me all you needed was two bullets. One to put 'em down. And one to keep 'em down. I only had one bullet. But it didn't matter, because I had perfect aim. And so did he. So we pulled the trigger together. Then she fell. Then she died."

"Your father killed that woman," Aggie said, rushing to my defense. But there was no one to defend me against. I had been there. I was the one who was blamed. I was the killer. I could feel the cold shape of a gun form in my hand. It felt heavy, and I was twelve again. Aggie shook me back to the present. "You were a little boy. You didn't know. It's not your fault."

"Mother wasn't home. And at first we tried to hide the body. Like it was a game or something. I remember we were laughing. But she kept bleeding all over everything, so we took her back outside and he called the police." More silence from Aggie. "They didn't talk to me after that. After he told the police it was an accident. That I had been playing with the gun without permission, and it discharged on its own. No one cared, Aggie. Even the cops seemed bored. They just let me get away with it. But my parents never really spoke to me after that. We just knew it was time for me to leave three years later. I'd run up a tab at the sheriff's office, and our house was much too crowded with Helen's ghost living there. My mother put me on a train, and that was it. That day I killed Helen, I killed everything."

"You didn't shoot her. Do you hear me? That was not you."

"You can start at any age, Ag. It's in the blood."

"No, it's not. This isn't you. It happened to you, but it doesn't own you."

"Then why do I carry it around? Why is she still standing there on the lawn with a hole in her throat? Why can't I forget? Why did I have to remember?"

Aggie didn't say anything for a long time. The building was still, empty, there was no one else in the city. "Sometimes you have to remember something before you can forget it."

"I'm sorry I put you through all this. I finally know what I didn't do. To Felly, to Cheng and Billy, but I'm still not sure who I am. Alone, I could figure that out. Or at least how to survive. How to keep on being whoever I was. But with you, out here in the open, I just don't know. There's too much space." I felt shy, a child, first day in a new school. I cowered at her brightness.

"We could find out together." She took my hand and stroked it on her face. Her skin was rough from sweat and tears and the chase.

"Do you want to? Can you help me figure it out?"

"As much as you've helped me, Jefferson. Remember. I love you." The kisses came, the room flipped, and with a final embrace, I pushed myself toward the door.

"We didn't stop anything, did we, Aggie? They'll keep putting on those heroin suits and flying here. We didn't make any difference."

"We didn't have a choice. We were just following orders." She kissed me on the nose I'd broken all by myself. Crazy. It hit me how crazy I had been. "The bad guys can regroup, but at least we pissed them off. And the captain and his ship of fools will be writing letters from prison for a long time."

"It didn't make any difference," I said again. We stepped into the darkened hallway. Laughter hurried toward us from the interrogation rooms.

"You made a difference to me."

I walked out, still waiting to reach my end. Ever feel like you're going to die? And then you don't.

Word to the wise. Just because you confess doesn't mean you are forgiven.

The next morning I went to eleven o'clock mass. It was packed. I crossed myself, bowed to the altar and found a seat on the side. Mobley was in full flight, his robe flowing wild beneath his hands.

" 'And at the resurrection, we shall be like angels.' That's what it says. At the resurrection, we're going to be like angels. Now, I reckon most of us don't know what that means. What is an angel? Have we ever seen an angel, touched an angel, spoken to an angel?" A little boy next to me said yes out loud. His mother gave him a Life Saver. "People think, they assume that because I am a priest, that I have an inside track to the angels. That if I want, I could get them to pull a few strings for good old Jessup T. Mobley."

I began to look more clearly at the congregation. I didn't recognize anyone. I looked at the little boy again, and he smiled. His mother smiled at me too. Not regular smiles, something else. A wave rolled over me inside and out. Mobley pushed on. "It's how God intended it to be. These are the words of his son Jesus Christ. Ye shall be as angels. Forgiven, set free, made new, resurrected human beings. Ye shall be as angels."

Mobley went on, but I couldn't hear him. There was a great flapping of wings, louder and louder. The air rushed against my skin, pews trembled, the altar shook, the pulpit broke loose and raised up in the cool, hot air. The crazy beating of wings, heavenly wings. Then I saw that the church was full of angels, glorious, unspeakable angels. They hung above, around, beside, within me. They flew to the corners of the sanctuary, played in the rafters, sang themselves from saint to saint. The wind blew out all the candles, yet the light blazed purple and pink, white and orange. They cupped me in their wings, folded and unfolded me, sealed my cracked head with a winged touch. I fell up into the air and spun there, a top, on top of whatever was left below. Breathing became dancing, thought was healing, motion was forgiveness. Up there with the angels, up in the air, an angel myself.

"Angels. Ye shall be angels. Amen." Mobley tucked his wings away and closed his Bible. The organist splashed out a tune as Mobley descended, and after the benediction, I stood in the Sunday sun to shake his hand. Only forty people had come for mass, but Sup didn't look disappointed.

"Boy, you have been gone too long. You're coming home for some of that Sunday special. And bring your girl. How have you been?"

"You missed me," I realized.

"Damn right, Jefferson. You're a good man. A good man I always miss."

"I'm a good man, Sup?"

"Future angel."

"I really liked your sermon. You haven't lost your flair. I could feel what you were saying."

"I know. I saw you dancing up on the ceiling."

"Can we go for a walk?"

"How about Audubon Park? That'll make me hungry for some gumbo."

It was May, but summer was already shedding the sweater of spring. The humidity lined up beads of sweat on Sup's forehead. Every step he took shook one off and another took its place. He had slipped into enormous sneakers and a T-shirt. He was ready for action. The park was loaded with college students getting tans, throwing Frisbees, drinking the day's first beer.

"Lapsed Catholics," Mobley said. "Whenever you see a tan white kid with bad grades here in New Orleans, he's a lapsed

Catholic." He laughed a minute, then stopped. "Did you see the pulpit shake loose, Jefferson?" I didn't want to talk about the pulpit or the angels. It was private. "It's not private," he said.

"I don't know who I am. I'm not a good man."

"You are," Sup corrected. "You are a good man. God made you a good man."

"But I made myself a bad man. There are things I've done. You don't know."

"I know you can't change what God's done. Eventually, it comes around to get you. You have no choice. Your days are up."

"I know." He was inside my head. It was all right.

"Are you afraid?"

"Of the end? I don't know. I wonder what it will be. When and where, but I'm still prepared for my punishment. I'm prepared to die."

"No one is ever prepared to die."

"I am. I've filled my hours with other people's tragedies to better prepare me for my own." There was a gentle, human pause.

"You understand that the glass is gone."

"I'm just waiting for the voices to take me there." I was ignoring him. "They're in charge now." Mobley stopped me by an oak and pinned my shoulders back, a captured butterfly. His eyes were planets, his face the midnight sky. He spoke in the language of a faraway star.

"You understand that the glass is gone. The glass in your head. The angels took it away."

"Jesus and Mary," I breathed.

"Pieces of Jesus and shards of Mary. The glass is gone."

"This isn't the end. I have to get to the end. There is a definite end."

"This is the end, Free. The end of you."

"The end of me." Sup started walking back. Back through the bathing suits and unopened books. I knew I wasn't supposed to follow him. The oak tree laid its branches down low to cover me. I could see the outlines, the strange movement of friends, of people in love. I couldn't hear them. Just the muffled sounds, a fading dog bark, a quiet hello.

"There's nothing there. Maybe it disintegrated. Maybe it's racing through your bloodstream as we speak." The thick-haired doctor at Charity seemed genuinely happy. He wasn't used to handing out good news. "I honestly have no explanation."

"No danger?"

"It doesn't look like it. Nothing serious. Your blood tests are normal, the skull fractures have healed. Your nose is crooked, but that gives you character. And you could use a better barber, but honestly, I can't believe it. It's as if it never happened."

"Hey, Doc," I said, holding back a right hook. "It happened."

There is a place where angels are born. I don't know who gets to visit, to see the wings first dance, to feel their breath fresh against his face. I don't know where the place is. Maybe it's everywhere it needs to be. But I've been there. I was taken there, and though I don't live there now, I carry it with me always. They say healing is a memory eraser. That you can never remember the pain once it's gone. No. There is some pain I will never forget, even though the blood has disappeared. I see it still, when I look into Aggie's eyes. When I see that she forgives me, that she loves me, that she is an angel in my midst. I feel it in her fingertips, touch it on her hip, taste it in a kiss. I can never forget where I've come from. I don't want to. I don't know where I'm going, but wherever it is, I go as a man with Aggie, not as a rhinoceros, alone.

It's Christmas in New Orleans. The nights have been cold. I'm staying warm. Last night I went to the Christmas Eve service with Aggie. Sup talked about the baby Jesus and Mary, the star the Wise Men followed, the shepherds keeping watch. Even Joseph, happy just to be involved, standing up at the altar. The crèche was silent. Two cows, a mule, Sup had somehow found a camel. There were the shepherds trying to get a closer look. The Wise Men offering gifts, the star floating in the air and a familiar-looking angel announcing the good news. Good News.

As we sang "Joy to the World," the Advent candles burned brighter for a moment, lighting up the faces of Mary and Jesus, together at last. She held the baby in her arms, a tiny promise, a chance, a shot at being free.

The congregation sang "Silent Night" without the organ, lifting their candles high in the darkened church, telling each other that Christ the Savior was born. I hoped for freedom. For the frightened people of Hong Kong, for the other rhinos on the streets of New Orleans, for the prisoners all around me, those with invisible chains. Those that never knew they'd been captured. During the last verse, I kissed Aggie on the cheek and stole up to the balcony. It was roped off, and I had it to myself. I waited there until the church emptied and the lights were turned off. I lit my candle and walked to the window.

The stained glass had been replaced. A whole new window had been installed. It was an exact replica of the hard curtain I'd escaped through. In the orange glow, everything was whole. I touched Mary's face and Jesus' tiny head. I heard the angel sing. As the window had been made new, so had my head, my life, my everything. But this time I knew who to pray to. I knew who to thank. With closed eyes, my lips and soul quivered. The answer was clear as an angel's tear.

"Merry Christmas, Free. Merry Christmas."

ABOUT THE AUTHOR

Todd Komarnicki is a screenwriter and playwright who lives in Los Angeles. *Free* is his first novel.

For information on how to volunteer
to help the homeless, contact

National Coalition for the
Homeless
162 Connecticut Avenue NW
Washington, DC 20009
(202) 265-2371